D1748342

Enemies of the Modern World

A triptych of novellas

Paul Cudenec

winteroak.org.uk

Copyright © 2021 Paul Cudenec. The author formally retains copyright over this work but permits non-commercial reproduction or distribution

Occitanie, France

ISBN: 978-2-9575768-0-7

"The most basic task ahead of us is to bring as many people as possible together around the conviction that the system has got to be destroyed"

Miguel Amorós

CONTENTS

1 Theo Carter   **7**

2 Swanboy   **145**

3 The Game   **251**

From 'Our Stolen Freedom'

For the last nine and a half years I have been living in prison. I eat prison food, I drink prison tea, I wash myself with prison soap and keep myself warm with prison blankets.

I am also very much against prisons. Not just this particular one, which is marginally preferable to the one in which I served the first part of my life sentence, but all prisons. I am against the prison system.

Does this make me a hypocrite, that I remain alive and in reasonable health thanks to everything which the prison system provides?

No, of course it doesn't. I didn't choose to be in prison. I would much prefer to be elsewhere, as you can well imagine. But I have no choice. I am stuck in here and so I am forced to make use of the material and infrastructure around me.

If I wanted to escape I would have to make use of prison cutlery to scoop away a hole in a wall or to fashion a primitive weapon. Even if I chose a less joyful way out, I would still have to depend on the world of the prison and use one of its very own blankets to make myself a hanging rope.

Before I was put in here, I lived in the outside world. The outside industrial capitalist world. I used its money, consumed its products, communi-

cated with others by means of its infrastructures.

I was also very much against the industrial capitalist system.

Did this make me a hypocrite?

I d'ont really kno who I am. I thout about this becoase of what Dad told me from a book he is reeding, which sounds rely interetsing.

The man says we need to kno who we are deep in syde us, which is stragne to me because I d'ont think there is somthing diferant in syde me that is not the Boy that everybody knoes and luves (NOT!!).

But if their is somwone inside me that is not the saym as waht pepole thinck, then who exsatly is it or waht is it becoase Dad says it mihte be from all of nacher and the hole yunivers.

That mussed be y Ozman can tern himsself in to a Bird. I wishe I cuod do that and jussed fly a way.

Undated

The other day, I stopped to look at the old yew tree down by the river near Merryford. It isn't dead yet, although you might think so from a distance. It is still pushing out sparse shoots of greenness, little tufts of vitality defying its destiny. And it came to me that I, too, am one of those little tufts. I have always felt within me, ever since I was a girl, an overwhelming sense not just of being alive but of thirsting to be more alive, still more alive, to be radiating with life, bursting, overflowing, exploding! Is this the 'feeling', for want of a better word, that pushes out the living tufts from the old trunk? What is that urge to be and to be more, to reach out, to embrace and to become? And what happens to that feeling, that desire, when it is thwarted by the world outside, by circumstances beyond itself, which it cannot control? For I have always also felt that frustration, that constant sense of being blocked, stifled, crushed by a thing surrounding me that I have often imagined as a cage. All those rules about what we shouldn't do, about how we shouldn't let loose the living within! Don't run, don't sing, don't scream! Don't touch, don't taste, don't dream! And then all those expectations about the person we should turn ourselves into, all the barriers they erect to define the limits of our possible being. Barbed wire fences around our souls! They tell us that the sunlight and the freedom we crave don't even exist. Have never existed. There is no great outdoors, no fresh air, no world of exaltation, they say. There is no reality beyond this cardboard-and-plastic replica so carefully built up around you to provide you with the impression of being alive. But I have always known this is a lie. A flimsy lie. And the green shoots of my life-energy have kept pushing against the lie, forcing it back, forever searching for a way round it, beneath it, above it or straight through it.

But what has that made me? What do you call a simple joyful will-to-be that for decade after decade is kept confined, imprisoned, frustrated? What do you call the driving impulse behind this becoming when it has been forced to keep smashing its innocent head against the concrete walls of incomprehension, of stagnation, of dullness and artifice?

This is not simple life-energy anymore. Life-energy constantly denied is forced to take on a different form and character.

1

THEO CARTER

There was something so clear about that Friday morning in May that it felt almost unreal.

From the moment that Theo was awoken by the joyful trilling of the blackbird in the copper beech outside his bedroom window, the morning seemed to represent something beyond itself.

This impression did not, for the moment, take the form of a conscious thought in Theo's mind but rather of an emotion. He felt happy. The day into which he had emerged felt like a representation of this happiness, this inner state which shone out on to everything around him and bathed it in the light of perfection.

Everything seemed exactly as it should, from the sharp sunlight in the kitchen, to the gurgle-growling of the kettle, the click as it turned itself off, the faint odour of the teabag, the heat of the mug in his hand, the humming of the fridge. There even seemed something just right about the way the toast got stuck in the toaster, about the slightly burnt crust.

The tattiness of his flat seemed perfect, the hall carpet beautifully worn and faded, the crack in the frosted bathroom window the touch of some master craftsman.

The metallic ringing of his footsteps down the outside staircase merged seamlessly with the rustling of leaves, the passing of traffic and the whine of a tube train pulling out of Wotton Park to create an exquisite symphony of the familiar, reassuring sounds which had accompanied his life for so many years.

Theo loved the fact that at 8.30am there was still a little chill in the air, he loved the energy that he still felt in his 50-year-old legs as he skipped over Yew Tree Lane and headed up towards Little Wotton.

He was so pleased to exchange a few good mornings along the way – with Faduma and her kids from over the road, with Frank who used to work at the newsagent's and with a pale little red-headed girl at the bus stop whom he'd never seen before but, with her eyes of brightest green and her quick smile of the most radiant humility, somehow seemed to embody all the vital energy he felt rising up through the city on this to-be-fateful morning.

The green man lit up on the pedestrian crossing just at the right moment for him to stroll across the road, traders rolled up their blinds at the very moment that he passed, two playful mongrels chased each other round the corner of Mafeking Road just as he reached its red-brick Victorian splendour.

It was all so perfect, so choreographed, that it felt like the opening scenes of a film. Every little incident, every little exchange – such as the way that Taavi was putting Theo's takeaway cappuccino on the counter as he walked in and the way that he, for his part, already had the right change ready to slap down beside it – spoke of a well-established daily routine.

The whole point of this cinematic introduction to Theo's life, which he had the strange impression of experiencing half as participant and half as spectator, was to imply a status quo, a general state of affairs that formed the background and foundation of whatever was to come next.

In one way, it spoke of permanence, of a lack of change that had allowed this reality to blossom to such a point of effortless perfection. But in another way it spoke of impermanence, for the context in which this reality was being presented was that things were very soon going to change. The essence of Theo's current life had come to fruition on this Friday morning in May, it suggested. Its perfection was a peak which could be neither sustained nor surpassed.

Again, Theo did not initially give shape to this reflection, but it nevertheless fermented in his unconscious mind and flavoured the way he was experiencing the start of his day. What should have been the innocent enjoyment of a fine moment of his life took on a bitter-sweet tinge, as is so often the case. Illusory perfection and permanence slip out of our grasp the moment we imagine we have secured them.

Finally, just as he reached Kelmscott Road and the final 100 yards before the Infoshop, this hidden realisation reached the surface of his brain and he found an inner voice talking him through the last leg: "Look, Theo, this is where you live, this place, this is where you have made your life. You have made it work here, you have found somewhere where you can stay still. It's been nearly 15 years now, Theo, in Wotton. Seven years since the Infoshop opened. Yes, you're good here, mate. You're stable. Feet on the ground. Growing roots. And Isha? No, she's gone now but it doesn't matter, that's the thing, it doesn't matter. You've got over her, you've moved on. That's quite something, eh? Look around, Theo, look at this road, these little shops, these people – see how that old bloke over the road just waved at you. Look at this treasure you've found. You're accepted here, Theo. You can relax. Be yourself. At last you've got a home".

If you detect, in this little interior monologue, a little too much in the way of self-reassurance, then you have glimpsed another side to the apparently self-confident professional community activist enjoying a moment of peak satisfaction. You have caught sight of the insecurity which often nagged away at Theo, the doubts about himself and the life he was leading which underlay his being at all times, even if he rarely allowed them to become visible to himself, let alone to others.

Theo's right hand gave the cappuccino to the left one so that it could fish the keys out of his pocket, as it did from Tuesday to Saturday each and every week. It rolled up the security blinds, swung open the front door and switched on the computer. Then, after Theo had flopped on to the sofa by the window, it resumed its coffee-holding duties as he savoured his first ritual treat of the day.

A quarter of an hour later, he had started work, checking through the emails and social media accounts. He liked to get this done first thing, before Jay turned up. Not just because Jay talked a lot, because he did, but because Theo liked Jay's chatter and wanted to listen to it and join in properly, rather than merely grunt little affirmations or notes of surprise while trying to concentrate on something else.

The first message he opened was from the Anderson-Butler Fund for Social Change, confirming that this month's funding had gone into the account. This was unsurprising but always welcome news. That chance encounter with Jeff from The Radical Impact Project, the evening in Camden where he had told him about his group of friends and their vision for a local initiative down in Wotton, Jeff's tip-off about the ABFSC and subsequent endorsement of his bid – all of that had made what he was currently doing possible. The timing had been exceptional, as well. The morning after Theo saw yet another job fall apart under his feet – this time because the cycle repair shop had been evicted for unpaid rent – news had come through that the bid had been approved in full. The funding was not massive in usual business terms, but, together with one or two other contributions they had managed to scrape together, it was enough to run the Infoshop and pay Theo, on what was admittedly a very low wage, to work on it full-time, plus some other part-time participation. The monthly email from the ABFSC served, therefore, as a prompt for Theo to offer a little silent prayer of thanks.

There was a lot of social media to sift through. In inspiration, the Infoshop was very much a frontline activist project, although that wasn't so obvious at the moment. There had been a deliberate idea of building a wide community network, based around the physical location, which could be activated in case of emergency. The nature of this possible emergency shifted in

Theo's mind from year to year. Sometimes it seemed it would involve evictions. Sometimes it felt as if the ever-present road-widening threat to Thorbury Common would spark a full-scale mobilisation. At the moment, given the political climate, Theo imagined that immigration raids would be the issue that called for a big response. It really felt as if fascism was lurking on the doorstep and he for one was not going to stand aside and let it in.

Theo, Jay and the others (what others? Nikki and Denise never came any more, Nathan was shacked up with his boyfriend on the other side of the city...) had pre-empted any such possibility by creating a network of social media channels that could all be used for one purpose if the need arose. Some of them were activist accounts openly linked to the Infoshop – Wotton Anti-Raids, Wotton Solidarity and Communities Against Capitalism, for instance. But they also ran accounts with broader appeal, such as the Little Wotton Friendship Network or Tuesley Borough Civil Liberties Society. There were also the individual accounts, where each of them tried to develop "characters", using humour and local references, to draw in followers who might have been put off by the political tone of their other entities. Several of these had fallen by the wayside, of course, but Theo had kept his part of the operation going and now boasted a considerable reach into Wotton and its immediate hinterland.

Theo looked up from the screen. Someone had just come in. It was Prateek from next door, wanting an update on the plumber who was supposed to be coming to sort out the leaking pipe in the passage at the back. This sort of thing – practical details of building maintenance, insurance, bank accounts, funding applications – bored Theo rigid. But he knew it had to be done. It was all part of the job that the Collective had created. There was nobody to complain to but themselves and nobody else who was going to sort out these tiresome minutiae on which the success of their political initiative depended.

Once Prateek had left, he went back to skimming through the incoming information. Mobilisation against the far right in Lancashire the next day. A few years back Theo would have been heading north up the motorway for that one. It would have been him who had been sending out the messages, phoning around, booking the minibus from the Community Hub. But for some time now he had stopped going off on that sort of excursion. Old age creeping up, maybe. Less desire for physical confrontation, for set-piece spectaculars. A total lack of enthusiasm for close proximity to row upon row of riot cops. No burning ambition to spend eight hours in a police cell and months on legal paperwork, interviews and preliminary hearings hundreds of miles away. Or, framed more positively, a total commitment to this project, to what he was doing here, which meant it was actually rather irresponsible and self-indulgent to go charging up and down the country in the search of a few anti-fascist kicks.

What else? Another vast swathe of countryside threatened by a high-speed rail line. He shared it, sighed, and moved on. Sometimes it was just too much. You couldn't get involved in everything.

Ah, this was something to look at later, at his leisure. A new in-depth exposé by investigative journalist Sally Shukra, exposing links between environmental and wildlife charities, the pharmaceuticals industry and the deep state. He read everything this woman wrote. Incredible revelations time after time, all completely backed up by references and links, but which never seemed to get an airing beyond a fairly small network on social media.

Some good news. Anti-militarist activists were still successfully occupying the roof of an Israeli drone manufacturer in Kent. A new green anarchist activist network was being launched in Slovakia. Locals had chased police and authorities out of a dozen cities in Mexico.

Closer to home there was a talk about Emma Goldman at the Liberty Library, an all-day subvertising workshop at a squat down in Croydon and a Refugee Picnic over in Friswell on Sunday lunchtime.

Right on cue, just as Theo finished his online perusal, his friend Jay walked in bearing nankhatai biscuits and, as ever, a flask of cardamom-infused coffee that he had made at home. The Infoshop was also supposed to be a café of sorts, but somehow those who ran the place always seemed to prefer to source their drinks from the outside.

"What a perfect fuckin' morning," said Jay, as they took up their standard positions on the sofa. If Theo didn't know him better, he would have imagined he had picked up on the same energy as he had. But Jay was always like this, always up-beat.

Jay had had a perfect night-before as well, it turned out. He'd persuaded his cousin to give him the evening off from takeaway food deliveries so that he could give a talk about Wotton Solidarity to the Polish Club down the road. Things hadn't always been easy with the local Poles. Some of them, a few years back, had been a bit on the racist side and been caught hanging around with some dodgy far-right characters. But this group seemed to have moved on and a new crowd had taken over the club.

"You couldn't meet a nicer bunch of people, Thee!" enthused Jay. "And they got the politics straight away. Mutual aid, unity in diversity, communities against central control. Nobody raised an eyebrow when I said we never worked with the council or the cops. They knew it all already! They're on board and they've got lots of ideas about what we can do with Solidarity – new projects, working groups on different issues, reaching out to some of the newer arrivals we haven't met yet..."

"Cool," said Theo. "Let's just hope all that energy lasts longer than one evening and wasn't just a side-effect of a few cans of *Tyskie* and a couple of shots of vodka. The last thing we need is to be saddled with a load of great new initiatives and nobody with the time or inclination to do a proper job with them".

"Ah come on, don't be such a cynical old git, Thee".

"I'm not cynical. I'm just saying. We've seen it all before, haven't we? What was she called, that Scottish woman who was going to transform the Kingley Vale Estate into an anarcho-communist free zone?"

Jay chuckled. "Ah yes. June. They were going to have their own currency and aim for total self-sufficiency within two years".

"Allotments on the roofs and goats in the stairwells, if I remember right".

"And trained bands of teenage snipers to see off the forces of imperial law and order".

"What could possibly have gone wrong?"

Jay laughed.

"And how long did that plan last?" asked Theo, knowing full well the answer to his own question.

"To be fair, she didn't have the chance. She got back with her fellow up in Dundee".

"Yes, after three days, Jay. Day one she arrives at her sister's, with tear-stained face and bulging suitcase. Day two she comes to our drop-in session and announces the coming insurrection. Day three she's on the overnight bus to Scotland. An extreme case, admittedly, but we've seen too many like that come and go, so you'll have to forgive me if I take people's great intentions with a pinch of salt these days".

"Fair enough, Thee," replied Jay. "But you'll see with this lot. They're not like that. There's this woman called Magda who's really..."

"Aha!"

"What?"

"So when are you seeing her?"

"Well... we said we'd meet up tonight to talk things through a bit, but it's not..."

"Of course not, Jay, of course not. But that's good news. Gives an extra bit of motivation to the struggle. Sexual energy channelled into activism. For the meantime, anyway..."

Jay ignored this comment then suddenly whipped out his phone. He was evidently eager to change the subject.

"Thee! Look at the Boy! Look at him!"

Theo took the phone being held out to him with a sinking feeling.

Jay was so proud of his one and only nephew, Azad, and his desire to share his enthusiasm with his friend was normal and understandable. But it was a bit complicated for Theo. Isha, Jay's sister, had been the love of his life. Still was, truth be told. Part of the reason they'd split up was because they couldn't have children. And now she had this child, Azad, with her new man, with whom she was living her new life down on Santa Sofia.

The photo showed a bronze-skinned and beaming boy of seven or eight, stripped to the waist and proudly holding aloft a line to which was attached a huge fish.

"What a strapping and good-looking lad he is, eh Thee?"

"Yes," nodded Theo. There was no denying it. "Just like his dad, I suppose?" he added, trying not to show any signs of the slight bitterness he felt within.

"Oh yeah," said Jay, totally oblivious to any such issue. "A definite resemblance. But don't you think..." he leaned over to have another look at Azad "... don't you think there's a bit of his Uncle Jay in there too?"

Theo burst out laughing. "Jay Mukherjee, the Noble Savage of Wotton High Street, hunter-gathering for kebabs and samosas in the darkest rain forests of the London Borough of Tuesley, is that it?"

"Oh fuck off, Thee!" said Jay, snatching back the phone. "I know I don't look like that, but that's not my fault, is it? The Boy's so lucky to be growing up on the island and not on some shitty housing estate. I couldn't do that, but he's doing it for me. And I can't wait to get over there and join him!"

"No!" said Theo, and his objection was felt. "Don't do it Jay! Don't abandon me! The two of us together, maybe, we stand a reasonable chance of bringing down the entire capitalist system in the UK, but me on my own...?"

"You should come with me, Thee! Get out of this country and find out what life is really about! And do you know what, mate, if it's revolution you're after then it's down there that it's going to happen. Santa Sofia and everywhere like it. The periphery. Places where they physically can't maintain that total control that we have to put up with. Places with next to no surveillance cameras, places where the nearest riot police are a five-hour plane trip away, places that will never have 5G or 6G..."

Theo smiled at the total impossibility of ever sharing an island with Isha and her boyfriend.

"I'm serious!" insisted Jay. "I just need to sort a few things out here, raise a bit more cash and I'm off like a shot. You can put a sign on the door for me. Gone fishing! Gone fishing with Nature Boy!"

"Maybe you could even persuade your new Polish friend to go with you, eh?" said Theo with a wink as Jay bounded to the door to take delivery of a small pile of post.

As his friend thanked the postie and brought the delivery over to the coffee table by the sofa, Theo automatically went and fetched the letter opener from the desk. It was one of Jay's Santa Sofia souvenirs, in fact – a splendid wooden dagger. It was maybe overkill for opening mail, but it did the trick with an added sense of cultural satisfaction.

The first few items of incoming mail were all too familiar to both of them. Bills that Theo didn't even bother to open and then the inevitable two fat envelopes from Switzerland containing ten copies of the Official Bulletin of the European Municipalist Federation. One was addressed to Wotton Infoshop and the other to Wotton Solidarity. They didn't always arrive in the same post, but in any case the response was always the same. Twenty new issues were placed, in one or two stages, on the magazine rack and twenty of the previous month's were dropped gently into the bin, unread and even unthumbed, except perhaps for the most cursory of glances from Jay or Theo.

It reminded Theo of when he used to work in the petrol station near his secondary school and the newspaper rack always featured *The Irish Weekly Herald*. Once upon a time there had been a lot of Irish people in that particular suburb, and the paper must have sold well. But they had all long since died or moved on – and the next generation of the families that stayed put had little interest in news of an ancestral homeland they only saw for the occasional holiday or family funeral. But nobody in charge seemed to have noticed this subtle social change and the *Heralds* kept arriving. One chap used to pop in from time to time to buy one, and stay for a little chat, and then even he stopped coming and they all went unsold.

The next envelope was a lot more promising, only because it was unfamiliar. A fairly heavy A4 package with a handwritten address. After a deft lateral swipe with the dagger, Theo pulled out the contents, while Jay sorted out the magazine rack which he had somehow knocked over in his haste to replenish the municipalist literature.

A note in biro. "URGENT! You must read this! This is dynamite! The people of Wotton are counting on you good people! Save our neighbourhood!"

Underneath was a stapled photocopied report which had evidently been produced by the borough council.

"What is it?" called Jay from across the shop.

"Green New Wotton — eco-trailblazers for a smart tomorrow!"

"Oh, wow! About time too! When you think about all that trouble we had a few years back just to get that cycle track put across the..."

"Shut up a minute, would you? I'm trying to read".

Theo was already frowning as he scanned the pages of the report and the furrow on his forehead only deepened the further he went. There was something here he didn't like at all. It was the way it was written, that smooth corporate language whose very oozing charm is a tell-tale sign that there is something particularly ugly to hide behind the verbiage.

"Fuck!" he said suddenly, and turned back and forth over the pages to make sure he was not mistaken.

"What?"

"They want to build a smart city. Here".

"Yeah?" Jay was back by his side on the sofa now, but having difficulty in grasping the reason for his friend's adverse reaction. "Whereabouts, exactly?"

"Here exactly!" said Theo. "I mean they're not spelling it out, but it has to be... look!"

He jabbed his finger at one paragraph "... ideally located to enjoy the benefits of contemporary urban diversity and well served by both

Wotton Grange and Wotton Park stations... blah blah... sub-standard housing and retail units unfit for purpose in the 2020s... waffle waffle... a major investment which will boost the local economy and the prosperity of the borough, the New Green Wotton Smart City development in partnership with Gaia Heaven, under the leadership of the visionary change-leader Howard Gear, will reset what is currently known as Little Wotton into something altogether Great!"

Jay looked at Theo blankly.

"You do get it, don't you Jay? They are going to demolish the whole of Little Wotton, including this place, my flat and yours, to make way for some fucking techno-capitalist glass and concrete nightmare, while pretending it's all about protecting the environment!"

Jay burst out laughing, wagging his finger at Theo.

"Oh no, no, no, my friend," he was saying. "Just hold your horses there. You're jumping to conclusions as ever. It doesn't actually say that, does it? And if something like that was going on we'd know about it by now, wouldn't we?"

Theo couldn't hide his frustration. "For fuck's sake, Jay! As of now we *do* know about it! This is the moment! This is *how* we are finding out about it! It's not gone public yet, but someone at the council, someone on our side, probably just a post room clerk or a cleaner, has slipped us an advance copy. A whistleblower. We've been tipped off by a whistleblower that they're going to raze the whole of our community to the ground for the sake of yet more fucking corporate profits!"

"Give us it here!" said Jay curtly and snatched the papers from Theo's hands. He fished his glasses out of a pocket, shuffled backwards into a comfortable position and very pointedly set about reading the whole document slowly through, making sure to start from the very beginning and to skip nothing. When he had finished, he read it all through again, not once turning in Theo's direction to meet his eye.

Only when he had put the papers down, removed his glasses and put them away again, did he actually speak.

"You're right," he said. "The utter fucking cunts. We've got to stop them, Thee. With everything we've got".

* * *

The first thing they had to do was to let people know what was happening. Theo and Jay activated all their contacts on all the networks they had been painstakingly building up over the years. There was massive interest, particularly from groups that they had tended to regard as peripheral to their political cause. The only real brush-off had come from a couple of local environmental groups which Theo and Jay normally considered their closest allies. These had obviously been influenced by the council's greenwashing of the smart city scheme. Kay from Thorbury Common Action! was a particular disappointment as she had a lot of clout in the area, though she did promise to look into the development plans in more detail.

There was a good response from the migrant communities, particularly from the Poles, thanks to the gusto with which Magda had thrown herself into organising. She had been liaising closely with Jay, to the extent of spending the whole night at his flat several times a week. Such dedication!

While social media and email lists obviously took centre stage in modern political organising, they didn't neglect old-fashioned face-to-face contact. They called in at all the shops, cafés, community centres, taxi firms and sundry places of worship in Little Wotton; they stopped more than ever to chat to people in the street; they held court at bus stops; they leafleted the local stations during the morning and evening rush hours and they held Saturday stalls in the High Street, setting up their table outside what had until recently been a branch of Barclays Bank.

It was principally thanks to this direct contact with the local population that Theo, Jay and

Magda quickly came to realise that there was overwhelming support for their campaign. It would be an exaggeration to claim that opinion was entirely unanimous regarding every detail of the proposed development, because real life is not like that. But it would be fair to say that nobody was impressed by the prospect of Little Wotton being demolished to make way for a Smart City.

Nobody they spoke to thought that a vast array of solar panels and 'replanting' at an unspecified distant site would in the least compensate for the loss of hundreds of trees that currently graced the area.

Nobody seemed in the least bit interested in the exciting new modern way of living in which 'Internet of things' sensors collected data on everything in your home and life and 'used these data to manage assets and resources in an efficient and planet-friendly manner'.

They did not embrace with enthusiasm the notion that 'today's enhanced reality' allowed individuals to 'combine biosecurity and responsible social distancing with full virtual connectivity'.

They did not seem convinced that 'predictive policing' would ensure a safer space for one and all, for some reason imagining that they might find themselves on the wrong end of this computerised approach to law and order.

People seemed to prefer the existing grass in

Victoria Park to the proposed greenery on the rooftops of the glass and steel Green New Wotton and were not over-enthused by the announced tramway line which would whizz residents back and forth to the well-paid jobs in the City which they seemed to be expected to have somehow landed by then.

In fact, many of them seemed to imagine that it was not only the Victorian bricks and mortar of Little Wotton which would be replaced, but also the population of which they currently formed part.

Where the development blurb talked about 'smart mobility in a smart economy, smart living and smart governance for the smart people of a smart tomorrow', they did not recognise themselves in this vision.

The notion that they and their families might soon be enjoying 'a high quality of life in a forward-looking framework of inclusive and sustainable economic development' seemed to many Little Wottoners to be a claim somewhat removed from the social reality they had so far endured.

Years of experience had taught Theo to be very wary of petitions. Politely asking those in power to change their ways was neither a realistic nor an empowering approach to a struggle, in addition to which people who had made the enormous effort of signing their name on a piece of paper often seemed to think that their duty to take action was thereby discharged, leaving them free to get on with their usual shopping or TV-watching with a clear conscience.

But those same years had also taught him that nothing draws a crowd of people to a stall like a petition to be signed, and everyone who queued up to add their name to the Save Our Wotton! plea to the council was, of course, also added to the campaign contact list. An impressive number also ticked the column saying they wanted to get actively involved. Quite a few had slipped them a donation for the good work they were doing.

The petition sheets were soon all over Little Wotton, everywhere from newsagents' to dentists' waiting rooms. And they were filling up with names.

Also very present were their posters advertising the campaign's launch meeting, which they had organised well in advance, so as to have plenty of time to raise interest. The money they were getting on the stalls meant they could afford to hire the biggest venue in the area, Carpenter Hall, which sat about 200 people.

Jay had been on more of a high than ever when he'd dashed into the Infoshop to tell Theo the hall had been successfully booked.

"They were great about it, Thee! Eric from the Committee has even changed the date of the history workshops so we can get in there a bit earlier to and set things up. We just need to get over to his place in Thorbury Common to pick up the key beforehand..."

Theo gave a wry smile and patted the collection of keys in his jeans pockets in a mysterious fashion.

"That wouldn't be strictly necessary, in fact!" he smiled.

Jay looked confused.

"Remember that Palestine solidarity evening we did there a few years ago? With the journalist from Gaza? I took the precaution of getting the key copied in case the Carpenter Committee came under some last-minute pressure from the local pro-Israel lobby..."

"Ah, you sly dog, Thee. But I can't see us having any problems with this one. Eric is planning to come along himself. And he wants some petition sheets for down his way. We can keep the key trick up our sleeves for another occasion".

On the back of all this momentum, the core group grew rapidly. Some of their fellow-campaigners they knew already, of course – Meera, Ralph, Jo, Dawn, Ella and Trevor. The latter had the great idea of buying a single share in Gaia Heaven, so they could keep an eye on what they were up to and have the right to attend their annual general meetings. Theo promptly did this.

Other allies in the struggle were new to them.

There was a young lad, Jack, who worked at the supermarket and said he'd moved into the area because he had such wonderful memories of spending the school holidays with his gran and grandad, who'd lived and died here. He wanted to fight for Little Wotton on their behalf and to keep his memory of them alive.

There were two friends, Nadia and Yana, who were already planning a big campaign HQ, where locals could come and drink tea, eat together, exchange info and plan their resistance. They had lots of mates with a squatting background and felt sure they could pull something together.

Theo could tell from Jay's expression as he listened to them at the stall that he had the same doubts as him about this. Squats always get evicted, particularly political squats, and they didn't want all their energy going into saving the "HQ" rather than saving Little Wotton. The squatting would come later, maybe, when the developers actually got round to trying to demolish houses, if they didn't manage to stop it before that.

There was also Bill, a cheery chappie in his 30s, who lived just outside the area but was keen to get involved in whatever way he could. As a self-employed carpenter, he was the proud owner of a van, which he said was at the disposition of the group, though for the moment at least Theo couldn't think what they would need it for.

After one pleasant evening of door-knocking on the Waverley Estate, Bill even offered to drop them all off on their doorsteps on his way home, which was good of him but entirely unnecessary. In any case, Theo, Jay and Magda were planning a few beers and a private chat at the Royal Oak.

There were quite a few people in the pub, even more in the smoking area out the back. It had stayed much the same over the years, this place, apart from the arrival of three big-screen TVs silently broadcasting 24-hour news with laughably inaccurate automated subtitles. As he stood at the bar, Theo was intrigued to hear that the Foreign Secretary had been "caught off his God" by a diplomatic incident in Paris.

"Cheers!" he said when he had joined the others in a little corner and was able to take a healthy gulp of a much-needed pint. "Here's to the campaign!" added Jay. "Na zdrowie!" said Magda, clinking glasses with the others. "Here is to the health of Little Wotton and its amazing people!"

"It's going pretty bloody well, isn't it, Thee?" said Jay, leaning back in satisfaction. Because he worked evenings, he had seen less of the doorstep reaction than the others and was highly encouraged by what he had encountered. "Pretty much everybody seems to be with us on this!"

Theo immediately found himself correcting for his friend's attitude.

"It's going OK, but it's just the start. We've got a fuck of a lot of work to do from here".

Jay laughed at this familiar note of caution. "Yeah, but still. We couldn't have hoped for much better, could we?"

Theo had to agree, despite his fear of jinxing the campaign with over-confidence.

"There's just one thing I'm not happy about," he said. "I don't think we know enough about the developers. People keep asking me who these Gaia Heaven people are, and I don't have a proper answer".

"Oh no, Thee..." objected Magda. She was now the third person in the world to address him as such. "You answered the question very well when we spoke to that man with the funny red face. You explained about the company, you said the name of the boss, this fucking Howard Gear..."

"Ah," said Jay, ever keen to help her fine-tune her English. "There we would place the expletive in between the two parts of his name... Howard fucking Gear!"

"Howard fucking Gear," repeated Magda. "Magda fucking Kowalska. Jay fucking Mukherjee..."

"... and Theo fucking Carter. You've mastered it. But anyway, yes, Thee, I agree with Magda that we have enough info for people to be getting on with. We can tell them about that hideous Gaia Heaven project in Arizona, the links to that Green Globe Finance Initiative, Gear's past involvement with that vivisection lab in Canada... what else is there?"

"Well, that's just it, Jay, I don't know what else there is or even where to look for it. I have a feeling there might be something more but with everything we're taking on I haven't got the time to look properly. It's bothering me that we're missing something big".

After a while, Jay and Magda went to the bar together to get the next round, because they were now a couple and that was the sort of thing that couples did. Before the novelty wore off, anyway.

Theo was left staring at the subtitled news. It was a minor politician addressing a press conference. "I have to report that, Sally, an agreement has not been reached..."

What? Who was Sally and why was his press conference directed uniquely at this particular woman? It took him a moment to adjust his brain and substitute the word "sadly". Sloppy pronunciation there, Mr Politician. Please speak more clearly so that the computer can understand you.

For some reason, the name Sally kept turning around in his mind, like a leaf caught in an eddy of water in a gutter.

But why? Sally... Sally... Of course! Sally Shukra! The source of all information on the "sustainable" capitalist mafia! She was bound to have loads of dirt on Green Globe, Gaia Heaven and Howard fucking Gear.

Theo reached the bar just in time to cancel his order and explained why to the others.

"Oh, come on Thee. It can wait till the morning. She's hardly going to be answering emails at this time of night, is she?"

"She lives in Chiapas," said Theo. "So this should be pretty much the ideal time to catch her".

In the event Theo didn't even want to wait for Sally Shukra to check her emails but direct messaged her on social media, where she seemed to maintain a steady presence.

After he'd sent the question, he put the kettle on and busied himself around the Infoshop, tidying up odd bits and pieces that had been left lying around.

It was always peculiar being here in the middle of the night, on those rare opportunities where he needed to urgently access the internet.

Theo was a smartphone refusenik and had, for the last couple of years, abandoned his previous habit of using a laptop which he ferried between here and home. He spent enough time online while he was staffing this place, without carrying the work on in into the evening – or finding himself wasting hours wallowing in the nostalgia of old TV series. Evenings at his place were about listening to music, strumming the guitar and reading novels which were intelligent enough to keep him interested and engaging enough to keep him awake.

After ten minutes he checked to see if Sally had replied. She hadn't. Ten minutes later, his tea finished, he looked again but there was still nothing.

He sighed, washed up his mug, switched off the main light and sat down by the window to watch Kelmscott Road after midnight.

A thin, stooped character in a long raincoat scuttled past the Infoshop, staring intently down at the pavement five feet ahead of him and not noticing Theo looking out.

An oversized fellow in a baseball cap painfully walked his small nondescript dog along the other side of the road. Or maybe the dog was walking *him* instead, faithfully ensuring that he occasionally shifted himself off the sofa and into the "fresh" air, if such a thing could be said to exist in this city. It was not clear if the man was waiting at every lamppost for the dog to perform his ritual or if the dog was merely passing the time while his companion recovered from the effort of walking another 20 yards.

Now the dog was squatting and delivering a more solid tribute right in the middle of the pavement. His owner looked furtively around to make sure nobody had seen. He obviously had no intention of scooping the poop and, indeed, was possibly physically incapable of doing so. As he scanned the surrounds he suddenly did a double take and stared uncomfortably at a green 4x4 parked outside the newsagents. Theo followed his gaze and saw that there were two figures sitting in the front. They looked as if they were eating something and plainly had no interest in the dog's doings, and the guilty owner continued on his way, somehow managing to find a lurching burst of speed until he had passed the car, at which point he reverted to his usual shambling pace. The dog rushed to join him, tail-a-wagging, clearly excited by this evidence of unsuspected reserves of energy in his human sidekick.

Theo wandered back to the computer and checked for a third time. Now there was a reply.

"Hi. It's pretty well hidden from view, but Gaia Heaven is basically SLI".

Theo couldn't help gasping out loud. SLI. Schlueger Lorenz Industries. Could this be true?

He'd read so much about them over the years that they had become, in his mind, almost a byword for evil, a global mafia with a toxic finger in every part of the world.

And they were behind this development? He

would have to check that Sally was right, of course, find the proof, then research all the dirt on SLI from over the years... His mind began to race. He couldn't imagine he would be sleeping much tonight.

He was just about to thank Sally for her info when her messages started flooding in.

This is what she had been doing while he had been waiting impatiently for her to reply – providing him, on a plate, with all the research he was mentally preparing to carry out on his own.

There were links showing how Gaia Heaven was connected to SLI and what tied them both of them in to Green Globe. There were biographical details of leading players including, he noted, Howard fucking Gear.

Sally had sent links to news stories on SLI projects and controversies in South America, Indonesia, Africa, Australia, Canada, Italy, China and Turkey.

He couldn't hope to keep up with the flow as she sent the info across and he just got a general impression of the contents from the headlines as they came in. He barely had time to copy and paste the URLs on to a text file. From time to time he clicked on something that had caught his attention but didn't even try to read anything properly.

Sally was on to the historical stuff now,

working backwards into the past. SLI and vaccine scandals; SLI and the cover-up over toxic nerve agents that had killed 180 US soldiers in an experiment that went wrong; SLI and agribusiness; SLI paying politicians to ensure big defence contracts went their way; SLI's alleged role in CIA 'drugs for guns' deals in Central America; SLI and its links to anti-Communist terror cells during the Cold War; SLI re-establishing itself in the US after World War Two; SLI apologising for its role in the Hitler regime; SLI's close connections with the inner echelons of the Nazi Party...

Finally here was Sally: "There you go, @WottonSol – hope this of use and good luck in your struggle!"

"Thank you so much, Sally," he replied. "This is totally excellent. Just what we needed! We are so grateful!"

He copied over the last few links on to the "Gaia Heaven" text file and saved it on to a memory stick for back-up. With all that information to hand, he could safely go home to bed and get stuck into sifting through it all tomorrow morning. The anxious feeling of an urgent need to research had been replaced by the warm satisfaction of knowing that the job was already more than half done.

He was just on the point of closing down the computer and locking up when he saw that a new message had come through from Sally.

"Oh and @WottonSol" it said. "Be careful how you go. We are dealing with some VERY dangerous people".

The parting thought meant it took half a bottle of Theo's emergency rum to get to him to sleep that night.

* * *

There was a difference of views as to what to do with the exposé of Gaia Heaven and SLI once Theo had finished writing it up.

Jay was all for presenting it to an unsuspecting world at the meeting at Carpenter Hall.

"Think of the impact, Thee!" he enthused. "You'll bloody blow them away!"

But, as Magda had pointed out, this would completely undermine the purpose of the event, which was to set in motion the practical organising that would be needed to take on the scheme.

It would make more sense, she said – and Jay was forced to agree in the end – to make a big splash with the revelations in the run-up to the evening and then to simply have photocopies of the report available for people to take home and read at their leisure. They really didn't want to get dragged into discussing the detail during precious organising time.

The report, "Exposed: Wotton developers' links to Nazis, CIA and terrorism", went up on all their various sites, blogs and pages and was reposted left and right by a dozen of their contacts. Sally Shukra, who was obviously credited with the research, shared it widely and it got online attention from New York to New Zealand.

All this was great but what Theo and Jay wanted most of all was a write-up in *The Tuesley Advertiser*. The coverage of their campaigns and initiatives in the "local rag" had fluctuated bizarrely over the years. To start with it had been impossible to get anything in there at all. Theo had imagined the editor to be an authoritarian right-wing character from a bygone era, probably a Freemason and a golfing chum of the good and great of the local business community. But then they had experienced a break-though moment with their campaign to clean up Victoria Park, which the *Advertiser* had adopted as a cause close to its heart. After that, reporters had started ringing them up on a regular basis for quotes on this and that and even turned up at events and wrote up a few paragraphs for the paper.

Gradually, however, they stopped coming. They always seemed to be so short-staffed that they barely left the newspaper office. Press releases from the council started going in the paper without any balancing comments from "opponents" such as Wotton Solidarity. When Theo cottoned on to this, he started sending them ready-made articles, imitating their own leaden and clichéd writing style, which for a golden period always made their way straight on to the pages of the *Advertiser*, unmarked by any unwelcome comments or contradictions from whomever it was they were criticising.

Inevitably that stopped. Someone high up must have put an end to it – or their secret friend inside the paper had moved on. After that, for the last couple of years, it had proved virtually impossible to get anything in there at all. Usually this didn't particularly matter any more, with the coinciding fall in *Advertiser* sales and the rise of social media. But on this occasion, for this particular campaign, Theo and Jay would have loved to have seen a mention and they made a particular effort in penning a version of their report which they thought stood a chance of making it into print.

Braced though they were for failure, they were not prepared for the article which actually appeared in *The Tuesley Advertiser* the day before the meeting.

"Fake news hits borough" was the page three headline. "Conspiracy theorists inciting fear warns councillor", the sub-heading added.

The gist of the piece was that 'extremists' were busily 'terrorising' the Wotton public with alarmist smearmongering conspiracy theories about developers working with the borough council on the innovative and ground-breaking New Green Wotton project. These 'sinister anti-green reactionaries' were peddling 'climate denial' and using 'hate speech' about American developers to 'whip up fears' among residents.

"Fuck me," said Jay when he had read it. "That is the biggest pile of shit I have ever had the misfortune to see in print".

Theo could only look at him blankly and shake his head in despair.

He scanned down the columns again. "Not even a mention of the meeting," he said. "The bastards".

Jay grabbed the paper back from him.

"Do you even think they wrote it themselves?" he asked. "I mean this all just looks so slick, so..."

Theo was nodding. "So familiar," he said. "It's that same style you see every time they're out to smear someone. Smug, superior, full of those little insinuations that they never actually spell out..."

"Because they're not true..."

"They're not true, but somehow you accept there must be some fire behind the smoke. Once they've got the idea planted in your head, it stays there".

* * *

If there was one head where the article's insinuations remained planted more firmly than elsewhere, it was Theo's. He had set off for a long walk to try and think straight, but as he did a tour of Victoria Park and headed down the little terraced streets behind the old post office depot, the hoped-for clarity refused to materialise. Instead, his mind was filled with a swirling fog of confusion, indignation and...

Theo was having difficulty in putting his finger on another emotion that was adding to the heavy mix when he suddenly became aware of the way he was walking. He was slouched, hands in pockets, head turned down towards the pavement, eyes safely averted from any chance encounter with another human being. He immediately pulled himself up straight and lifted his gaze. Shame! That was what it was! He was feeling ashamed at how his campaign had been depicted by the newspaper, ashamed that people in the street might believe that he was "anti-green" or xenophobic in some way. But why? Why would he care less about the smears being dished out by the mouthpiece of his political opponents?

The truth of this matter went, in fact, all the way back to Theo's childhood, although he himself was not aware of this – indeed, his lack of awareness of this dimension of his make-up was part and parcel of the problem.

Theo had never known his father and his mother had never given any indication of who he might have been, shaking off any juvenile inquiries by insisting that he knew full well he hadn't got a dad and could he please just finish clearing the table so she could get on with her packing work.

Theo had found out, through his mum's Uncle Reg, that the mystery man had been paying maintenance for his upkeep throughout his childhood and old Reg had once even provided a name, 'John Kidder', only to claim a few years later that the man had been called 'Nick Osman' and then, just before he passed away in a home for Alzeimer's sufferers, he remembered that it was in fact 'George Hood'. None of this was of much help.

When his mum had died, five years back, Theo had expected to find physical proof of the man's identity among the boxes of papers which filled what had been his bedroom in her council flat, but she had ruthlessly thrown out anything relating to him and his searching had led nowhere. The only clue was an envelope of souvenirs – bus tickets, postcards, a town plan, a duplicated itinerary – from a church youth club visit to the Peak District, near somewhere called the Green Chapel appropriately enough, nine months before Theo was born.

But the absence of an identifiable father had

not, in truth, caused Theo any psychological problems. The state of affairs seemed quite normal to him and when he heard tales from other boys of their own fathers and the misery they inflicted on their families, he felt privileged, honoured by fate, to have escaped any such patriarchal hell. It had never even struck him that his mother might one day present him with a stepdad, a surrogate father. She was always too busy for that sort of thing, never showed the slightest interest as far as he knew.

The real problem arose from the very low income on which he and his mother were obliged to live. The daughter of a Geordie dock worker who had moved down to London to seek work in the 1930s, Maria was a proud woman who refused take advantage of the social security on offer in late 20th century Britain. She insisted on paying her own way, taking on piecemeal packing work which she could do in the evenings, when young Theo was tucked up in bed and, later, supplementing this by working as a waitress in an old-fashioned café next to the tube station.

She made do, but only just. Theo's clothes were either hand-made or hand-me-downs, invariably hand-repaired, patched and adjusted. She always made sure she bought him shoes that were made to last, in a size too large so that he could grow into them. She cut his hair herself, as she did her own, in fact. Their meals were healthy and simple. Nothing pre-cooked or fancy. Maria instilled in her only child a moral obligation to make the most of what they had and to waste nothing.

This presented no issues for Theo until he was 11 years old. The boys and girls on the estate, the ones he played with in the park under the railway bridge, and those he went to primary school with, all came from similar, if not identical circumstances. He fitted in.

The trouble came when he passed his 11-plus exam and was allocated a place not at the local Dunbridge Secondary Modern, where nearly everyone else he knew would be continuing their education, but at the Florian Grammar School for Boys, which was a half-hour bus ride away from home in what was, for Theo, unknown territory.

Maria had been delighted with this academic success, of course, but her face had turned a shade paler than usual when she learned of the cost of equipping her son appropriately for his step up the social ladder. A yellow-and-purple-striped blazer, with school badge to be sewn on; grey trousers; white shirts; a matching school tie; PE shorts and singlet in house colours; officially-approved plimsolls; rugby shirt, shorts, boots and socks... even without the optional extras of school scarf and house tie, this was going to make a major hole in the Carter household's finances.

This social mismatch affected Theo directly at his new school. While everyone may have been equipped with the same uniform, differences in wealth always find a way of showing themselves. For Theo, the immediate concern was his school bag. All the other boys seemed to have brand new, very fashionable sports-type bags, mainly with Adidas or Puma branding all over them. He turned up with an old-fashioned brown briefcase which his mother had been very proud to have picked up for a reasonable price from a little second-hand shop near London Bridge. It was well-made, of good quality leather, and with any luck, she had reckoned, it would see him through the entirety of his days at Florian Grammar.

It broke his heart now, when he remembered how, scarcely three weeks after the start of his first term, he had begged his mum to buy him an Adidas bag like all the other boys had. That must have hurt her so much, must have somehow symbolised for her a rejection not just of the briefcase she had so carefully chosen and bought for him, but of the personal ethics that lay behind it. He was spurning common sense, frugality, long-term thinking, a sense of quality, in favour of the shallowest form of consumer-cowardice, a peer-group induced craving for the branded baubles of corporate conformism.

Theo could still recall with total clarity the strained, tight, expression on her face as she looked up from the sewing machine on the kitchen table and told him that she could not afford to buy him a second school bag and that, even if she could, there was no way she was ever going to buy that sort of plasticky rubbish.

He remembered throwing the little briefcase towards the sink with a gesture of despair and disgust and how, to his horror, it had sent two dinner plates crashing and shattering on to the lino. He remembered his mother holding on to him with her hands on both his upper arms, gripping him tightly and looking at him with an expression which, as he had even realised at the time, combined anger with hopeless dismay at what he seemed to have turned into.

And then he had told her. He had told her about the sneering comments from the other boys. The comments that had turned into kicks, the teasing that had turned into bullying. He told her, hot tears filling his eyes, how, every morning before the teacher arrived, somebody would steal his briefcase, pass it around his classmates as he scurried to retrieve it. They would stuff it in someone's desk, hide it inside someone's bigger bag, throw it up on to the top of the cupboard behind the teacher's desk, from where he would have to retrieve it with the hook-equipped wooden pole used to open the top windows. Invariably it would be covered with dust, or with chalk because one of his tormenters had used it to wipe the blackboard, or with mud because the game had ended with somebody throwing the bag out of the first-floor window on to the edge of the playing fields below, to great cheers from, it had to be said, everybody in the class apart from Theo. And then he would have to retrieve the bag from wherever it had ended up and skulk away to the art room, if it was empty, or to the toilets, and wash off the dust or chalk or mud under the taps and dry it on the big roller towels.

All of this he did surreptitiously, because he didn't want anyone to see, because he was ashamed of who he was and what was happening to him, ashamed of the weakness that had made this possible and which prevented him from being able to bring it to an end. When he got back to the classroom and the teacher was already there, he never explained what he was doing, where he had been, but accepted the admonition for being late, yet again, and the detention that went with it. And then the detention added another layer to the torment, because he couldn't let his mum know he had been in trouble, because that would be letting her down, so he had to make up excuses about missing the bus or going to the shops with a friend in order to cover up his lateness in getting home. This made him feel worse than before. Even more ashamed of himself.

And as Theo told his mum all of this, through his tears, he saw that she too was crying and her gripping of his arms turned into an embrace, a hug, as her motherly love shared and absorbed his pain.

She bought him the Adidas bag, of course. And another one, two years later, because it had fallen apart already and its shiny whiteness had quickly turned to cracked grey.

But Theo's problems had not ended there, even if the bag-related bullying came to an end and his victim status faded into more of a general, dull, anonymity.

There remained a social gulf separating him from his classmates, who all seemed to come from either well-off families, or fairly comfortable families, or from hard-up families who were prepared to spend what little money they had on creating the impression of wealth. Their whole way of existing was alien to Theo, their sense of complacent well-being in the world, their confidence in themselves and their future. They seemed to always have money to spend, on new digital watches, or trainers, or records. They *had* to be seen to have money to spend, in fact. Their self-image depended on it.

The issue of records complicated this story a little, because in truth there was more to Theo's dislocation from his contemporaries than his mother's lack of financial resources. Theo liked to tell himself, looking back, that he had never had enough money to buy records. But if he had really been motivated, he could probably have found a way to get hold of some. He could have done a paper round when he was younger. Later on, he could have used some of the money he earned working at the garage, instead of saving it all up for the dream of "travelling". He could have borrowed other people's records. Hung around record shops. Listening to the radio would have been a start. But he didn't, because he couldn't be bothered. That world – of singles and albums and charts – just did not interest him.

The problem was that it *did* interest the other boys, with an increasing obsessiveness. By the time Theo started his third year at the school, it was all anybody seemed to talk about, in fact. There was no way Theo could join in these conversations, because he had literally no idea what they were on about. He started to feel like a dumbstruck social leper.

It was here that Theo developed the self-defence mechanism, the persona, that was to stand him in good stead for decades to come. He started to formulate his social exclusion in more positive terms by actively rejecting the world from which he was shut out. He was a teenager, so this formulation was initially very clumsy, even though the vague outlines of the man he was to become can clearly be seen emerging through the confused mists of adolescence.

"It's all fake anyway," he announced suddenly one Wednesday morning in December when a group of classmates were speculating as to what would be the Christmas Number One.

They all turned around and gawped at him in surprise. He hadn't hitherto been part of their conversation.

"What's fake?" asked Roberts, a rat-faced little lad.

"The charts," announced Theo as nonchalantly as he could. "Apparently, it's all made up. Nobody really knows how many records are being sold. The industry just invents it. Men in suits taking us all for a ride".

"How do you know that, Carter?" asked Hutton, a tall, rather gentle-looking boy whose face betrayed genuine alarm at this revelation.

"He doesn't know anything," muttered Roberts. "He's talking bollocks!"

The rest of them looked at Theo with expectancy. He realised this was going to be a pivotal moment. This would have to be good.

"Inside information," he replied as smoothly as he could and, pre-empting the objection which he could already see poised on the tip of Roberts' tongue, he continued: "Look, I shouldn't really be telling you this, but my half-sister is going out with someone very high up in the record industry. He let the cat out of the bag a couple of weeks ago and she told me, only I wasn't supposed to tell anyone else..."

The other boys' jaws dropped in astonishment. They had fallen for it. This was partly because they were only 14 years old, quite innocent and closeted, and would never have imagined that somebody their own age could have lied to them quite so outrageously. But it was also perhaps because, deep down, they knew there was a fundamental truth in this account. The "charts" *were* all for show. It *was* really all just about money. This was what Theo told himself afterwards, as well. This was only *technically* a lie. OK, he didn't even have a half-sister, let alone one with access to the secrets of the music business, but he felt confident that if he had, and she did, this *would* have been what she would have reported.

From this point on, Theo managed to convert his social and cultural apartness from handicap into trump card. He was the class cynic, the cool outsider, the rebel who had seen through it all at a precociously early age. Increasingly, this posture took on a political tinge. Theo was the anti-establishment one, the dissenting one. He was a fierce critic of authority, of advertising, of road building. He spoke out against jingoism, racism and Apartheid. He was known for hating the Tories, the fascists, the army. His left-wing politics became not only the characteristic by which he was known by his schoolmates, but the characteristic by which he knew himself. His whole sense of self-identity was founded on this.

Theo had become used, over the years, to being called a "leftie", a "red", a "hippy" or a "commie". He had become used to being told to "get a job", "get a haircut" or "go back to Russia", even though he had a job, had just been to the barber's and came from London. He could cope with all that because it came with the territory. These insults, this hatred from his political enemies, merely confirmed and strengthened his left-wing identity.

But when *The Tuesley Advertiser* suggested that his campaign group was xenophobic and anti-environmentalist, Theo was deeply wounded. This was an attack on his whole sense of who he was. The image and self-image with which had been protecting himself since his schooldays had to remain intact, otherwise he would be inundated with all the repressed pain and shame of being a weak and useless nobody.

* * *

"Sleep well?" asked Jay jauntily when Theo turned up at the Infoshop the next morning, take-away cappuccino in hand, as ever.

"Yeah, not bad," he replied, although this

wasn't true. He didn't want to infect anyone else with his malaise.

"How about you, Jay?" he asked in return as he sat down, knowing that the answer would be positive.

His friend looked enraptured to be stapling together an umpteenth copy of the Gaia Heaven exposé for that evening's big meeting. He was always so bloody cheerful, this man! He beamed well-being from the core of his self, under all circumstances. Theo had asked him once how he managed it, not without a trace of envy. Jay had put it down to his family. He had grown up in a loving household, surrounded by brothers and sisters, with cousins living next door and grandparents just down the road. He had all the deep-seated security that Theo lacked. The only problem these days was that his family was dispersed all over the place. He certainly longed to be closer to Isha and young Azad, but even this absence was put to good use, thanks to the magic of Jay's underlying good humour. The idea of his move to Santa Sofia had become a comforting source of strength and inspiration through the trials and tribulations of everyday life in the UK.

"Like a log!" Jay replied to Theo's question, with predictable positivity.

"A snoring fucking log!" added Magda as she stood up from behind the photocopier, where she had been sorting out the latest paper-jam.

Jay smiled at her with such affection that you would have imagined she had just flattered or praised him in the most tender of terms.

The worries of the night began to fade away for Theo as he slipped back into his daily routine in the presence of his friends and comrades. They had built up a real momentum for tonight's campaign launch and, as he scanned through social media and email accounts, Theo could see no sign that the *Advertiser's* poison had done anything to slow it down.

His heart briefly skipped a beat when he saw there was a message from Kay of Thorbury Common Action! She was already hesitating about supporting their efforts – could it be that the newspaper report was the final straw?

"Hi guys," she had written. "Just wanted to let you know that that filthy local rag's attempts to drag you into the mud have totally backfired on them as far as I am concerned. Their story finally made me read all your stuff properly and I am 100% on board, so are Jeff and Lisa. We are going to have a quick committee meeting just before yours, so we should be able to announce publicly tonight that TCA! is adding its weight to the campaign, if that is OK with you. See you later, in solidarity, K".

A great warmth seemed to flow through Theo's entire body as he leaned back in his chair and savoured the prospect of sharing the news with the others. Things were going to be all right after all.

* * *

There was lots of stuff to take over to Carpenter Hall, not least a huge Save Our Wotton! banner which Magda and her friend Lena had been working on all week, and on which the paint had only just dried in time. Around the bottom of the lettering was a depiction of the neighbourhood, with its trees, terraced houses and little shops, plus a diversity of residents. Above, in the sky, lurked a huge bulldozer with the initials TBC and GH on the side, its massive blade raised and poised to crush all that pretty local life into nothingness.

There was also the Infoshop projector and screen, for a slide show of historic scenes of Little Wotton for people to digest while they were waiting for the meeting proper to get underway.

What with the boxes of leaflets and posters as well, this had seemed like a good moment to take advantage of Bill's van and he duly pulled up in the street late in the afternoon, leaving plenty of time to load up, get the key from Eric at Thorbury Common and then go on to Carpenter Hall to set up.

"Should be a good turn-out tonight, eh?" said Bill, as he helped them slide the banner on to the shelving in his van, which was emblazoned with the name of his firm, Croon Carpentry. He had evidently taken out all his work gear and given the vehicle a good clean-out for their sake. "How many are we expecting?"

"221!" replied Jay instantly. "200 seated and 21 standing at the back!"

"Hope people don't get put off by that stupid article. Some idiots swallow any old crap they read in the papers. My Melinda for a start!"

Theo shook his head. "I don't think so, Bill. We may lose one or two, I suppose, but we'll pick up some us well; people with minds of their own who don't like being made fools of, which is just the type we need".

Bill chuckled. "Yeah, we'll need them for the next phase, that's for sure. For the action. What do you think it's going to be, lads? A demo? Picket? A bit of nocturnal naughtiness?"

"I am hoping for some of the latter," said Jay with a sidelong grin at Magda, "though I'm not sure it will officially be part of the campaign!"

She kicked him in the shin, which made him smile even more.

"Ha, ha," said Bill. "But seriously, how do you see it shaping up after tonight?"

Theo abandoned his heroic attempt to pick up two boxes of leaflets at once and contented himself with taking just the one.

"Who knows?" he said. "That's the beauty of

democracy. We'll see who comes along and what they're up for and take it from there. Ask me again in five hours' time!"

Jay's phone rang and he answered it.

"Hi Eric!" he said brightly, "How's things? We're just on our way over, actually, we... Oh".

A dark cloud passed over his face.

Theo felt the blood drain from his head.

"What is it?" he whispered, but Jay was listening and just waved him away.

"Listen Eric," he said, after a while, "I think it would be a good idea if you could have a word with Theo, who's with me here".

He looked at Theo with an expression that did nothing to relieve the tension and handed him his phone.

"Hello Eric," said Theo. "What's happening?".

What was happening was that Eric was cancelling the meeting.

"I am so sorry Theo," said the chairman of the Carpenter Hall committee. "This is totally out of my hands now. You know that I'm very much behind the campaign and have no truck with any of that nonsense in the *Advertiser*. But we've had threats, which means that I have to go to the police and when I go to the police I have to tell the Board in Manchester, they have to tell the insurance company and so on. We can't expose Carpenter Hall to this sort of danger. Or the neighbours for that matter. We'd be responsible if anyone came to any harm!"

"No you wouldn't, Eric," said Theo calmly. "The people who caused any damage, or hurt anyone, would be responsible for their own actions. It's as simple as that. Victims are not responsible for coming under attack!"

"Oh, Theo," said Eric with genuine distress in his voice. "It's not as easy as that. We know in advance, you see. We have had the chance to take evasive action. We have a duty of care to the public and..."

"Don't give me that, please!" retorted Theo, less calm now. "Wouldn't you say that you have a duty of care to the public not to let their town be knocked down by a bunch of rapacious capitalist sharks?"

"Look, I really am sorry Theo, I..."

"OK, I get it. Thanks for phoning, Eric. We'll sort something out. Bye".

Theo rang off and gave the phone back to Jay.

"Fuck!" he shouted. "Fuck! Fuck! Fuck!"

The others were standing and looking at him with alarm. He filled them in with what little detail they hadn't already gathered. This was ridiculous, he said. Was it really that easy to stop a public meeting? Anonymous phone calls from what was probably a non-existent group threatening to stop the 'reactionary' meeting by any means possible, accusing the Carpenter Hall of hosting 'hate speech'. They hadn't even had to turn up!

Jay was looking at him with a strange glint in his eye.

"So no key for us then, Thee?" he said in a rather expressionless way.

"No," said Theo, tacitly endorsing Jay's implication that there were some things better left unshared with others.

"But you know," he said. "I think we should take the stuff down there anyway. We can have the meeting outside. On the steps and on the pavement".

"I heard it might rain," said Bill. "And I don't think there's room for 221 people in front of the door".

But Theo was adamant, Jay obviously agreed and Magda supported her friends, so the decision was made to go down to the hall, pretty much at the last minute so as not to alert anyone, and set up in the open air.

Bill popped off down the High Street on foot for an impromptu visit to the bookie's, Magda put the kettle on for some tea and Theo and Jay went for a walk round the park to discuss how they were going to handle all this.

In truth, Theo came into his own at moments like this. He was always in a state of mental vigilance and this was one of those rare occasions when this was totally appropriate. All the tension and energy which caused so much anxiety and inner turmoil when trapped inside him was channelled directly into action and thus transformed into something positive and enabling.

Because of this, he radiated good energy as the early arrivals started turning up outside Carpenter Hall. He wasn't calm in the usual way, that was sure. These were strange circumstances that were pushing their carefully-constructed local campaign on to a new level. He knew full well that what they were about to do would mean the end of any kind of relationship with Eric and the possibility of using this place again. But he also knew that the issue at stake was important enough to merit the sacrifice. What was the point of theoretically having access to a venue, anyway, if the rug was liable to be pulled out from under your feet at the first whiff of controversy? Theo knew he was doing what had to be done and, accordingly, he was calm in a different way, in an enhanced and transported way. He was tingling with the electricity of defiance and revolt and this communicated itself, even physically, to everyone who came up to shake his hand. The bad news about the hall became good news about the fact that they were carrying on regardless.

A quarter of an hour before the meeting was about to start, Jay sidled up to him and tugged at the sleeve of his jacket.

"Don't look now, Thee, but our friend Eric is over the road, checking us out".

After a moment or two, Theo stole a surreptitious peek. Yes, there he was, pulled up at the bus stop, staring over at them and talking on his phone. Nobody else seemed to have noticed him, fortunately.

Theo turned to chat to Trevor, who had just turned up with a magnificent placard showing a capitalist 'bankster' trampling all over Little Wotton, but was interrupted by the furious honking of a horn. The number 333 to Tooting Broadway had just arrived and Theo looked round to see Eric's Volvo hastily pulling out of the lay-by in which he had been illicitly parked.

Jay had noticed as well and they exchanged a meaningful glance. This was the ideal moment to spring the next stage of the plan.

Theo couldn't help smiling to himself as Jay started frantically patting the outside of his trouser and jacket pockets, as if his phone had started ringing and he couldn't remember exactly where it was. He was a born actor, that man. He eventually fished it out and moved, head down, away from the growing crowd of protesters, as if to seek out a quiet space for an important conversation. He nodded, spoke, nodded again, smiled, put his phone away and strode over to Theo, announcing in a voice loud enough for everyone to hear: "It was Eric! They've changed their mind! We can have the hall!"

A little cheer and a patter of applause went round the group.

"Fantastic!" said Theo. "So we need to go and get the key?"

Bill stepped forward. He looked a little flustered, for some reason. "We can go in the van, if you like?" he volunteered.

"No, no," said Jay. "It's fine. He's going to bring it down himself straight away. I'm meeting him round the corner, in the car park behind the shops".

He started heading off, then turned to add with a mischievous smile: "I said he could just pull in at the bus stop, but he wasn't having any of it. Said it was against the law and he could get in trouble from his insurance people!"

Now there was a real buzz about the evening. The hall denied, the cancellation defied and the cancellation apparently cancelled had made the atmosphere much more lively and optimistic than would have been the case if none of this had happened.

When Jay returned, at a trot, bearing aloft the key that Theo had given him earlier, there was a rousing cheer and soon everyone was at work getting out the chairs and decorating the platform ready for the start.

In the meantime, the public were flooding in. It didn't take long for all the seats to be taken and people started perching on the stacks of little tables around the edge of the hall.

A dozen young people, carrying some sort of rolled banner, made their way to the very front and sat down, cross-legged, on the floor beneath the platform. Theo tried to work out who they were. They were obviously from some kind of campaign group – an environmental one judging by the look of them – but he didn't recognise any of them.

People were still coming in to the hall, although they were clumping around the door and making it difficult for others to join them. Theo looked around with what almost amounted to satisfaction, except for the fact that the uncertain circumstances of their use of the hall would not allow the slightest hint of complacency. Everyone he had expected to be there seemed to have come: there were people from the estates and people from the posher end; people from the Bangladeshi, Polish and Somali communities; there were politically-minded people he recognised from various left-wing events around this part of town and others who were simply familiar faces from his daily routine. Right at the back, sitting by herself on a radiator near the door, rucksack and violin case propped up beside her, was even the little red-headed girl from round the corner, who shone out such vital radiance. Theo himself had handed her a leaflet a few days back, so he was particularly pleased to see she had made it.

He exchanged a few words with Jay and Magda and they decided to start the meeting. Eric would no doubt be back at some point and the further they could advance before then, the better.

Theo spoke first, outlining the plans for the smart city and, briefly, the unwholesome big business interests behind it. Magda, Trevor and Dawn were already handing round copies of the report he had written up from Sally Shukra's research.

Then he handed over to Jay, who explained the need for powerful community action to challenge the project, which was coming from a place of combined state and private power ("They're the same thing anyway, these days!" objected a voice from the serried ranks) and was not going to be easily halted.

He explained that those who had called the meeting in no way wanted to form a rigid, centralised organisation that would make decisions and tell people how to resist. That way nothing would ever get done and everyone's outrage would be thwarted and diverted into petty internal disagreements.

Instead they proposed that today they formed an umbrella group called "Save Our Wotton!" and agreed a simple set of guidelines excluding any kind of racist or discriminatory language and, also, any possibility of collaborating with the authorities. This group would simply be used as a flag of convenience, but the actual campaigning work would come from the bottom up.

"I know a lot of people don't like working in groups, and that's just fine. Individuals can be part of Save Our Wotton! and do their own thing their own way, if they want, as long as they don't break the guidelines. Personally, I find that campaigning is a lot easier, a lot more efficient and a lot more fun if you do it with other people, so what we really suggest is that you get together with others – people you know, who live in the same area, have the same interests or whatever – and form your own action groups to spread the word and mobilise people in the way that suits you best.

"We haven't got all the time in the world to fight this, the wheels are already turning, and we need to transform all the anger we are feeling into action. The best way to do that is for you all to get on with it, full throttle, without waiting for me or some stupid steering committee to give you permission! And there is no need to depend on us or anyone else to distribute information. Do it amongst yourselves, in every way you can. You're going to use social media, of course, but not just that. We all live in the same place. We can talk to each other, put up posters, leave leaflets – that is something we can provide for you, if you want – and basically become a many-headed hydra that our enemies, that is to say the people behind this horrific scheme, will never be able to stop!"

All of this went down well, with a few inevitable quibbles, and the broad plan for Save Our Wotton!, henceforth to be known as SOW!, was approved with a near-unanimous show of hands. Jay looked across at Theo with a smile. Everything was going to plan.

Theo took back the mike and announced that the next part of the meeting would be devoted to specific proposals for action, large-scale actions in which everyone in SOW! was invited to take part. This would be the key part of the evening, the moment when this struggle would really get going.

"I'd like to kick this off by proposing..." he began, but had got no further in announcing the picket of a "preliminary consultation meeting" on the plans at the Town Hall when he realised the group of young people at the front had stood up *en masse* and were clambering up on to the stage. One of them, a lad who could have been no more than 18 or 19 and was already trying to grow a straggly kind of boy-beard, shot him a furiously hostile glance as he hauled himself up.

They unrolled their banner right in front of Theo, cutting him off from the rest of the hall, and a young woman with blue-dyed hair started shouting through a megaphone. She was obviously in a state of some agitation because her voice was impossibly shrill and, combined with the fact that she held the megaphone far too close to her mouth, this made her quite difficult to understand, but Theo, as he slipped off the side of the stage to get round in front of them, heard her declare that what was happening this evening was "disgusting" and "frankly offensive".

In a few seconds he had achieved his immediate goal of being in the right position to see what was written on the banner. When he read the wording, he literally stepped back in surprise and had to hurriedly apologise to Maureen from Little Wotton WI, whose toes he had crushed.

"Stop the Fossil Phoneys!" it declared in chunky orange lettering on a purple backdrop.

And at exactly the same moment that the voice in Theo's mind formed the phrase, the woman's voice on the megaphone pronounced the last two words, lending them a peculiar stereophonic resonance.

"Fossil Phoneys... Spreading lies... Twisted conspiracy theories... Climate deniers... Links to the oil industry".

Glancing around, Theo saw that two of the disruptive guests were handing out leaflets in the aisle for people to pass along the rows and he managed to intercept one of them. The headline,

"THEO CARTER: FOSSIL PHONEY WORKED FOR BIG OIL" sent a physical jolt through his body. He felt his legs become weak and his head become light – it felt as if he was in danger of collapsing. But he was maybe saved from this humiliation by the need to focus on another disruption, at the back of the hall, which was turning heads away from the chaos on the stage.

It was Eric, who had managed to push himself through the knot of people blocking the door. Red-faced and beside himself with indignation, he was glaring at Jay and jabbing an angry finger towards him.

"No right!" he was shouting. "You people have no right to be in this hall! This is an absolute outrage!"

It must have been bad enough for him to come back to find the crowd inside his hall, let alone to come across the very conflict that had been the cause of his worries.

"This sort of behaviour is totally intolerable!" he yelled. He seemed to want to say more but had evidently run out of words, so moved on to his punch line.

"I've called the police and they'll be here any moment. You're going to have to explain yourselves to them!"

With the grimmest of expressions on his face, which had suddenly turned from red to a greenish shade of white, he pushed angrily through the group at the door and left the building.

Applause swept across the hall. For a second, Theo was appalled. Had they lost the support of all these people, who were taking Eric's side against them? But then he realised that only he and Jay knew that Eric had not actually let them use the hall and only he and Jay knew to whom Eric's tirade had been addressed.

As far as everyone else was concerned, the finger pointing accusingly towards the stage was indicating the intruders, not the organisers, and it was on their account that the police had been called.

This was evidently the impression gathered by the saboteurs themselves, because the blue-haired woman jumped off the stage and the rest of them followed her through the hall and towards the exit, tossing their remaining leaflets out at the public as they went.

There were boos and catcalls as they passed. Eric's little outburst had inadvertently united people against them. When the blue-haired one was nearly at the door, head held high and haughty in an attempt to retain her dignity, she suddenly stumbled and crashed to the floor. Theo thought someone behind her must have tripped her up and apparently so did she, because, as she got back to her feet, she turned furiously to confront the presumed offender.

But this turned out to be the sweet little redhaired girl, who not only was the last person likely to have done anything like that, but also had her legs tucked up neatly beneath her on the radiator and so was quite obviously incapable of having stuck out a foot. Unnerved and somewhat humiliated, the woman led her little gang out of the venue.

Any relief that Theo might have felt at the departure was dispelled by the sight of the leaflet he was clutching in his hand. He read quickly through it. They said he was the "leader" of the campaign and were accusing him of being in the pay of the fossil fuel industry with a vested interest in opposing an environmental project. "Carter seems to have forgotten to tell anyone he is a former employee of one of the big oil companies who have brought us to the point of climate collapse". What nonsense! They said he was "parroting the paranoid climate denial rantings of conspiracy theorist Sally Shukra", who was a "notorious apologist for dictators and anti-democratic fascist regimes across the world".

He glanced nervously around the room to check if people were looking at him with obvious signs of suspicion or rejection, but detected instead an impatience to resume the meeting, so he climbed back on to the stage with Jay and they carried on from where they had left off.

It was agreed to go ahead with the picket of

the preliminary consultation meeting about the Gaia Heaven project a fortnight later. In fact, Theo, Jay and – particularly – Magda were hoping for a bit more than that. A mass occupation of the Town Hall was how the event was already shaping up in their minds. Maybe just for the one evening or maybe, if there were enough of them, they could keep it going for 24 hours or more? But this wasn't the sort of thing to discuss in public.

Various other smaller events were also okayed, although Theo felt people were going into too much detail about minutiae which they could easily sort out on their own.

He looked at his watch and wondered when the cops would turn up. He and Jay had a little whisper and decided it would be best to wind things up, while the atmosphere was still positive. So they did just that, to an enthusiastic round of determined applause.

Trevor wandered up on to stage to pick up his placard, which had been propped up on the back wall for decoration. He wanted to know if there was any truth in what the leaflet said about Theo having worked for an oil company, just out of interest. Not that he would be bothered if he had, he was at pains to add, because he himself had once worked with Jimmy Savile and that didn't make him a child abuser.

No, said Theo. He had no idea where they

had got that from. He noticed that he was now also addressing a white-haired gentleman in a smart waterproof jacket and flat cap, who seemed to be trying to attach himself to the conversation.

"Unless I do have a past life in the oil industry", quipped Theo, "but I've just forgotten all about it in the meantime!"

"Aye, that you have!" interjected the old chap, who turned out to have a strong Irish accent.

"Sorry?"

"You've not forgotten that you used to work at the petrol station out past the hospital? Near that school you went to? I used to call in for my *Weekly Herald* and pass the time of day with you, before we moved over this way. Never forget a face, me! Although I have to admit I didn't remember your name, errr..." He stole a glance at the 'Fossil Fascist' leaflet in his hand. "Theo! I'm Frank, by the way".

Theo shook Frank's hand with warmth and no small degree of confusion.

"Yes, of course... Blimey, that's going back a bit. But it's hardly working for the oil industry in the sense they are implying. And how would anyone know about that?"

Frank tapped the side of his nose. "Records! It's all on record you know, somewhere or other, in the company files, at the tax office, you name it. All you need is the right access and everything is there for you. The question you might want to ask yourselves is who exactly has that kind of access?"

They tidied the hall, loaded Bill's van, locked the front door and had just pulled away into the traffic when two police cars, lights-a-flashing, swung round the corner from the High Street and screeched to a halt outside the hall. An hour and a half. Not a bad response time for this part of town.

Inevitably a group of them ended up down the Royal Oak – Theo, Jay, Trevor, Meera, Jo, Bill, Nadia, Yana, Jack, Magda and a couple of friends of hers whose names Theo did not catch.

They were in celebratory mood and Theo allowed the optimism to flow with the alcohol, not on this occasion expressing his inner reservations about the dangers of over-confidence and subsequent complacency. He also managed to hide – from himself as well as from his fellow campaigners – any adverse effects on his inner calm from the stage intervention and leaflet.

When he got home, he pretty much collapsed on to his bed and fell asleep within seconds, with any cause for anxiety thoroughly drowned out by the late evening merriment.

But three hours later he was wide awake and in a state of something approaching sheer panic. Words seem to be plastered up in huge lettering all around the inside of his brain, flickering and buzzing and with harsh neon accusation: "Climate denier", "Fossil Phoney", "Big Oil". He saw his name on the leaflet duplicated and distributed a thousand times – "Theo Carter, Theo Carter, Theo Carter" – and was filled with the chilling realisation that he no longer knew who that was. Was it all a lie, everything that he believed about himself? Was he living a delusion? Were those young people actually right?

Obviously the nonsense about his long-gone job at the petrol station was neither here nor there, but was there still a kernel of truth in the fact that he belonged to that world, the world of yesterday, the world as it was before those youngsters had even been born. Had he been left behind by the direction the world was taking, failed to adapt to the new reality around him? Was he an old fossil, raging hopelessly against the passing of the years, the coming of new generations with an experience and opinion of the world that was simply unfamiliar to him? Was he a 2020s version of Old Jim, a dimly-remembered neighbour from his childhood, who had held out against the onrushing modern era by saying "no" to electricity, gas and telephone and had died of hypothermia when he fell down the stairs one Christmas Eve, broke his leg and must have lain in agony for hours, as his feeble cries for help went unheeded, his coal fire died away and the winter cold crept down from the unheated upper floor to envelop his body and steal away his soul?

Was he, Theo, not a revolutionary at all, but a reactionary? A hater of change? A denier of progress? An enemy of the modern world?

He tossed and turned in his bed, desperately trying to push away these unwanted images and thoughts, but the more he did so, the more he entangled himself in a web of self-doubt and self-hatred. He was back at Florian Grammar, back to the feeling of being nobody and of feeling ashamed of this emptiness within, this lack of substance. The identity that he had so diligently built for himself, and which had sustained him for so many decades, was dissolving into the fevered darkness. All that was left was his 13 year-old-self, an embryo within that had never evolved, just wrapped itself up in layer upon layer of illusion.

A crowd of classmates was surrounding him, taunting him, throwing his old leather school bag from one to the other in sneering, mocking, jollity. He recognised rat-faced Roberts, Hutton and the young man who had glared at him with such hatred on the stage earlier that night.

"Phoney!" they chanted, jubilantly. "Phoney! Phoney! Phoney!"

* * *

Theo was late in to the Infoshop the next morning, after his disturbed night, and Jay was already *in situ*, doing some photocopying. Young Jack was also there, browsing the literature.

He was pleased to see both of them, for different reasons: Jay because his enthusiasm and good humour always made him feel better and Jack because his youth gave Theo a sense of responsibility, pulled him away from his own personal anxieties into an understanding of the role he had to play, for the sake of others.

After the usual pleasantries, Theo headed for the computer, but as he logged in he noticed that Jack was lingering awkwardly a few feet away.

"You all right there, Jack?"

"Yes... it's just that there's something I want to talk to you about..."

Theo spread his palms in front of him. "I'm all ears!"

Jack looked embarrassed, not knowing how to explain himself.

"Maybe not in here..." he said, looking meaningfully around the room, his eyes lingering particularly on the computer.

Jay, who had heard his words and not seen the visual cues, called out: "You're quite right Jack, I'm not to be trusted with sensitive information!"

This supposedly humorous intervention only

intensified Jack's awkwardness, but Theo managed to smooth things over, with the upshot that he and Jack went for walk around the block, without mobile phones, with the promise that Theo would fill Jay in later on.

"So... What's on your mind, mate?"

"It's about those people that came to the meeting last night, the ones that went on the stage... I recognised one of them".

"Really?" This was interesting.

"Yeah, the one with the blue hair. I was at school with her, where I used to live, in Hampshire. She's called Pippa, but I can't remember her second name for the moment".

"And was she always such a pain in the arse?"

"Well, no, that's the odd thing. She wasn't that type at all. She didn't have blue hair, of course. And she was pretty straight, serious, one of the rich kids. Her mum used to come and pick her up outside in a massive 4x4 and take her home into the countryside, somewhere. She only stayed for a couple of years and then she went off to some private school to make sure she passed all her exams".

"So you don't know what she did afterwards?"

"Not first-hand, no. But my ex-girlfriend bumped into her in Winchester a couple of years ago and apparently she said she was on some sort of training course for the government, something to do with the army or security that she couldn't really discuss. That's all, really. I know it's all a bit vague, but I thought you ought to know".

Theo nodded grimly and patted him on the shoulder. "Thanks Jack. You're right. We can't necessarily do anything about it, but it's important to have some kind of idea as to what we're up against. If you do remember her surname, let me know. And if you get a chance to ask your ex about what exactly this Pippa said to her in Winchester, that could be useful".

Again, embarrassment overcame the young man.

"I'm not going to be able to do that, I'm afraid, Theo. She was pretty angry with me when we split up and she's totally blocked me on everything! And also..."

He trailed off, obliging Theo to shoot him a questioning glance.

"And also, since we've gone to some lengths to keep this conversation secret, it would make sense not to mention it on messaging or whatever, don't you think?"

Theo smiled. The lad was a step ahead of him. He mentally pencilled Jack in as the future full-time Infoshop organiser.

They went back to base, where Jack picked up his phone and headed off for his shift at the supermarket. Jay was on the computer and Theo wandered over to him with the intention of luring him outside for a secure debriefing on Jack's information.

But Jay was busy reading something. And frowning.

"Shit," he said. "Have a look at this, Thee".

It was an email from the Anderson-Butler Fund for Social Change, but not the usual monthly confirmation of funding. It was a personal message from Josh, one of the co-ordinators.

"Hi guys. We would really like to link up with you for a catch-up meeting, to discuss how the project is working, how you see the future going forward. Nothing to worry about, but the sooner the better from our perspective. Josh".

"Nothing to worry about", repeated Theo out loud. The very phrase gave cause for concern. As did the subsequent "but".

"Shall we get this over with as soon as we can, Jay? We could go and see him this afternoon, if he's free".

Jay agreed immediately. Days of fevered speculation as to what was wrong were not a particularly enticing prospect.

Josh from the ABFSC got back straight away and suggested a rendezvous in a café in Haringey Green Lanes.

The two Wotton activists didn't discuss the

reason for their trip as they headed north in the tube train. They talked about the previous night's meeting, about the people they had met there, about how they were going to organise the protest at the Town Hall. Theo was dying to tell Jay about Pippa but, with respect to young Jack, refrained from talking about her in earshot of the general public and their mobile phones.

They were well ahead of schedule and took the long way around to the meeting point, through Finsbury Park. They sat on a bench in the sun, watched a crazy dog running round in circles and it all seemed like a rather pleasant day out.

But as soon as they reached the café, a Turkish or maybe Kurdish joint on the main road, they realised that this was not going to be a bundle of laughs.

Josh, whom they'd both met on a number of occasions, had planted himself in the far corner with his laptop open in front of him. Next to him was a young woman, whom neither of them recognised, with matching laptop.

After Theo and Jay had ordered their coffees, they headed over to join them and noted that both of these individuals wore grim, tense, expressions.

This didn't stop them from smiling and greeting the arrivals, although Theo noted that the usual comradely hug had given way to a brief handshake.

Josh – a pale fellow in his late thirties – seemed to feel obliged to indulge in lengthy conversational foreplay, asking both of them about their health, their families and what they thought of the weather. His colleague, Chloe, said nothing at all, but tapped away at her keyboard occasionally, as if taking notes.

This continued in a meandering sort of way until Jay mentioned, inevitably, their current campaign. At this point Josh lowered his gaze in obvious discomfort.

When he looked up again, it was with a pained look on his face.

"Actually, guys, that is what I really need to discuss with you today," he said.

"Oh yeah?" replied Theo. He had known this was coming. "Why's that?"

"Well," said Josh, "we have been hearing a lot of concerns about the tone and content of this campaign of yours and we thought we really needed to hear your side of things".

"Concerns?" said Jay. "Who from?"

"From many different sources, Jay, including people inside the Fund".

"And what is it that concerns them?"

Josh sighed, as if the answer was so obvious he really shouldn't have to spell it out.

"People are worried – we are *all* worried – that you are promoting conspiracy theories".

"Theories?" said Jay. "What theories?"

"Gaia Heaven" piped up Chloe out of nowhere. "Howard Gear. All that bullshit about sinister businessmen ruling the world".

"Hang on," said Theo, feeling as if he was sliding into a parallel universe. "That's not bullshit, or even a theory, it's documented fact. And sinister businessmen ruling the world pretty much sums up capitalism, doesn't it?"

Josh was shaking his head, while Chloe tapped furiously away at her laptop.

"No Theo," he said, as if addressing a retarded infant. "Capitalism is a network of social and economic relationships. It's not about pointing the finger at certain individuals who you claim are pulling all the strings, because that just falls into the hands of..."

"Anti-semitism!" snapped Chloe, all traces of friendliness now erased from her features.

"Oh come on", gasped Jay. "You're having a laugh, aren't you?"

"No, I'm deadly serious," said Chloe. "This whole story of a secret group of rich bankers or financiers being behind everything you don't like in the world is a classic anti-semitic trope".

"But SLI worked *with* the Nazis!" objected Theo.

"And that's another classic anti-semitic trope," said Chloe with a bitter little smile, tapping away once more. "Hitler as a Jewish Frankenstein's Monster who got out of control".

"Bollocks!" said Jay, who was getting visibly riled by the conversation, while Theo was managing to rein in his feelings – perhaps because Jay was expressing them for him. "You're just using this anti-semitism trope business to shut down anything we say".

"Well done!" smirked Chloe. "Anti-semitic trope number three – anti-semitism is not real but just invented by the Jews to stop people criticising them and exposing their evil plans!" She noted the offence on her laptop.

Jay looked at Theo despairingly. He was lost for words.

Theo decided to address Josh, who had so far been marginally less hostile.

"I really think these concerns are unfounded, Josh. After all, we are openly anti-capitalist and it is hardly unusual for anti-capitalists to criticise capitalists, even if you disagree with the way in which we have done so".

"That's true," said Josh. "And if it was just that, we wouldn't have asked for this meeting. But there are a couple more issues we need to talk about".

"OK," said Theo, leaning back on his plastic seat. "Like what?"

"Well firstly, and this is a continuation of the conspiracy theory issue really, we were disturbed to see that you attribute the research in your article to Shukra".

"Sally Shukra, yes," said Theo. Why did Josh insist on tersely using her surname alone? "She didn't write the piece but she did provide the leads for pretty much all the information".

Josh raised his eyebrows and felt obliged to tap some notes into his laptop. Chloe, meanwhile, was pretty much hammering away.

"You do realise she's a notorious conspiracy theorist, don't you?" said Josh.

"Notorious?"

"Yes, notorious. She's accused pretty much every NGO and political group on the planet of being in league with big business and the CIA, she has fuelled all that hysteria over GMOs and vaccines, she thinks calling for renewable energy is falling into the hands of the capitalists, she has defended dictatorships..."

"Defended dictatorships? What are you talking about?"

"She does it all the time. Just a few months ago she wrote an article saying the Iranian atrocities weren't real. That it was all an imperialist plot".

"It's always the Americans, with her", chipped in Chloe. "Totally anti-American. Just racist shit".

Theo noticed that Jay was looking worried. He hadn't really read much of Sally's stuff, so he might even be taking all of this seriously.

"Look," said Theo. "She isn't defending dictatorships, she's opposing war. She's exposing the excuses the so-called West is constantly cooking up to bomb and occupy other parts of the world!"

"Excuses?" shrieked Chloe. "Are you actually agreeing with her?"

Theo paused for a split second. He looked at Chloe and Josh's accusing faces. He looked at Jay, who was waiting expectantly for his response.

He knew what answer he was *supposed* to give and he knew what answer he *had* to give.

"Yes, I do agree with her," he said firmly. "I read all her work and I am convinced that her investigations are useful, accurate and incredibly important".

"Well said, Thee," said Jay.

The other two were busy typing.

"So, not just a conspiracy theorist but an atrocity-denier!" muttered Chloe between her teeth.

Theo now wanted to get this meeting, this interview – this trial? – over with as soon as possible.

"And what was the other outstanding issue, Josh?"

"Ah!" Josh looked slightly surprised that he had bothered asking, having already pleaded guilty to heresy.

"We are also concerned about the anti-environmental tone of your campaign. Here at the Fund we are totally committed to moving into a carbon-neutral and sustainable society and..."

"But it's not green, is it, what they're planning?" interrupted Jay. "It's just more capitalism, worse than before, more glass and concrete and surveillance and private property, all dressed up as being environmentally friendly to sell it to the public".

"It's all just a conspiracy..." murmured Chloe, her bitterness more audible than her words.

"Let's get this straight, Josh," said Theo. "The Infoshop is 100% anti-capitalist, anti-racist and pro-environmental. There is nothing in this campaign which conflicts with our principles, and your principles as I understand them. In fact, I would say we are defending our principles more than ever in what we are doing now".

Chloe snorted.

"That's not how we see it, Theo," said Josh, gravely.

"So what are you saying, then?" said Jay. "That you are going to stop our funding? Is that it?"

Theo was glad his friend had had the courage to get to the point.

Josh and Chloe exchanged glances and there was a moment of silence, during which Theo became intensely aware of the middle-eastern background music, the smell of fried food and coffee, the rumble of traffic outside the open doors of the café.

"No," said Josh. "Not necessarily. But in order for the Fund to continue supporting the Infoshop project we will need you to remove the Gaia Heaven article from wherever you can, to cease from further propagation of conspiracy theories, to sever all links with Sally Shukra, to publish a statement which Chloe has prepared explaining why you have done so and, finally, to abandon your ill-conceived campaign against the smart city project".

Theo and Jay needed barely to exchange the briefest of glances before heading silently out of the café and into the loud city street.

* * *

If the trip up to the café had been light-hearted and chatty, the journey back down could only be described as morose.

They barely exchanged a word, apart from the occasional repetition of "unbelievable", "bastards" and such like, and when they caught each other's eye the response was inevitably a forlorn shake of the head.

After they reached Wotton Park, each went his own way without any mention of meeting up again – Theo straight home to his flat and Jay to his cousin's takeaway, ahead of his evening shift.

A great tiredness had descended on Theo since the end of what was undoubtedly their final meeting with the Infoshop's principal funders and he had thought of little more on the train home than the prospect of lying on his bed and falling asleep.

But when he finally reached the promised land he found that the desire had left him. After 20 minutes of rest he was wide awake and filled with the burning desire not to sleep but to go outside and to walk.

He gave no thought at all as to where he was going, apart from a general instinct to avoid the roads heaviest with rush-hour traffic. He took the back streets, the hidden roads and less-frequented avenues, cut across scruffy little patches of grass, paying close attention to where he stepped; slipped through alleyways and access roads, dived into subways to cross and recross the dual carriageway.

And what was he doing all this time? He was thinking and he was not thinking. Or rather, he was thinking in an entirely unstructured way. He was not consciously pulling thoughts out of his mind so as to rationally assess a situation or come to any decision. He was not setting himself a problem to be solved and working through the various possibilities. No, he was just letting everything inside him come to the surface in its own, chaotic way, without trying to impose any overall sense of order. Emotions, memories, opinions, resolutions – all of these swirled around in glorious confusion in Theo's head as he strode through the streets of his home town. He walked and walked and as he walked this cloudy whirlpool began turning more calmly, more steadily and the waters of his imagination started clearing.

If anyone had traced the route Theo took – perhaps they did! – they would have seen that it took the form of a spiral. After the first broad sweep round the borough, it turned in to complete more or less the same circle in a tighter, shorter, version and then, finally, looped around for a final descent into what had presumably all along been Theo's unconscious destination – the off-licence.

Only with his mind cleansed and his flat well stocked with beer and rum could Theo really face the evening ahead of him.

He started off by playing, as amateurishly as ever, his guitar, which had the benefit of slowing down his drinking rate as his hands weren't free. But later he switched to listening to music and got stuck into his supplies

Inevitably, he drifted off, only to awake some time later with the word "phoney!" ringing in his head. He must have had that bloody dream again.

Theo could take no more. He put on his trainers, grabbed his keys and marched out of the flat again.

It was completely dark now, it was no doubt very late, and he was aware that the closing of his front door and the clanging of his footsteps down the metal staircase were jarring the nocturnal calm and, despite the state he was in, hoped he wasn't waking his neighbours.

But his mind was mainly focused on one idea only – to get away from the torment in his head. How much walking would it take?

He didn't turn right after the railway bridge, like he usually did, but carried on briskly up the main road, strangely quiet at this hour.

He marched faster still, as if the taunting inner voices were hot on his heels, and deliberately crossed the road to head up a tree-lined avenue he didn't remember having taken before, feeling that the novelty would help keep the metaphorical wolves at bay.

Theo walked and walked, in what was this time pretty much a completely straight line. And somehow he became so immersed in the mere act of walking that nothing else came into focus, apart from a lingering feeling that something unpleasant was trailing behind him and would catch him up and overwhelm him if ever he slowed or stopped.

He was still on the same avenue, lined with privet hedges and London plane trees. It seemed to be going on, and up, for ever and he was now being surrounded by a light mist, as if on the hills.

The large detached houses on either side of the road became more sparse, with patches of parkland just visible through what was becoming a proper fog, saturated with the glow of the street lamps.

The road became yet steeper and the fog yet thicker. Theo could no longer see more than a foot or two around him and had no idea whether there were still houses to either side.

When there were no more street lights in view and the pavement beneath his feet had turned into a rough gravelly surface, he concluded that he had obviously wandered into some kind of park, although which one he could not currently imagine.

He was forced to slow down a little, because he could not properly see where he was stepping, but kept solidly on in a straight line, convinced that his course was the right one.

It was his inner sense of balance, rather than his sight, that told him the incline was levelling out and he had reached some kind of hilltop. The ground became softer and damper under his feet – he was now walking on grass. There was, again, an upward slope and Theo found himself mounting what was evidently a small mound.

He came to a halt on the top and turned slowly around to examine his surroundings. Nothing but thick white-grey walls of fog in every direction. He looked up, straight up, and saw, to his astonishment, a small circle of clear blue sky above the swirling mist. What? Was it morning already?

At that very moment, something quite remarkable started to happen. The fog around Theo began to melt away, at great speed, revealing the hitherto-hidden world beyond and leaving him gasping and unsteady from astonishment.

He was indeed on a mound, a green mound on a green hill. The hill stretched down in woody slopes towards a plain, through which wound a sparkling blue river. Turning to the right, Theo saw the river widen into the sea and there the horizon was ripe with the coming of the sun. He watched, spellbound, as the undersides of small clouds were lit up by the rays of something which for him, was still out of sight. His eyes remained fixed on the distant line between sky and sea, waiting. Then a pinpoint of light appeared, as if someone was pointing a powerful torch in his direction. This point of light grew larger, larger and larger still and soon revealed itself to be nothing but the very outer edge of a mighty beast of fire, which hauled itself slowly and proudly into the morning sky, forcing a mere mortal such as Theo to turn away through fear of being blinded by its untold brightness.

He looked around him, at the hills, the trees, the river, the countryside stretching out around him in every direction, now bathed in sunlight.

"Where the fuck am I?" he said out loud.

Where was his city, his world, his reality?

And all at once he knew that this *was* his reality and his world, that this was where he belonged.

He started to turn around on the spot, slowly at first but then faster and ever faster, drawing up all that essence into his swirling self.

He felt its strength rise up into him through the greenness of the earth mound and flow down into him from the sun.

Its strength was all around him and within him. It was *his* strength as well. He was this world and this world was him.

With that certainty, Theo turned to face the pack of dream-demons who had chased him from his bed and one single glance from his radiant eyes saw them shrivel to nothing.

Then he lay down on the green mound, curled up in a ball, and slept.

* * *

When Theo awoke it was in his own bed, and

much later than usual. He had no memory of his excursion and was disconcerted to find his trainers soaking wet. How had that happened? Having uncovered an old pair at the back of the wardrobe, he made his way down to the Infoshop.

Jay was already there and had clearly been impatiently awaiting his tardy arrival. He looked uncharacteristically agitated and didn't waste any time on niceties.

"Thee, there's something I wanted to ask you – you never did tell me what it was that Jack had to say to you..."

That was true. The right moment hadn't presented itself. Theo proposed a walk round Victoria Park to discuss it all.

He was surprised by the look on Jay's face when he had passed on the information – thirdhand information, now – about blue-haired Pippa. All the remaining confidence and *joie de vivre* seemed to have drained away. It must have been the cumulative effect, combined with the Josh and Chloe meeting. Jay looked frightened and defeated.

"This is so fucking heavy, Thee," he said. "We're getting attacked by fake activists working for the state, sabotaged by the people who fund us and are supposed to be on our side... What next?"

"We knew all along it wouldn't be easy," said Theo, somewhat nervously plucking a twig from a bush as they passed, and twirling it around in his hand.

"Yes, but this is..." Jay sighed. A sigh of unmistakeable despair.

Theo stopped, turned to his friend and placed a friendly hand on his shoulder.

"What is it, Jay, what is it that is really getting to you?"

Jay raised his hands in the air.

"It's my dream, Theo! Everything I have been working for! Going to live in Santa Sofia. Being with The Boy. Living a proper life away from all this shit! I don't want them to take that from me! I know I don't earn much with my hours at the Infoshop and I don't depend on it like you do, but it helps me save for the day I get out. I don't want to use up all my money staying here to save Wotton if the dice are totally loaded against us. I don't want to risk losing the future I deserve if there is no way we can win this thing. I don't want to be worn down, Thee. I don't want to be crushed! I want to live!"

Theo started walking again, head down, and Jay followed him. Finally his thoughts came to the surface in the form of words.

"What I'd say to you is this, Jay. Obviously this fight is going to be harder than we ever imagined. Obviously we are taking on people with huge amounts of power who are not simply going to roll over and go away because of a bit of negative publicity or community opposition. Obviously we are not going to be able to keep leading this campaign, at least in the way we are now, on a long-term basis. But that doesn't mean we give up, because this thing is too important for that. What was the point of everything we have been doing for the last seven years if we don't stick to our principles on this one? That's why we've lost the funding, because we put principles first, so why would we back down on the campaign? But we have to adapt what we are doing to the new reality".

Jay was shrugging his shoulders. "But what new reality, Thee? We don't even know what we are up against, here, I don't see how we..."

"Shhh!" countered Theo. "Let me finish. Please. Jay".

Jay sighed and listened.

"We have got enough in reserve to keep paying the rent on the Infoshop for another three months or so, I reckon. So we don't have to pack it all in just yet. But what we need to do is to take full advantage of the months that we've got left, gamble everything we've got on them, turn them into the red-hot phase of the campaign, the decisive stage. We have got to make this scheme so controversial, so politically combustible, that it can't just go straight through, that it will have to be called in by the Mayor of London, and the Secretary of State as well hopefully, even if it is all theoretically in line with their 'sustainable' city plan..."

"Yup," said Jay. "Sounds good in theory".

"So we have really got to make the most of the Town Hall demo. I know we were already going to try and pull something off, but it's going to have to be a bit more than that. What I've been thinking is that we divide into two groups. The main event is the public protest, of course. You and Magda could take that side of it on, Jay. That would all be completely above board, you wouldn't get nicked. Another group of us, me and some people we trust, would keep out of sight and away from the protest, round the corner behind the car park. At a pre-arranged moment, you lot create a diversion. Perhaps you announce that you're all going to go inside to the meeting, which is what they will be expecting. The cops will rush over to stop you and block the main doors to the Town Hall. We'll seize the moment to come out of hiding and make a dash for the back door, which is a fire exit really, but is always left open because that's where the staff are allowed to come out and smoke. We're not right next to the council chamber there, it's true, but I can picture the way to get there and with all the kerfuffle out the front they won't be able to react until it's too late".

"And then what, Thee? What will you do when you get there?"

"We'll trash the place. Do as much damage as possible. We'll start with the projector and the screen where they'll no doubt be showing Gaia Heaven propaganda, then we'll rip up their paperwork, chuck their jugs of water all over the place, fight off the security, scream our heads off, break a few windows while we're at it... Basically do all we can to make sure everyone hears about what they're doing and knows that there are some very angry people out there determined to stop them".

"You're joking, Thee. You'll end up in jail".

"Yep, I will. And not just me either, which will be the hard bit, finding people who are really up for it. But it's got to be done, Jay. We've got to up the ante straight away, bring it all to a head, because we're not going to be able to wage the long-term war we had in mind. As for me, what have I got to lose? This is everything I've got. The Infoshop and Wotton. They're taking the first away so that they can get rid of the second. They might as well take me with them".

"Thee," said Jay. "I don't want them to put you behind bars. We need you on the outside".

Theo turned away and looked out across the park. A dad was helping his small son learn to ride a bike on the far side. Kids were kicking a ball about. Mums were pushing buggies. It felt almost unreal to see ordinary everyday life going on around them.

"But need me for what? That's the question, Jay. This struggle needs me, yes, but it needs me to do what I know I have to do".

There was only silence in response and when he turned round and saw Jay's face he realised that he had understood.

* * *

The first part of Theo's plan was perhaps the most problematic. He had to find a few other people willing to take the same risks as he was prepared to take. And he needed these to be people he could absolutely trust.

He did toy with the idea of trying to do it on his own, but quickly gave this up. One person alone can't 'storm' a meeting. He would easily be restrained by security in the council chamber, or even by councillors themselves, perish the thought, and was not likely to be able to wreak much havoc. He would still be arrested, but the incident would be a mere footnote, not the trigger for resistance which they needed.

He didn't want to ask Magda because Jay would need her support and comfort. He didn't want to ask Jack because he was someone who could pick up the reins of the campaign in his absence.

He thought about the others in SOW! – about their personal circumstances, their way of seeing things, the likelihood of them being willing not only to be arrested for a good cause, but to have caused a fair bit of damage beforehand. Obviously this was not something he wanted to talk about to too many people, so it was important to make the right choices.

What about Bill? He was always full of fighting talk. But no, the others would need him and his van to get the props for the picket down to the Town Hall – banners, placards, table for the petition and leaflets. Besides, Theo had a strange and irrational feeling that Bill was not entirely trustworthy.

Trevor, for all his enthusiasm, would probably draw the line at getting arrested. Meera would no doubt say 'yes' but she had her children to think of and Theo felt it was irresponsible even to ask her.

Nadia and Yana, the would-be squatters, seemed like a good bet. Maybe they would welcome the chance to get physically involved in a different kind of way?

They actually called in to the Infoshop shortly after Theo had this thought and he took the opportunity to raise, in general terms, the prospect of direct action and to sound them out regarding their potential participation.

He quickly found out that this would not be possible because of their status in the UK. Getting arrested would probably lead to them being thrown out of the country and he couldn't ask them to risk that.

Who did that leave, from what he considered the core group of the campaign? Jo, Dawn, Ella and Ralph.

He approached each of them in the same way. He made sure they were talking alone – if necessary inventing some pretext for taking them out of the Infoshop or out of their homes, in the case of Ralph and Ella. First of all he started chatting generally about the campaign, then threw in what could be taken as a joking reference to 'trashing' the preliminary meeting on the development. Four times he was relieved that this provoked a positive response.

Next, he adopted a more serious tone and spoke about the likelihood of ending up in court. Here, alas, he lost Ella, who started talking about people needing to hold on to their jobs or face homelessness and starvation.

Dawn, Ralph and Jo were all of the opinion that sometimes certain things just had to be done. They were all through to the next stage, which involved a walk around Victoria Park, without mobile phones, during which a practical proposition was made. To Theo's delight, they all said 'yes'.

He found each of them highly impressive, in their own different ways. Dawn was a strong, feisty woman in her early 70s who had somehow managed to keep hold of her powerful energy long beyond the point where many people had consigned themselves to a life of slippers and TV. She had been involved in anti-war activities in her younger days and had no qualms at all about the prospect of being arrested for doing the right thing.

Ralph did not look at all like the type to be involved in direct action. A quiet man in his late 30s, always neatly dressed in a corduroy jacket and sometimes a tie, he had, so far as Theo could judge, little in the way of social activity. A chronic illness, which he never named, prevented him from working and he appeared to spend most of his life at the public library. It seemed to Theo that Ralph's sense of values came from his reading rather than from his life experience and that something inside him yearned to take action which would launch his abstract value system into the physical world.

Jo was the youngest of the team. She had told Theo previously that she was 28, although she looked more like 20 to him. She had already been heavily involved in community politics, on the other side of the city, having been at the forefront of a campaign against police racism and brutality after her cousin was killed by cops. She had put up with no end of shit from the local constabulary and had eventually had been forced to move down to Wotton to get away from them.

She was not someone to be intimidated and was not in the least afraid of confrontation.

All in all, Theo told himself when the last of them had verbally signed up to the plan, a great team.

As the preparation for the demo approached, and people began to talk more concretely about how they were going to organise it, Theo realised he needed to invent a reason for his absence, and that of Jo, Dawn and Ralph, from the start of the protest. It seemed so wrong to lie to his own people, but there was no way around it. He decided to say they were going to do a banner drop from the railway bridge on the main road, taking advantage of the fact that the cops would all be gathering outside the Town Hall, half a mile away.

Everyone thought this was a fantastic idea, to his slight embarrassment given that it wasn't going to be happening. And when Nadia and Yana turned up with a huge plastic banner they had 'liberated' from a garden centre on their way back from a trip to Canterbury and enthusiastically set about creating a beautiful and colourful Save Our Wotton message on the reverse side, he had to offset his guilt by making Jay promise to put the banner up at a later date, by which point he himself would, presumably, no longer be available.

Theo and Jay hadn't had any further heart-to-heart conversations since that walk in the park. There wasn't any need. There was a calm, and yet sad, understanding between them that made itself felt in the form of brief exchanged glances, of passing quips and smiles, of a certain more substantial warmth in all the little functional everyday phrases that punctuated their days. A mere 'there you go, mate' accompanying a mug of coffee took on a kind of velvet ritual solemnity, a brief 'thanks' was delivered with obvious meaning and behind each 'see you later' was a genuine, audible, gratitude that this was indeed the case – for the time being.

These busy days of organising passed all too swiftly until suddenly Theo found himself waking at 4.30am, with a lump in his throat, to the morning of the protest.

Because everybody who was gathering at the Infoshop was a little over-excited, Theo's peculiar state of mind went unnoticed. Nobody was in the least surprised to see him pacing up and down, popping out and back into the street, checking the time. He and Jo had been out the night before to stash the banner for the alleged drop in the nettle bed next to the railway bridge – a strange gesture since both of them knew it would not be needed, but one which meant they would not be lumbered with the object itself on the day.

He had arranged to meet her, Dawn and Ralph in front of the DIY Centre rather than at the Infoshop, in case they were followed. He had mentally planned a tricky little route to take him to the rendezvous, cutting through the entrance hall of the clinic on the edge of the old hospital, and his keenness to get going was struggling against his determination not to arrive too early and make himself too visible.

When the time finally came, he wandered, as casually as he could, over to Jay. "Right", he said. "I'm off. Bye, Jay".

"Good luck, Thee!" whispered Jay and, on a sudden impulse gave him a great bear hug.

The brief walk to the meet-up was initially a liberation – he was moving, using up all that energy! – but Theo's joyful state of mind was quickly ended. The gate to the clinic car park was locked. He quickly scanned the notice fixed to the gatepost by the health authorities – something about a contagious infection closing the facility – but his mind was already trying to work out how he was going to get to the DIY Centre. This was now a huge dead end and he was going to have to retrace his steps in a major way to get round the blockage.

Theo always walked fast, but now he was almost breaking into a run as he made his way around the backs street of Wotton. He had allowed plenty of time for them to reach the Town Hall but he hated being late for anything. He didn't want to let the others down.

He was mentally phrasing his excuses when he arrived at the roundabout by the DIY Centre – and was stopped dead in his tracks.

Across the road were three police cars and a police van – into which were being loaded Ralph and Dawn. His eyes rapidly swept all around and on the far side of the roundabout spotted a knot of activity. There were some cops over there and they seemed to be holding someone down. He strained his eyes and saw a familiar mop of curly hair on the pavement. It was Jo.

Without a second thought, Theo turned back the way he had come. It would help nobody for him to make himself known to the police and to try and defend his friends. They had nothing on them – they couldn't because nothing had happened yet – but the police were well capable of making up some story that would keep them locked up for the rest of the day.

But what should he do now? What was the point? There was nobody there to help him. He would have to go through with the plan on his own, the best he could. He would have to go in there like a berserker in order to have the sort of impact they needed, the impact that would create waves and bring the struggle to a head while they still had the Infoshop from which to coordinate it.

In the meantime, he had to get off this busy road. The cops would surely be looking out for him as well, if they had nabbed the others.

He nearly jumped out of his skin when a male voice shouted at him from a few feet away.

"Theo! Want a lift, mate?"

Theo turned round and saw a white van with "Croon Carpentry" on the side. It was Bill.

For all his doubts about the man, Theo was actually pleased to see him on this occasion and clambered up into the front of his van.

It turned out Bill had seen the commotion atced Jo. Theo explained about the others.

"Fuck, so what about the banner drop?" asked Bill. "You can't do it on your own".

"No", agreed Theo. That was true, if hypothetical.

Bill screwed up his face in an exaggerated frown. Evidently he was thinking.

"I could do it with you!" he announced a few seconds later.

"Thanks Bill, but we need you for the protest," said Theo, kindly. "How else would we get all the gear down there?"

"No, no, I was thinking about that!" said Bill, eagerly. "It's not me you need, is it, it's this van! And I've got it insured for anyone to drive. All we need is someone with a licence".

"Really?" said Theo. Jay had a driving licence – he couldn't do his deliveries without one.

But there was another problem, of course. It

wasn't a banner drop he was planning, but the town hall action. And he had already decided not to ask Bill, because his instincts told him he was not entirely to be trusted.

Did he stick with that hunch – which was no more than that – or did he seize the opportunity to recruit a replacement for the others and try to salvage the day?

Theo thought about the next possibility for an intervention of this kind – it could be months away. He thought about how long they could keep the Infoshop open without funding. He thought about what would happen if he himself tried to force his way into the council meeting, how quickly he would be overpowered, and then he pictured the scene again with this big bulky bloke at his side.

He had no choice.

"Bill, there's something I have to tell you. We were planning a different action, a really full-on thing at the Town Hall. But I don't know if it's the sort of thing you would be up for?"

It turned out that it was exactly the sort of thing that Bill Croon was up for.

Ten minutes later, Theo found himself installed deep within the shrubbery at the edge of the Town Hall car park, hidden from the CCTV cameras.

It was a beautiful morning, as Theo had had time to realise, now that he had stopped rushing around. While he waited for Bill to drop off the van and catch him up, he soaked up the birdsong, the sunshine, a certain freshness of the air that had managed to waft into the metropolitan sprawl.

But there was something that jarred in all this, for Theo. He felt as if he was looking at the illusion of a lovely English summer day, rather than the real thing – an illusion that was shortly to be shattered. For him at least.

There was a whistling behind him. He spun round and saw Bill, some 30 yards away, trying to find out where exactly he was. He gave him a wave and his new primary accomplice crashed through the bushes to join him. Christ, he didn't really have to make all that noise, did he?

"They had already started loading up when I left," Bill reported in a loud whisper. "So they won't be long. Jay and Jack are bringing the van, Magda and the rest are going to walk down". He nodded towards the road and added: "Looks like it's going to be a good turn-out!"

Theo followed his gaze. A straggle of half a dozen people, carrying home-made placards, were making their way towards the front entrance of the Town Hall. This was the fifth or sixth group they had seen passing, from this direction alone.

"Let's hope so!" he said. "This is one of those moments when it all hangs in the balance".

As Theo finished his sentence, the air was ripped apart by a great booming explosion that seemed to physically shake every bone and nerve-ending in his body.

He turned to look at Bill. "What the fuck?" he asked. Bill shook his head.

And then the screaming started. The screaming and the wailing – dreadful, despairing howls of pain, of shock and of horror.

Theo ran, with Bill a pace or two behind. He ran towards these terrible sounds and, as he rounded the corner and reached the street at the front of the Town Hall he was faced with the most horrific scene a human being could ever imagine.

Blood, confusion, limbs, heads, guts, pain, death, torment and grief.

And amidst the piles of the dead and the writhing, sobbing, wounded, their placards and banners all torn to shreds and mingled with the burnt flesh, stood the twisted, smoking remains of a white van. Bill's white van.

* * *

Nearly a year later, those images were still burned deep into Theo's retina as his plane taxied at Heathrow Airport, ready to head off to Santa Sofia. But, strangely enough, as the greyness of the London suburbs was enveloped by the greyness of the London clouds and the jet emerged into the sunny blueness beyond, the reality of that darkest of days began, finally, to slightly fade.

Theo moved his foot gently against the bag he had slotted under the seat ahead of him, reassuring himself yet again that the urn carrying Jay's ashes was still there and still intact.

It hadn't been easy to raise the money for this flight – the low-cost firms, already struggling, had been killed off by the economic shockwaves from the Wotton Bombing and the general panic and state of emergency it had unleashed – and it had taken for ever for Theo to get permission to leave the country, as one of the initial prime suspects for the atrocity, apart from Jay and Jack, of course. Unlike Theo, they had never been able to defend themselves and insist on their innocence and it had certainly suited the authorities to declare the case closed and both the perpetrators dead.

To say that Theo felt guilty about their deaths, and about the deaths of the 25 others outside the Town Hall that morning, not to speak of the dozens of injured, would be an understatement of fantastic proportions. Theo had been almost crushed by his role in the events. Even though he had not purposefully done anything that could be said to have caused these deaths, he could not help thinking that he had committed a mistake of monumental folly in telling Bill, or the man they had known as 'Bill', about his plans, even the cover story of the banner drop, and in letting him hand Jay the keys to his van and the responsibility for its lethal load.

Magda had told him that it would have made no difference, that the bastard would have found some other way of tricking others into driving his van to the scene, but Theo could not clear himself of blame. Why hadn't he followed his instincts? The little clues must have been stacking up for weeks and his unconscious mind had added them all up and come to the correct conclusion, even if his rational brain had decided to override this knowledge. He should have positively warned Jay and the others to be wary of 'Bill', to take care not to be manipulated by him.

And why had he never even got round to looking up 'Croon Carpentry' on the internet, or the phone number underneath on the side of the van. Neither of them were real, of course, and the same was apparently the case for Bill Croon. He disappeared from Theo's side seconds after they arrived at the bloodbath and was never seen again. It quickly became common consensus that no such person had, in fact, ever existed. The more campaigners came forward to say that they had met him, the more their statements were derided and presented as proof by the authorities and the complicit media of a concerted and ridiculous attempt by 'the extremists' to blame the whole affair on a mythological character of their own invention.

Such was the scorn poured on the very idea that there ever had been a Bill in the Save Our Wotton! campaign, that the phrase 'Bill did it!' had started to enter the English language as a clever way of saying 'it wasn't me!' when it most plainly was.

The van itself turned out to have been stolen from Crawley in West Sussex some four months previously. Jay had a cousin in Crawley, whom he used to visit from time to time, and a CCTV still of him walking out of Crawley railway station, allegedly on the day of the theft, was presented as conclusive evidence of his key role.

When Theo worked out that Jay could not have been in Crawley on the date suggested, as he had not only put in a shift at the Infoshop, but had also attended a dentist's appointment, listed on the Infoshop calendar in fact, nobody took him seriously. What was he suggesting? That the police would have forged the time stamp on the CCTV image just to incriminate Jay! Absurd! Paranoia! And yet the same people who were so quick to cry 'conspiracy theory!' at evidence in Jay and Jack's favour were all too eager to believe that the letter from the dentist was a forgery or that, because he had been happy to host a copy of the campaign's petition in his surgery, he was himself an active participant in the terrorist plot.

The air hostesses had arrived with the trolley and the man beside Theo was ordering a beer. Theo turned away and looked out of the window. He didn't want to *see* an alcoholic drink now, let alone consume one. Partly, this was because he felt his dependence on alcohol had played a part in allowing all this to happen. He hadn't been sharp enough, on the ball enough, to have seen the warning signs and taken preventative action. But he also now feared the release of pent-up emotion that came with drinking. Previously this had been a positive, in many ways, in that it had cleared out feelings that might otherwise have festered. But now Theo knew full well that he was struggling to keep a cork in the bottle of suppressed guilt and rage that would risk destroying him if it was ever allowed to disgorge its toxic contents into his conscious mind.

The battle against the Gaia Heaven project was lost, of course. What kind of moral high ground could you claim when everyone believed your group had wanted to ram an explosive-laden van into the Town Hall with psychopathic disregard for lives of even your own supporters? Worse still, battles against all smart cities seemed to have been lost as well. The bomb had transformed them overnight into symbols of all that was good, moral, forward-looking and life-affirming and all those who opposed them as inherently callous, unthinking, barbaric and potentially murderous.

How quickly everyone had rushed to distance themselves from their contaminated campaign and everything it stood for! Green groups took up the claim made by the blue-haired one and her gang that SOW! had been anti-environmental from the start. Genuine eco-citizens were fully behind the sustainable future promised to us by the 'clean' technology of the brave new ultra-connected era, they said. Left-wing groups declared that the 'denialism' and 'conspiracy theories' spouted by Theo, Magda and their handful of remaining supporters were proof that they had 'drifted alarmingly into the hate-filled politics of the far right' and had been fundamentally opposed to Progress, that eternal beacon of hope.

Sally Shukra had weighed in on their behalf from Chiapas with a forensic dismantling of the official case against Jay and Jack, but since she had already been declared one of the dangerous 'anti-semitic conspiracy theorists' who had 'radicalised' the offenders, her intervention ended up being used to further confirm their guilt.

Needless to say, the Anderson-Butler Fund for Social Change crept out of the woodwork to point out that they had detected the early warning signs and had cut off funding for the Infoshop when they had realised the direction the campaign was heading. Their only regret, they said, was that they had not acted sooner.

On the other side of the political spectrum, the colour of Jay's skin meant that, for them, the bombing confirmed everything they had always said about 'foreigners' and the people, like Theo, who pandered to them. Nobody at all, it seemed, was prepared to speak up in defence of Jay and Jack's reputation, in support of Theo and the other 'suspects', or to echo in any way their criticism of smart city plans which would see all sense of community as we knew it abolished, in favour of empty electronic lives of total surveillance, control and social isolation.

The cloud below had cleared now to reveal the delicately rippled surface of the blue ocean. Theo tried to push Wotton from his mind and focus on the task in hand, the long-planned gesture that had been the lynchpin of his attempts to stave off insanity and persuade himself that life was worth continuing. He was taking Jay back to where he had wanted to be, to where he had dreamed of being, and where he could now stay for eternity.

There was a price to pay for Theo, of course. Not the financial price of his return ticket, nor the price of the lost pride at having pleaded with Jay's family to be allowed to take his ashes to Santa Sofia, and then to have had to ask for their help with the cost of the trip, nor even the price to his nerves of the endless bureaucratic delays to his permission to leave the UK. The biggest price would be the emotional one of seeing Isha again, after all these years, and witnessing at first hand how happy she was with her new life, her new man and the child which he, and not Theo, had been able to give her. But then, maybe that was all part of this process for Theo. If there was no price to pay, no suffering to endure, then there could be no inner redemption.

He had long held in his mind's eye an image of the encounter at the arrivals lounge on Santa Sofia. There would be Isha, Azad and what's-his-name (he had made a careful point of refusing to remember what this man was called) waiting for him and he would have to make a great point of shaking the fellow's hand, looking him in the eye, giving Isha only the most superficial and polite amounts of attention, so as not to make it blindingly obvious to one and all that he would remain forever besotted with her.

Azad was a different matter, of course. Theo would be bringing to The Boy all the love that his Uncle Jay had wanted to bring him. He would tell him about Jay, about what he had been like, about what he had said and done, about how he had longed so much to spend the last decades of his life on Santa Sofia with him and Isha.

Theo must have fallen lightly asleep at some

point, because the next thing he knew was a feeling in his ears that the plane had started its descent to Santa Sofia.

He peered out of the porthole. For the moment there was nothing to be seen but water, which got closer and closer until he could see the sand banks beneath the azure surface and it felt as if the wheels of the plane would skim the white crests of the waves.

And then a brief strip of sun-baked sand followed by a great outpouring of greenness, a pulsating and overwhelming abundance of vegetation that scarcely seemed plausible for someone raised on the meagre rations provided by recreation grounds, mowed lawns, grass verges and railway embankments.

The perimeter fence, the runway, the bumping and braking, the taxiing, the doors opening and the thick sticky wall of jungle-smelling heat which nearly knocked Theo backwards as he stepped out.

There was a slight hold-up at passport control, a whispered conversation and some pointing at the computer screen. They looked in his bag and wanted to know all about the urn, where he was taking it, who he would be staying with. It was to be expected, of course. After all, Jay Mukherjee was a notorious terrorist.

Theo almost missed Isha when he eventually wandered out into the arrivals lounge. He had been looking for a family group, in fact, but there she was alone, standing up from a table at the café and walking towards him.

She was older, of course, but no less beautiful in Theo's eyes. Even more so, in fact. He felt suddenly helpless in the face of the great flood of emotion that was sweeping through every cell in his body.

"Hello Isha!" he said, holding out his hand awkwardly to her, as this seemed the correct thing to do.

"And hello Thee," she replied, taking his hand and gently, briefly, shaking it, with an amused look on her face.

He felt intimidated by her presence – her existence even.

"So..." he said, looking around the hall, "did you come with...?"

"Azad?" she chuckled. "No, you wouldn't catch him dead in a place like this. He's off fishing with his mates".

"And how about...?"

She looked quizzically at him.

"So where's your partner, Azad's father...?"

She burst into laughter. "That bastard? How would I know? Last time I heard he was in Melbourne with some little Japanese girl. We split up three years ago. Didn't Jay tell you anything?"

"Oh," said Theo.

As they left the airport and headed for Isha's village, as she chatted, laughed and smiled, as she told him how well he was looking, as she took one hand off the steering wheel to press it on his when he was telling her about the hard things he had lived through, he was aware that something very precious, something that had been frozen for such an endlessly long time, had began to thaw and flourish anew.

When the time came for him to return to London, he knew that he couldn't.

The years that followed were like a dream for Theo Carter. He had touched happiness in Wotton, only to lose it in such traumatic circumstances, but now he fully embraced it in a manner that he could never have imagined possible.

Sometimes he felt as if it was not his own life he was leading at all but someone else's that he had stolen – Jay's, in a way, though he would obviously not be sharing a bed with Isha, as Theo was.

Sometimes he felt as if it was not even real, instead a kind of afterlife or illusion, but then something would crop up – an infected mosquito bite, a splinter in the foot, a dose of the runs – to reassure him he was very much within the organic imperfection of the real world.

From the perspective of the civilization he had fled, Theo was living a 'miserable' existence, a subsistence lifestyle that would be termed 'poverty'. They grew vegetables, picked fruit from the forest. Azad taught Theo how to fish in the rivers and the sea and how to fashion and adapt the long wooden fishing spears used by the locals. They traded produce with others, helped each other out and exchanged gifts of know-how and resources without calculation.

Their simplicity was not austerity. Their freedom was not isolation. The earth in which they grubbed was not dirt, but the only gold truly worth having.

They had no televisions, computers or mobile phones. Why would they need any of that? They had life, love and sunshine.

"You're very different from when I knew you before, Thee", said Isha, leaning against him in the long grass as he stroked her long black hair, streaked now with flashes of grey and white. "There was always something in the way, back then. A tension, an anger inside that made you quite uncomfortable to be with, a lot of the time. You rarely seemed properly relaxed, like you are now".

"I know," said Theo. "It was a battle. It was always a battle to know how to cope with all the shit happening around you, constantly changing, constantly pushing towards you, cornering you. How can you be yourself in a world designed to *prevent* you from being yourself? How much do you adapt and conform and how much do you resist? How can you reconcile those two contradictory impulses – self-preservation and defending the well-being of everyone and of everything?"

"Other people manage, Thee," said Isha, gently. "Other people find a path that lets them carry on living, without throwing all their principles out of the window".

"So did I," Theo reminded her. "I found that balance with the Infoshop. For a while. But it couldn't last, because this thing is always encroaching further and further. If we were just talking about a static state of affairs then, yes, I could have got used to it and put up with it, even if I knew it was not what I really wanted. But that's not how it is. They never stop. They never leave us in peace".

"Really?" said Isha. "You're not at peace here, Thee?" She lifted her head and gave him an affectionate kiss on the nose.

"Here, yes, of course, but we were talking about back there, in that other world. You must have felt the same, deep down, or you wouldn't have come here, would you?"

"Hmmm". She thought about it. "I think it was more of a positive choice. I don't think it was that I couldn't cope. I had created my own little world there. That's what people do. I had my friends, my job, my interests, my books, my music. I had you, too, Thee, for a while... But you never really fitted into the rest of it, did you? You never let me lose myself in my safe personal space, you always had to remind me of the big dark reality out there..."

"And I was wrong? There was no big dark reality?"

She turned and looked at him and from the welling in her eyes he could see she was thinking of her brother.

"Yes, of course there was, Thee. I know that now. I probably always knew that, but I didn't want to, if you know what I mean. I wanted to feel safe, be happy, make the most of being alive!"

"We're doing that now, I think".

"Yes, we are Thee", she said, and pressed her lips to his.

"Mum! Thee!" They were interrupted by Azad's voice. He had come back from his latest fishing expedition with something to show them.

"Over here, Az!"

He was bounding over towards them bearing, on the end of his pointed wooden stick, the most splendid and enormous fish.

As he excitedly filled them in with all the details, Theo marvelled at the way this lad now stood astride childhood and manhood. Physically he was strong and imposing but his enthusiasm, and the simplicity with which he spoke, were those of an adorable child. His voice, cracking between treble and bass, itself seemed to express that vulnerable vitality, that touching innocence of a fresh new incarnation of the human species stepping out into whatever world awaits him.

Azad loved hearing about his Uncle Jay. He loved hearing about the times that Theo and Jay had spent together. He bellowed with laughter at the little anecdotes Theo told him, even when he had heard them a dozen times before. Azad knew roughly what had happened, of course, but Theo tried not to dwell too much on that side. He tried to keep it light. He wanted The Boy to feel, above all, the love that Jay had so often expressed for him. Theo also did not tell Azad too much about what life was like in London, the sort of everyday existence they had known. He didn't want to corrupt him with even knowing anything about all that. He wanted him to stay untainted and natural.

All was well in the village. Everyone had each other, even when they fell out over various everyday trivia. Theo had Isha and Azad. Isha had Azad and Theo. Soon, when he was not even 16 years old, Azad had Daksha. And then Daksha had Jay. Little Jay.

One morning, when Theo emerged from their wooden cabin to start a fire and to fetch water from the spring, he looked down the gentle forest slope to the sparkling ocean and drank in the happiness. The day into which he had emerged felt like a representation of his own inner state, which shone out on to everything around him.

As he walked up the hill with his wooden pail, his tread was light and carefree. But what was this, on the edge of the forest? Some workmen, by the looks of it, not locals. What were they doing?

As Theo approached, he saw that the men were building a fence, a very large fence topped with a double row of razor wire. And on to this fence they were attaching large notices, printed in angry red: 'Nature Protection Zone. Keep out! World Preservation Trust'.

"What's all this?" he asked the nearest worker.

"Can't you read?" he said, pointing at the sign. "This all has to be protected. Nobody can come here now".

"And the spring?" asked Theo. "How are we going to get our water with this fence here?"

"That's not our problem, mister. We are just doing our job. Maybe you need to pay your water bills like everybody else!"

For the first time in years, the anger was rising again in Theo and, fearing where it might take him, he walked round the end of the fence-in-progress and marched on up the path towards the spring, ignoring their shouts of protest.

On the way back, with his pail full, he had to take an even bigger detour to get round the barrier.

"You won't be doing that again!" the same man shouted at him as he passed. "They are sending people to protect the land! You'll see!"

In a strange state of calm fury, Theo made breakfast for Isha and Azad, told them what had happened and then headed down to the road to hitch a lift into town. He needed to go online.

Half way through the two-hour journey, they were forced to bump over into the rubble on the side of the road to let past a convoy of military-style trucks coming in the other direction.

"Is that the army?" he asked his companion, who was probably more or less the same ripe old age as the battered and dust-covered old Japanese car he was driving.

He tut-tutted. "No, no, not military, not government. Those are private security! Not people's army but private army!"

Could they be heading for the village? Was it something to do with the fence? This made Theo's mission all the more important.

The little phone shop and internet cafe was right on the main market place and the bright orange curtain that served as the front door did nothing to keep out the hubbub of passing scooters, shouting traders, barking dogs and laughing children.

Theo knew in advance exactly what he needed to punch into the search engine. 'World Preservation Trust' and 'Sally Shukra'.

Within seconds he had what he was looking for: "The World Preservation Trust," wrote Sally, "is at the forefront of this new pseudo-environmental imperialism, essentially privatizing huge swathes of the planet, and displacing indigenous people living close to the land, to create its ill-named 'Nature Protection Zones'. Copious evidence shows that this is nothing more than a cover for seizure of land for purely corporate interests, whether that be the interlaced carbon-offset and logging industries, or the mineral extraction essential for the so-called renewable energy sector. This connection is confirmed by the funding partners listed on the WPF's own website, which include the likes of GloboMine, Carbon Exponential and Gaia Heaven, which I have previously shown to be part of the SLI empire".

A shudder of black electricity ran down Theo's spine. He stayed staring at the page, as if paralysed, for a full five minutes before he made his next move.

This search was more complicated and took a lot longer, but he got there in the end, via all sorts of obscure government, commercial and geological sites on a global and local level. It was clear that Santa Sofia, in particular the area where they lived, had recently been identified as a potentially crucial source of lithium, so badly needed to fuel the electric batteries of the brave new 'sustainable' world.

Theo usually liked to chat a little with the locals when he took a ride into town. It was so much easier than with English people. They didn't hide behind an image of who they wanted you to think they were, who they thought they were expected to be. They were just who they were and, as a consequence, Theo too could be just who he was with them, without that feeling of being constantly judged, assessed and socially graded.

For this journey back to the village, however, he was uncharacteristically silent, to the point that the young couple, bringing their farm truck back from the market, broke off their lively conversation about the psychological health and mores of the man's mother to ask Theo if he was feeling all right.

He told them he was tired and then, in the spirit of openness, explained that he was worried about this 'nature protection zone' and what it would mean for their community. Their total lack of concern, their sincere conviction that all was for the best and nothing bad could possibly happen, actually rubbed off on him for a while and made the last part of the trip bearable, as they zig-zagged their way around the hilly coastline in a cloud of summer dust.

But when they reached the edge of the village, the knot was retied in Theo's guts. There were dozens of people out in the road, gesticulating and surrounding half a dozen 'private army' vehicles. As Theo hurriedly thanked his driver and climbed out, a young 'soldier' stood up in the back of one of these, pointed a gun towards the heavens and let off a rattle of shots.

There were screams and people scattered in every direction. Theo dived into a side street and hurried off towards home as fast as he could, even though running was pretty much beyond him now, especially uphill.

Another shock awaited. There were neighbours outside his home. Two elderly ladies were cradling Little Jay in their arms, stroking his hair, enveloping him with maternal warmth. The infant looked up at Theo and his look spoke of incomprehension and terror. One of the women, Fatima, waved her finger silently at him as a sign to wait. "I'll fetch Isha," she said.

Seconds later, Isha emerged from the cabin, hair dishevelled and eyes wide with anguish and red with tears. She fell into Theo's arms. "It's Azad, Thee. They've killed Azad. They shot him. He's dead!"

It was the 'private army' of course, sent to defend the 'protection zone' from the people who went there for their water, for their fishing and their hunting. A group of locals had taken no notice of their warnings and had carried on as usual, and so these corporate mercenaries had opened fire, with Azad being the one to bear the cost. It didn't matter to them. These people's lives were worthless. There would be no repercussions.

As he gazed down at the lifeless body of this noble young man, all that primal human strength and vitality destroyed forever by a single bullet through the brain, the tears did not flow from Theo's eyes.

Instead they flowed backwards and fed his soul, his blood and his heart with the knowledge of what he had to do next for Azad, for Isha, for Jay and for Little Jay. For everyone and for everything.

* * *

Howard Gear was on top form at the Gaia Heaven annual shareholders' meeting close to London Bridge station.

Simon, his personal assistant, couldn't help thinking that there was something actually perfect about him this morning. His immaculate grooming, his dignified white hair offset against his smooth, bronzed, face – he looked ten years younger with his chin fixed. Simon allowed himself to bask in appreciation of his boss's expensive new suit, his brilliantly shining shoes, his gleaming (if not entirely natural) teeth. His posture and his delivery both radiated supreme confidence, steely determination wrapped in the velvet assurance of inevitable, unassailable success. He couldn't wait to get him back to the hotel room.

The speech was going down particularly well with an eccentric old duffer in a sports jacket and flat cap sitting in the front row.

He roared out his approval when the CEO spoke of his plans to roll out 30 more smart city projects following the enormous success of the pioneer New Green Wotton scheme and the subsequent developments in Birmingham, Manchester, Sheffield and Edinburgh.

And he even got to his feet, with the aid of his walking stick, when Gear enthused about his company's inclusive and global vision, which involved nurturing and aiding the global south, and at the same time preserving our natural capital, by means of innovative protection zones and associated sustainable industry.

"Well done to you, Sir!" he bellowed, in an old-fashioned upper class accent. "It's about jolly time somebody stood up for the countryside! Marvellous forward-thinking stuff, what!"

"Who the fuck's this geezer?" whispered Harry to his security second-in-command Mo as they watched proceedings from the doorway.

Mo shrugged. "I dunno. A shareholder. He turned up at the last minute".

"You checked for metal?"

"Of course".

"Did you double-check with the watchlist?"

"The watchlist? For him? You've got to be..."

"Do it. Now".

The great business leader Howard Gear was coming to the end of his speech now, thanking everyone for coming, thanking the venue for their hospitality, thanking the backroom staff who had prepared everything so perfectly.

Mo was back, looking embarrassed and agitated. "I think we've got a problem," he said, showing Harry what he had discovered.

The applause was ringing out across the conference suite. The catering staff were manoeuvring the canapés and glasses of fizzy white wine into position in the side room.

Harry almost choked as he took in the information. "For fuck's sake!"

The old fellow was on his feet again, fumbling around with the end of his walking stick, advancing towards the stage, holding out his hand to congratulate the speaker in a more personal way. Exchanging an amused glance with Simon, Gear stepped forward to meet him, arm extended and ready for the handshake.

"Stop!" screamed Harry at the top of his voice as he and Mo launched themselves into action.

Gear looked up in astonishment and at that very moment the old man deftly manoeuvred his walking stick so that the newly-exposed addition of a wooden dagger from Santa Sofia, once used as a humble letter opener, thrust its way under the CEO's ribcage and right through his vampire-heart.

From 'Our Stolen Freedom'

For most of my life I believed that radical social change could be brought about by broadly political means.

I quickly saw through the illusion of their democracy, of course, and abandoned any notion that the system would allow us to vote away its control and power.

But still I imagined that this type of activity could form part of a breakthrough, that the pressure put on the system by increasing electoral challenges would force it to make mistakes, show its hand, destroy its own enslaving illusions.

Perhaps over-influenced by the Spanish Revolution of the 1930s, and other historic uprisings, I lived in the hope of a mounting pressure of revolt which would culminate in people taking to the streets in huge numbers and sweeping away the structures of domination.

As time went on, this idea of 'revolution' became more and more of an in-joke between me and my comrades, more of an abstract holy grail than a concrete goal.

But still I was sure that if we organised politically in the right way, and with sufficient determination, we could one day manage to bring it about.

Now, I no longer believe it is possible to com-

bat the system in the strictly political realm.

What has changed?

Firstly, and most importantly, the system has developed its powers of deceit beyond even the level imagined by George Orwell or Guy Debord in the last century.

It has taken control of 'reality' as perceived by the vast majority of people. It fills their mind with a false version of the world, a full-spectrum spectacle, designed specifically to hide the truth as to what is happening around them.

How can you talk politics, make a political case, to someone who essentially does not live in the same world as you, who bases all their reasoning and judgement on falsity, on circumstances and events which have been invented and fed to them so as to keep them in a condition of manipulated ignorance?

The gulf between the rebels and the people they hope to mobilise becomes impossibly vast.

Any provisional success in establishing common ground, in overcoming the obstacles created by lifelong conditioning, can be swept away in an instant.

The system merely concocts yet another spectacular crisis, event or threat and the people you thought you had won over go fearfully scuttling back into the arms of authority, begging it to use its power to protect them and their families.

Because you refuse to swallow the system's lie

and naturally seek to analyse and expose its deceit, you yourself are conflated with the threat in question, regarded as complicit in its menace, irresponsible in your disregard for the official alarmism, insane in your refusal to accept what all those around you now accept, unconditionally, as truth.

The rebels find themselves, yet again, isolated and powerless in the face of cynically-induced mass delusion.

A second factor is, of course, the technological structures developed by the system, which make meaningful political organising, which was still prevalent until the 2020s, almost impossible.

There is total surveillance of all forms of electronic communication, of course, and of our real lives by means of the devices we use for this communication. Surveillance cameras watch us everywhere, smart systems track our moves, drones and satellites watch out for us, enabling the system to enforce the latest restrictions it has decided to place on our movements.

When large numbers of people do gather together in the streets, this same technology, plus an array of militarised weaponry, is used to push them off again, using the levels of brutality required to deter any recurrence.

And then of course, to loop back to my first point, there is all the apparatus of lying which steps in to deny that the protests are happening, or to distort their significance in some way, or to paint those involved as threats to the very people in whose interests they are acting.

This is not to say that I believe the system is all-powerful and that the people as a whole could not physically rise up and bring it down. This is why I rated the psychological aspect of its power as more important than the purely physical. But the combination of effective mind control and these physical infrastructures of repression together make a traditional revolution very difficult to imagine.

Does this mean I am without hope? On a personal level, yes, of course. I have no hope at all that I will ever see the sun, the sky and trees again and little hope that I will manage much longer to smuggle these words into the outside world through the small and temporary human crack in their wall which has opened up for me.

But I do have hope that the death-system can be brought down. How this might be done, I will explain on another occasion.

Sumtimes evrithing that hapens duznt feel reel. Amm I woching a show or plaing a game or is this my achual lief? Y cant I chaynge enything or mayke enything happen and jussed have to sitt and woch and sai nuthing?

Wat is the piont of beeing born if u are'nt alowd to doo wat u want to do or sai wat u want to sai?

Undated

I was thinking again about the tufts of greenery on the old yew and realised that it isn't a very accurate metaphor for what I am feeling. The tree, you see, is old and dying. It is an individual tree and individuals of all kinds come and go in time. This is an entirely natural process. But the tree of which I am part is a collective one, one which contains all the coming-and-going of individual trees. The tree is humankind. Nature. Our world. And it isn't right at all that this tree is dying. There is nothing inevitable about it. It is supposed to keep living for millions and millions of years. So the defiant surging-forth of greenness from that trunk is not just some final, futile, display of lingering vitality. It is an attempt to halt the decline and the decay. That is what I have always felt I have to do. I need to be alive myself, but that living-in-spite-of-it-all is also meant to wake up the wooden flesh around me, to stir the sap in every branch of this tree, in every twig, every leaf, in its trunk, its roots. In fact, come to think of it, that is partly what I mean by being alive, this taking-part in something so much bigger and so much more important than my own short-lived individual role. Being truly alive is to become more than oneself. We surpass and expand ourselves by becoming aware of our belong-

ing to a greater reality. And more than that, we live our lives as part of a greater reality. Or, at least, we try to. Because this is one of the forms of livingness which is blocked by the corpse-cage in which we are trapped. It won't let us be our individual selves, because our sense of freedom and empowerment threaten the dead hand of its complete control. It won't let us be our collective selves, because our collective sense of freedom and empowerment poses even more of a threat to the security of its prison. Indeed, these two forbidden sources of being are one and the same, when you get down to it. The joyful secret at the heart of our individual sense of life is our belonging to a wider being. And it is only by feeling our own individual meaning in a collective context that we can ever come to treasure our own self and life. The 'I' is only happy when it is also a 'We' and the 'We' draws its strength from being a coming-together of 'I's.

So the life-energy within me is, in reality, the life-energy of the collective which finds its expression through me. As an individual, I feel that its aim is to let me, personally, live fully, wildly, courageously. But that is only half the story, because this life-energy, transformed as it has been by adversity and necessity into something angry and potent, also seeks to liberate and unleash the living of the collective – of humanity and our Mother Nature.

2

SWANBOY

Alfie Duckworth wasn't a happy 12-year-old. He wasn't actually conscious of being unhappy because, for him, his life was simply normality. But on an unconscious level his body and his mind – which are, despite modern superstitions, the same entity – were both deeply aware of the drabness of his existence.

Every day of the week he was dragged out of his dreams by the rather abrasive voice of his mother, Donna Duckworth, demanding that he report at once for breakfast duties.

Every day of the week saw the same frantic dash to get dressed, washed and fed before being bundled into the back of Donna's company saloon to be dropped off at Hogton Manor Middle School, known on Saturdays and Sundays as Hogton Manor Juvenile Safety Centre.

The smell inside the new car made him feel sick. The lurching of the vehicle and whining of the electric motor made him feel sick. Wearing a mask and being trapped inside this metal box made him feel sick.

These short trips set the tone for the standard days of his childhood: grey and vaguely toxic days in which the best he could do was to stop himself from physically vomiting.

Alfie Duckworth wasn't a popular boy. He was awkward, gangly, with oversized hands, feet and nose. His lips bulged out from his face in a rather comical way. Inevitably he was called Duckface at school. He had always been known as Duckface, as far back as he could remember. Maybe the nickname had been passed on from one group of children to another by the infantile grapevine, even when he had changed school. Or maybe it was just such an obvious and easy insult that it would spontaneously pop into the minds of any random group of a certain age.

Alfie wasn't much liked by his teachers, either. He was dyslexic and this was frustrating for them. Mr Gums, his English teacher, kept reminding himself that just because the boy had enormous difficulties in spelling the simplest of words, this did not mean that he was stupid. At the same time, however, he could not help whispering in his own ear that Alfie's dyslexia did not in fact exclude the possibility of him also being rather dim. The only time Alfie had ever got into actual trouble at school was for talking during class, but at the same time the teachers were always complaining that he was too quiet. Mrs Tadiss, his Biology teacher, even wrote in his report that he needed to "come out of his shell", which Alfie took as another cruel twist on the duck theme.

Alfie had got used to being disliked by pretty much everyone. The name-calling generally became water off a duck's back, if you'll excuse the expression. It did hurt him, though, when pretty Debby Thomas called him 'ugly' with a malicious joy that twisted her features into an unrecognisable picture of spite. It also hurt him when other boys leant round his plastic shield in class to flick his ears from behind, when they crossed into his zone in the exercise yard just to trip him up and laughed as he got awkwardly back on his feet, more worried about the damage to his trousers than the bloodied caps of his knees, because his mother would never see his knees.

Days at school became days to simply endure. That was how it was. The evenings weren't much better. His mother would make him 'help with the housework', although he invariably ended up doing the lion's share. She had even trained him to lay the table and pop a ready-meal into the microwave, or make a dessert with the 3-D printer, while she busied herself on her nuphone: there was barely a moment when she was not either scrolling, messaging or talking on the thing.

After that he had to load the dishwasher, do

his homework and unload the dishwasher until, after a few minutes of TV, Donna declared that it was time for bed as he had an early start in the morning.

Alfie quite liked being in bed, in fact. He enjoyed just sitting there, with the light still on, doing nothing. He was really the kind of child who would have liked to have read for hours in bed, to have been transported off into a fairy world of his own imagination by the power of the written word. But he couldn't do that, as it was all too slow and painful, so instead he just let thoughts well up within him and enjoyed whatever images appeared in his mind.

Even here, he had to be careful. Donna had come in to say goodnight once and seen him just sitting there. This had worried her – 'freaked her out' she had told her friends at the gym. It was like he was in some kind of 'catastrophic trance', she had insisted, to general nods and frowns of sympathy all round.

She had arranged a video link-up with a doctor, who turned out to be so old and useless, bordering on incompetent, that he had failed to understand the problem and had declared that daydreaming was 'perfectly normal behaviour' for a boy of that age.

But Alfie could not afford to take any chances after that, and he started taking his phone to bed with him, as any decent modern child would. He had little use for it, in fact, having nobody to talk to, no desire to catch up on the latest insults and mockery being heaped on him by his peers and little patience with the various games that should normally have kept him entertained, as his clumsiness made it impossible to master them.

He would sit and wallow in his innermost unformed thoughts, as before, but clasping his phone, and when his mother came in for lights-out he would tell her with the sweetest of smiles that he had been 'chatting with his friends' or that he had managed to reach level 2 of Torture Bloodbath.

"Lovely," she would purr, putting on her disposable plastic gloves in order to tuck him up neatly for the night. Maybe the little fellow would turn out to be quite normal after all.

Donna Duckworth wasn't a happy 39-year-old. She was very conscious of her own unhappiness and liked to tell other people about it. Her listeners would have seen tears of self-pity in her eyes as she spoke, had it not been for the fact that she invariably wore sunglasses, even indoors.

The main source of her unhappiness was that she perceived her life as being unhappy for no fault of her own. The blame all lay with Alfie's father, Robin. She had been very impressed with Robin when she met him, at a friend's wedding reception, fourteen years previously. He had just started work as a secondary school teacher. He was good-looking, charming, generally did what she wanted him to and looked a good bet for keeping her in a reasonable state of modest affluence for many years to come. When she became pregnant, semi-deliberately if truth be told, she certainly went along with the idea of marriage and was able to fulfil her dream of tying the knot in Las Vegas, the glamour capital of the world's most marvellous country.

But, afterwards, things had quickly gone downhill. Robin was not really cut out for the modern educational system. He was constantly being reprimanded for not ticking the right boxes, not filling in the right paperwork in the right way, resisting the use of e-teachers in a manner considered close to technophobic. "Yes, of course education is all about reaching out to the students," Mr Azin, head of history, had told him. "But not just any old how! There are rules to follow, Robin, rules that are there for a reason! You and I just have to put our trust in those rules. It's not our job to make the rules, to question how the rules are made or to decide unilaterally, as you seem to be doing, to completely bypass the rules in a misguided desire to 'get the kids interested in history' as you put it. For Christ's sake, Robin, this is the 21st century!"

Robin had become disillusioned with teaching, spent months off work with depression and ended up quitting the profession.

He had only been unemployed for a short time, in fact, but, together with the sick leave, this period had left an indelible stain on Donna's opinion of her husband. From that time on, he was a worthless good-for-nothing, an idler, a 'total loser'. She had taken up a job as a secretary in a PR firm to fill in a short-term financial gap and ended up liking it so much she didn't want to pack it in when Robin started working as a taxi-driver.

The fact that she earned slightly more than him gave her an inflated sense of superiority and allowed to look down on her spouse in a way that she found fairly therapeutic for her own mental state. She managed to be indignant and resentful of almost every move the poor man made – the fact that he was still in bed when she left home in the morning was used in evidence against him, time and time again, even though this was because he didn't finish his shift until the early hours.

There was a connection between her low opinion of Robin and her concerns about Alfie. On one level, it was because she was worried that the boy would turn out like his father. She sometimes caught her husband in moments of reflection, 'staring blankly into space', and became fearful that this shameful disposition might have been genetically passed on to her son. On a secondary level, both males were victims of a certain prejudice that Donna had inherited from her mother, Betty, who had fallen in love with a US serviceman based in the UK, only for him to disappear without trace the moment she fell pregnant. Men, for Betty, just could not be trusted and Donna never quite shook off this inherited gem of wisdom.

It wasn't that Donna didn't like men at all. Her hormones saw to that. In fact, it was her liking for a man that had kept her in the job she had taken as a stop-gap when Robin gave up teaching. And it was *his* liking for *her* that had seen her promoted to a ridiculously elevated status in Lionel C. Warnock Communications. All right, let's not be coy about this. For some time now, she had been having an affair with her boss, Lionel himself. Lionel represented everything Donna liked about men. He gave her respect bordering on adulation, sex, money, expensive meals and weekend trips away disguised as business duties. She could claim her visits to the tanning salon on expenses! When Donna complained, as she often had, about the unappealing size and shape of her breasts, her husband had invariably trotted out some corny line about loving her the way she was. Lionel, however, had taken action and paid for plastic surgery.

Lionel wasn't a drain, like Robin was. She didn't have to clear up after him, remind him about household tasks or listen to endless accounts of the latest tedious and moth-eaten old book he had been wasting his day reading. OK, her boss was a bit older than her, but he kept in shape at the gym, dressed well and even if she knew it was a toupee, had an impressive shock of jet-black hair. And he had energy! He was a go-getter, a shaper and maker, an 'up and at 'em' kind of guy. He had friends and business contacts with exotic names like Klaus, Uri and Roberto. He was even famous, for being the first man in Britain to have had three vasectomies! The first two had been reversed when he began new relationships with women who wanted children with him, but then inexplicably changed their minds. Lionel was successful! He was a winner! What a contrast with that miserable misfit of a man she had had the misfortune of marrying.

Alfie was sitting outside on the plastic lawn that his mother had been proud to have had installed the previous summer. It was so much more convenient than those dirty old weedy things you had to keep cutting. He was gazing up at the vapour trails drifting across the suburban sky and tracking the occasional drone passing in front of the pylons.

"Alfie!" It was Donna, from the back door.

"What are you doing?"

"Nothing," he said. "Thinking!"

"You what?"

"Thinking!" he repeated.

She was right beside him by now, jabbing an angry finger at his face.

"If I get any more cheek from you, my boy, there'll be no Nu-Meat Crazy Capsules in your lunch box for the rest of the term! Hasn't your e-teacher got any homework for you to be getting on with?"

"Nope," he lied. "I've finished it".

"No games to play? No credits to be won? Snap out of it and do something useful with your life, for Christ's sake, my boy, instead of sitting here doing nothing like some useless pile of..."

She nearly uttered the word 'Robin' rather than 'rubbish', presumably out of force of habit, and even though she had avoided the slip, she glanced guiltily up at the window of the bedroom where she knew her husband would currently be rousing himself.

She slipped on a glove, grabbed Alfie by the arm and whispered fiercely in his face: "Now, look after yourself, be a good boy, take no notice of your father and remember to be ready and smart for six o'clock, because Lionel has got a surprise lined up for us!"

Alfie would have liked to have been able to have guessed, from the expression in his mother's eyes, just what kind of surprise this was likely to turn out to be, but all he could see was a distorted reflection of his own sullen duck face in the shiny black plastic behind which she hid her soul.

As Donna made a last sweep of the kitchen and living room before departing – furiously spraying disinfectant over tables, chairs, door handles, light switches and fruit bowl – Alfie went through the motions of going online.

But when the front door had safely clicked shut – plus double-locked from the outside because you never knew – and the sound of her car had safely disappeared from earshot, he put the device to one side, leapt to his feet and flung open all the downstairs windows.

There was always a guilty side of his mind that pictured the swarms of evil black microbes that his mother had assured him would flood into the home if ever they had the chance, settling cunningly on every nook and cranny and lurking for hours, days or months, waiting for the chance to propel themselves into his throat, his lungs or his brain.

But, like the stink of disinfectant, this cloud of unease was invariably swept away by the delicious oxygen-rich breeze that filled the house in his mother's absence.

Alfie sat back on the sofa and looked out of the window, waiting for his father to come downstairs.

Robin Duckworth wasn't an unhappy 40-year-old. He wasn't exactly radiantly happy, either, but he kept himself sane by retreating from the world around him as much as he possibly could.

The existence and presence of Alfie also saved Robin from unhappiness, although the life that the boy lived and the effect it was having on him was one of the aspects of reality from which he often felt the need to flee.

As soon as he reached the bottom of the staircase, Alfie was at his side, as was always the case when they were home together, without Donna.

"Hi Dad!" he smiled and the two of them enjoyed a warm hug – something not permitted in the presence of the mistress of the house due to the well-known dangers of transmitting infection.

"What have you been reading?" asked Alfie, trying to turn around the book clenched in Robin's hand so that he could see the title.

"It's called *Being Yourself*," replied his father, showing him the cover, which depicted the outline of a human head filled, on the inside, with an image of the night sky.

It was an old book of course, a remnant of the pre-normal. Neither title nor artwork would make it past Safety Check these days, regardless of the content. Irresponsible individualism and emotional mysticism had both been proven to contribute to unproductive social maladjustment.

"Why is the sky *inside* the person's head, not outside?" asked Alfie.

"Well..." said Robin, as he stood on a stool to reach the packet of tea from its hiding place on top of the cupboard – he didn't care if it was 'unhygienic' and could not abide the scalding hot fake-sweet chemical fluid his wife insisted on imbibing.

Alfie was looking at him expectantly.

"Well," Robin continued, "I haven't actually read much of it yet, but I think I can see where it is going. The writer says it is important to know who you really are..."

The boy was frowning.

"What is it, Alfie?"

"But we all know who we are. It comes up on the screen".

"Yes, but that's just the surface – your name and all the details of your life stored on the Global Community Cloud. He's talking about who you are inside yourself, deep inside yourself".

"Ah..." said Alfie, but he was looking lost.

"What he is saying, the man who wrote this, quite a long time ago now, is that if you look deep enough inside yourself, you will find that you are actually part of something much bigger, that you are part of nature, for a start..."

"What, animals and trees and things?"

"Yes. Animals and trees and human beings. We are all made up of the same stuff, when you look at it".

Alfie gave a little shudder. His mother had brought him up to believe that 'nature' was dirty, messy, unsafe, nasty, dangerous, teeming with infection. The idea that there was anything like that *inside him* was therefore somewhat alarming.

Robin saw his face and laughed. "You know, Alfie, once upon a time you used to like all of that. Do you remember the walks we used to do together? We'd get the train to Lower Erding and head out into the woods?"

"Did we?" His face looked blank and then it started to come back. "Oh yes!" He smiled. "There was a long windy path going down to a stream and a little wooden bridge that I was always scared was going to collapse under me!"

"Yes, that's right. Do you remember? And it felt good, didn't it, to be there with all the trees and birds and grass and earth?"

Alfie nodded and all of a sudden a great wave of nostalgia came over him, a flood of desire that had long been held down and locked up.

"Why don't we do that any more, Dad? Can we go there again?"

Robin was shaking his head.

"Not since the last emergency. You need a good travel ranking to be allowed that far now. I don't stand a chance..."

Alfie's brief moment of hope had been extinguished and Robin saw the sparkle fade from his eyes.

He put his arm round his son and gave him a little squeeze.

"But you know, Alfie, the trees and the birds and the stream are still there, and we are still part of the same world as them, even if we are stuck here and can't see them for ourselves. That's what the man's saying in this book. And what I can see he is going to say next is that we are made up of the same stuff as the whole universe, in fact, and that if we look closely enough *inside* ourselves, we will find the same thing that we would discover if we looked far enough *outside* ourselves. So that's why the picture shows the stars inside the person's head. Do you see?"

Alfie thought for a moment and then nodded.

"I think so. Thanks Dad".

He remained silent and pensive for a moment or two while his father prepared his breakfast, then spoke again.

"Dad?"

"Mmmm?"

"Do you think you could read me some of that book?"

Robin stopped what he was doing to focus on

his son. He thought about how to explain.

"I could, Alfie, if you really wanted, but I am not sure that you would like the way he explains things. It really is a book for grown-ups, and even maybe for grown-ups from the old days, because he uses a lot of words that are difficult to understand. Even I have to look them up sometimes!"

This made Alfie laugh out loud. The thought of his father not knowing the meaning of a word was so patently absurd.

"I can try to explain it a bit better, some time, if you like. When I have finished it and know everything he's saying. Or I could tell you about some bits as I go along, maybe?"

Alfie nodded. "OK, thanks Dad".

Robin turned back to the fridge.

"Dad?"

"Yes?"

There was no sign of impatience on Robin's face and, indeed, none in his heart.

"Could you read me something else? One of your books from when you were a boy?"

"What now? This morning? Haven't you got any homework to do?"

"No, I've finished it," lied Alfie again.

"Really? Good for you! Well, OK then. Yes, we'll go up to the attic in a bit and see what you fancy!"

A while later, the two of them settled down

in the living room to begin the chosen volume, which went under the title of Osman the Old.

This told the story of an ancient wizard, a one-eyed and white-bearded fellow in green robe and hat, who had once been much loved and trusted by the people of The Valley. However, these carefree and happy folk had been tricked into surrendering their land and their freedom by accepting the 'protection' of an evil Crown Prince and Osman was forced to flee into the hills, where he lived in a vast cave within a hidden rocky ravine.

As the centuries passed by, Osman was never forgotten by the people and it was to him that they invariably turned whenever they were in greatest need. Generation after generation were able to see off the worst of the cruelty and despotism of the Crown Prince and his descendents with the help of The Old Green Man.

Alfie sat entranced as Robin read chapter after chapter recounting the crucial magical interventions of the sage of the wilderness. It was a joy for his father to be able to give him this pleasure, although he also felt sadness that the boy's reading skills did not allow him to explore worlds like this on his own. There were endless videos and talking books available for kids, of course, but all of the dull and sanitised modern variety, amounting to little more than fictional renditions of global educational guidelines.

In one episode shared by father and son, Osman the Old had visitors from the nightmarish New City which had been built by the Crown Prince's regime on the ruins of Aldham, the charming market town which had thrived for thousands of years on the banks of the River Var.

An apparently sympathetic young couple came to visit him in his cave and told him they were dedicated to fighting injustice in the Valley and, indeed, everywhere.

They told him that their friends had been transformed into fish by a black magician in the pay of the regime. These fish had been trapped in a deep well in the courtyard of what had once been a monastery but was now a prison. The walls were so high that they could not even get near the well, let alone rescue the fish.

"Osman, you are so wise and deep and green," said Lulas, the young woman, caressing the outer edge of his gown. "We are sure you can find a way to help us".

Touched by their faith in him, Osman transformed himself into a kingfisher, flew to the city and dived from the sky into the well, with the idea of picking up the fish in his beak and rescuing them.

But the flattery had made him careless and, too late, he saw as his bird-self entered the well that there were no fish inside.

At the same moment, there was a great

crashing thump above his head – accomplices of the treacherous couple had dropped a huge stone slab on to the top of the well, trapping him inside.

Quick as a flash, Osman turned himself into a ball of blazing fire and when he descended into the water it all fizzled and evaporated into steam. The steam, containing Osman, rose through the tiny gaps in the seal at the top of the well and drifted up into the air to join the clouds.

The clouds were blown east into the mountains, Osman fell to the earth as a thousand drops of rain, pulled himself together and returned to his cave.

The lying couple, who had been in the pay of the Crown Prince, were long gone, of course, and Osman resolved, from that day on, never to trust anyone who praised him.

"Blimey, is that the time?" said Robin. "I've got to go to work!"

When he was alone, Alfie went up into his father's bedroom – Donna had long since given up sharing a bed with her husband – and saw the other book on the bedside table, the one with the stars inside the person's head.

This image, and what he heard about the contents, again stirred up something inside him and so, in accordance to what he had been taught, Alfie fetched his MeLog and created a new entry in the My Thoughts section. He wrote a few painful sentences and then saved it – not to the device itself, of course, but to the Global Community Cloud where the inner thoughts of every child in the world were collected and analysed.

"Alfie!" shouted Donna through her mask, when she arrived back through the front door, which she was appalled to find had not been double-locked by her departing husband. "Come here, my darling!"

Alfie obediently trotted out into the hallway towards her outstretched arms, which were holding a very thin film of plastic, with which she immediately engulfed her son.

"Turn around! That's it! Pull it tight! Move your foot in! Right, now count to ten!"

When she was pulling it off him again, she asked him if he was all right. He was looking a little breathless.

"Yes, fine thanks, Mum".

"You'll see, it'll do you the world of good! It's a new thing! HygieneWrap! It's coated with fifteen different types of disinfectant and nano-antibiotic. Fifteen! Kills all those horrible germs on your skin and your clothes".

Alfie smiled. She was so caring.

"Right boy, mask and gloves! We're going out!"

As soon as they got out of the car at the other end, Alfie saw that Lionel was filming them. This was no surprise as the man was obsessional about this. He filmed them eating meals, he filmed them walking in his garden, he filmed them filming him. Alfie had inadvertently once noticed over his shoulder that he was watching a video of Donna when she was getting undressed to go to bed and it made him feel queasy to imagine where Lionel might actually draw the line.

It was quite a treat that Lionel had laid on for them. They were going to something called 'the pantomime'. Apparently, in the old days, loads of people, far more than was safe, used to pack together, right on top of each other, to watch other people standing in front of them on a sort of fake screen, pretending to be in a film. During what is now the Winter Pause, they used to put on special shows for kids that made people laugh a lot, according to Lionel, who remembered it all.

Now one of these shows was being put on at the Edu-Screen here in Hogton, in the summer, but much better, explained Lionel, although Alfie had trouble understanding what was going to be happening.

Donna reassured Alfie that everybody would be properly separated and that it would not just be people pretending to be on the screen.

"So it's a proper film?"

"Yes," said Lionel. "And no. Because the film

shows people doing it like they used to. It's as if you were at one of the old pantos! And you have all the audience reaction, as well. Total genius. Just like being in the old days, but one hundred and ten per cent safe!"

It was a very strange film. There was a lady pretending to be man, men pretending to be ladies and lots of people disguised as ducks. Alfie initially smarted at this, imagining for a moment that this outing was some horrible joke at his expense, but soon realised that the Ugly Duckling was, in fact, the hero.

After it had finished, the way out was at the other side of the building and they had to walk through the park to get back to the car. Normally you needed to pay credit to go through, so Alfie was quite excited.

"Don't touch anything!" shouted Donna after him as he dashed off down a path towards the sound of running water. "Try not to breathe in too much!"

As Alfie rounded the corner, he saw before him a pond, a huge and magnificent pond in his eyes, with an ornamental bridge and weeping willows all around. And there, right in the middle of the water, heading straight towards him, was a swan. Alfie had no memory of ever having seen a swan in real life before. It was twice the size he had imagined and a hundred times more beautiful. As if basking in his admiration, it lifted and spread its wings slightly as it approached, providing a whole new dimension of majestic power. Alfie was spellbound as he watched the bird, soon joined by a companion, glide effortlessly round the pond, dipping at the water as it went, occasionally plunging its long white neck into the water in search of food.

"Alfie! Alfie!"

He gave himself another 30 seconds with the swans and then ran fast to make up the time.

Donna was looking impatient. Lionel had gone on ahead and seemed to be filming a litter bin.

"Mum! Look!" he shouted, lifting his arms a little and trying to swerve gracefully as he advanced. "I'm a swan!"

"What?" she said. "What did you say?"

"I'm a swan!" he repeated. "That's what I am inside. That was what I always was. That's the nature in me. That's what I can turn myself into, any time I want!"

Donna was looking at him strangely.

"Lionel! Come here a moment!"

Her lover became quite animated when he heard what Alfie had said. He seemed to break out into a slight sweat, turned away and when he span back around had a glint of excitement in his eyes.

"Alfie," he said. "Listen to me, boy. I want you to do that again. Just the same as what you were doing before, OK? Only this time I'm going to film you".

"Right back to the pond?" asked Alfie hopefully, but he wasn't going to get away with that.

So he did it again, maybe even more smoothly this time, but slightly more self-consciously as well, even though he was well used to Lionel and his ways.

There was an intense whispered conversation between Donna and Lionel in the car going back to his house, but Alfie didn't catch much of it because the music was so loud and nothing more was said over dinner.

Later on, when he and his mother pulled up outside their own home, Donna pulled down her mask for a minute to speak to him, which meant this was serious. She said that she and Lionel were very touched by his idea of turning into a swan and they might be able to help his dream come true. But in the meantime he was to say nothing to anybody about it, especially his father. Did he get that?

He did, the mask went back up and they went inside for the usual bedtime spray-round.

* * *

Roberto Nezuri was enjoying the dusk view from his vast penthouse home. There was a sense of profound visual satisfaction in the way the grid of the city streets lined up perfectly with the steel frames of the windows. Beyond that was the sea, sprinkled with hundreds of wind turbines. The horizon, too, formed a completely straight line in total harmony with everything else in front of him, disproving once and for all the foolish claim that 'nature' abhorred linearity and that there was something 'unnatural' about order and aesthetic hygiene.

With the slightest of gestures with his little finger, he made his synthetic-leather armchair swivel round to face the wall, whose surface was all but filled by a massive image of a Roman legion taken from one of his favourite films. Thousands of men, perfectly in line, perfectly self-disciplined, perfectly distanced from each other and perfectly obedient to the collective interests of the Empire. The sight sent a frisson of almost erotic pleasure through Nezuri's body.

"Tea, mother?" he asked, partly as a way of pulling himself out of the moment.

He waved his little finger again and the chair span a little more. He could not help feeling proud every time he saw this figure. She was more beautiful, more dignified, more perfect than ever she had been in the flush of her youth.

He smiled. She noticed and smiled back.

"Oh yes, Bobby," she said. "That would go down very well indeed!"

"Katie! Two teas, one black and one with a

little milk and half a teaspoon of sugar", he said and a minute later the KatieBot brought them in.

"There you are, mother!" said Nezuri.

"Oh thanks, Bobby. You're so kind – and so clever to have invented all of this! I really am so lucky to have had a son like you to look after me!"

Nezuri smiled and tried to enjoy the compliment. But, as ever, there was something else there, blocking the way, that he had to express.

"You didn't always think that way, though, did you mother? You didn't always think you had been lucky to have a son like me?"

"Why, whatever do you mean, Bobby?"

"All that business with my brother, Marcello. Everything that happened then".

"Oh, goodness! You know I'd completely forgotten about that, Bobby! It really is of no importance at all! It was all such a long time ago!"

"You're right, mother, it was a very long time ago. And I'm relieved that you don't think about it any more. But when you do think about it, when I do remind you about it, can you say that you have actually forgiven me, mother?"

"Yes, of course, Bobby. Of course I have forgiven you. I have always loved you. You were always my favourite, you know. My little Bobby Babie Blue I used to call you, and – heavens! – I do declare that I was still using that name when you were all of twelve years old".

"And then you stopped, didn't you mother?"

"Did I, dear?"

"Yes, you stopped because you didn't love me any more. Because I had done something unforgivable that meant I could never be your Bobby Babie Blue again. The thing with Marcello".

"Oh, goodness! You know I'd completely forgotten about that, Bobby! It really is of no importance at all! It was all such a..."

"Mother. Off!" said Nezuri and the android froze in mid-sentence.

Damn. She was looping. This still wasn't working properly. There was a lot more programming to be done.

* * *

For a few days after their outing, nothing changed in the life of Alfie Duckworth. His mother barely spoke to him, except to tell him to pull his mask up properly in the car. Most of the time she was busy messaging or chatting on her phone and even when he gathered, from the slightly hushed tone and the way she kept looking in his direction, that she was talking about him, she did not share the content of her conversation.

Donna didn't work on Sundays, apart from the usual emails and so on, whereas Robin could not afford to take a day off from his taxi driving. Alfie noticed that his mother seemed particularly impatient for her husband to leave the house and was also paying her only child a lot more attention than normal. She even cracked open a new crate of disposable gloves just so as to be able to pat him on the head as he did his homework with his e-teacher at the kitchen table.

He was not altogether surprised, therefore, when, as soon as Robin's car had safely disappeared round the corner of the close, his mother summoned him into the living room. He saw at once that she had already laid out a child-sized sit-mat on the central cushion of the new electric-pink sofa, its colour carefully chosen by Donna herself to match the masks worn by the elegant couple walking along a beach in evening dress featured in the framed print on the wall behind.

Alfie plonked himself down in his allotted place, put his e-teacher interface down beside him, and found himself directly facing his mother, who had drawn up an armchair to be positioned in front of him. Something out of the ordinary was going on here.

"Alfie", she said. And then, remarkably, she took off her sunglasses. She instantly became quite unfamiliar. The usual emotionless impenetrability was gone and Alfie was confronted with the unnerving sight of a pair of hazel-brown eyes sharpened by intensity and expectation.

"Alfie, I have got some important news for you. You are going to become a swan!"

Alfie looked blankly at her in total incomprehension.

"For real! We're going to make your dream come true! That's what you are inside, remember! I can't stop watching that video, Alfie! A swan! That was what you always were!"

"*Who*," said Alfie's e-teacher. "That was *who* you always were. Use *who* rather than *what* when referring to a person or persons".

"Turn that off for a moment, couldn't you, Alfie?" snapped Donna, and the sunglasses went back on.

"And so?" she asked him, the good humour suddenly absent from her voice. "Got nothing to say?"

"What do you mean?" asked Alfie, genuinely confused by all this. "What sort of thing should I be saying?"

"What sort of thing? Well, let me see, 'thank you' perhaps? 'Thank you mum for wanting to make my dreams come true, for wanting to make me become what I was meant to be, for wanting to make me famous...'"

"Famous?" This was all so bizarre.

"Yes, Alfie, famous! It's not everyone that gets turned into a swan, you know! It's not everyone that has this opportunity! You'll be the first, Alfie, the first person in the world to break through that barrier that says we are born human and we have to stay that way, caged into a body that doesn't suit us. You'll make history, Alfie! Everyone will want to know about you! Everyone will want to meet you! Everyone will love you! You'll be a star, Alfie! A celebrity! You'll be on the telly! And you'll make us very... You'll make us very happy, Alfie, because you'll be successful. And very rich, when you're older, I expect".

The last part of his mother's monologue passed Alfie by, because one phrase kept turning around in his head. "Everyone will love you!" Could that be true? Was it possible? Could his mother turn him from a despised and useless nobody into somebody that people actually sought out and appreciated?

He saw the swan from the park, how it glided across the water with such sublime elegance. He tasted again the strength of his own spellbound admiration for this bird and he imagined that same adulation being directed, by unknown others, towards him, towards Alfie Duckworth.

When he looked up to face Donna, there were tears of joy in his eyes.

"Thank you mum," he said. "Thank you so much! But how are you going to do it?"

* * *

It turned out that Lionel was, inevitably, set to play an important role in Alfie's transformation into a swan.

"He knows more or less everybody that matters!" explained Donna to her son, as she listed some of the allies already drafted in to ensure that he found his personal bliss.

It seemed that Lionel had made a point of nurturing every useful contact he had made during his long entrepreneurial career and even from back when he was still a student of Business and Marketing Philosophy, compiling his acclaimed 'Ethical Defence of the Built-In Obsolescence Strategy for Growth'.

Alfie was highly impressed by the quantity of important-sounding names Donna excitedly counted off on her fingers as she explained the extent of Lionel's reach.

But he couldn't help noticing that none of them actually seemed to be in the business of turning schoolboys into wildfowl. There were think-tank chiefs, government advisers, TV executives, publishers, journalists, army officers, sustainable growth experts, charity bosses and behavioural change specialists but no vets or feather-implanters or whatever was going to be needed to perform the task at hand.

His ears did prick up when his mother uttered the words 'scientists', 'doctors' and 'World

Health Organization' and he even dared interrupt her flow to seek reassurance.

"Are they the people who will be doing it?" he asked.

"What?" she said, in a flustered manner. "Doing 'it'? What's 'it'? And what 'people' are talking about? Really, Alfie, you need to express yourself more clearly!"

He thought for a moment and composed his question more thoroughly.

"Those doctors and scientists and health people you were talking about. Are they the ones who are actually going to turn me into a swan? That's what I was wondering".

Donna stared at him for a moment and then suddenly her features seemed to soften a little, although it was always hard to tell what was really going on behind those dark lenses.

"Oh Alfie," she said. "I know you must be feeling very impatient to get on with it, now you know it will really be happening, but that's not how the world works. This is all new, you see, my dear. This has never happened before. We need to make sure that when we go ahead, when we turn you into a swan, the world is ready for that. We need to make sure that people understand what's happening, how important it is".

"Will that take a long time?"

"Oh no! It won't take long! Not with all the weight that Lionel has got behind us! That's why all these people are so important, Alfie. They are influencers, people who change opinions, change the world. With them on our side, we can't go wrong!"

"So who is going to actually change me into a swan?"

"It'll be surgeons, of course. Doctors. Drug experts. People with qualifications and white coats. People you can trust".

"And is there a place where they do that sort of thing?"

"Alfie! Haven't you been listening to a word I said? Of course there isn't a place just for that, not at the moment. It's all new! But there will be! That's one of the things that Lionel and his friends are working on. Once people realise what a great idea this is – how *important* it is for the health and happiness of children like you – then there will be money to build special clinics and hospitals to take care of you all..."

Alfie was frowning now. "But you said it wouldn't take long, mum! Building a new special hospital is going to take ages and ages!"

Donna leant slightly towards him. "Don't be silly, Alfie, they won't need to build a new hospital just for you. You will be different, because you're the first. You'll see. It'll all come together".

The very first step in it all coming together turned out to be the shooting of a documentary about what was about to happen.

Lionel's usual level of filming was not of the standard required for this endeavour, which was to be shot in the very latest UHD6++ format.

The film crew turned up at the house the next Sunday afternoon, when Robin was again at work. There were three smartly-attired young men, two very tall and one very short, together with a frantically cheerful woman who was introduced as 'Melanie, the make-up girl'.

Lionel rolled up a few minutes later and Alfie overheard him asking the team whether they thought they should be 'reshooting the park scene' with the proper equipment.

"Oh no," said Tariq, the short one, who was evidently in charge. "I think that segment's great as it is. It's got 'authentic' written all over it. It just oozes amateurishness!"

"Cheeky monkey!" said Lionel, who prided himself on his film work.

With that question out of the way, the crew got on with the job. First of all they wanted to film Alfie going about his 'everyday' life, which for their purposes seemed to involve walking constantly up and down the stairs and in and out of the living room and the kitchen.

They had to keep reshooting scenes when Donna noticed there was something out of place in the room, which would reflect badly on her housekeeping skills, or when Tariq judged that Alfie wasn't looking sad enough.

"The idea is..." Donna whispered in his ear at one point, "that being trapped in your human body is making you miserable. We need to show you how you are now, unhappy in your life as a boy, so that later we can see how happy you are to have become a swan!"

Alfie nodded.

"I mean, it's true, isn't it, Alfie, that you are unhappy with how you are now?"

He nodded again. Yes, it was true, but it was also quite exciting having these film people here and making such a fuss of him, which was probably why he was not looking quite as dejected as they would have wanted him to.

Just to make sure the message was clear, Tariq sat Alfie down by the window in his bedroom and asked him to look 'wistfully' into the distance. When it transpired that Alfie didn't understand the word, he told him instead to stare at the pylon at the bottom of the garden and think about some lovely place he had visited years ago and which he might never see again.

Alfie thought of the wooden bridge over the stream in Lower Erding and the resulting facial expression was declared by Tariq to be 'utterly fantastic'.

Next came the interview section. Melanie dabbed at Alfie's face with some kind of powder and he was then sat at the dining table. All sorts of lights were pointed at him, and Tariq's colleague Albert asked him lots of questions about his 'feelings' and 'things inside' and his 'deepest desires', which Alfie answered to the best of his ability. Albert had a unnerving habit of staring intently straight into his eyes, with a look of complete and serious concentration. He nodded furiously at everything Alfie said, leaving him with the unfamiliar impression of being the most important and interesting person in the world. As a consequence, he found himself speaking in a way that he was not used to, except perhaps sometimes with his dad. This felt very liberating until the point where, as he talked about wanting to be free to be himself and to decide his own life, he noticed Donna shuffling a little anxiously from one foot to the other at the far end of the room and realised that he wasn't saying exactly what she wanted him to. So he said that he wanted to be a swan and was gratified to see her break into a warm and appreciative smile.

After that, the third young man, Dmitri, was brought in to take 'stills' of Alfie. He was very pale, very tall, and had a permanent half-smile on his face, which in the end made him seem slightly melancholic. Or maybe that was all part of the job he was doing, because in direct contrast to everyone who had previously taken photos of Alfie, he kept reminding him not to smile and to 'show us the pain'.

With all the whirring and clicking that was

going on, he seemed to have taken hundreds of 'shots' before he finally announced that he was 'done'.

This all took a very long time and when the team filed out of the front door with Lionel and Donna, Alfie assumed that this was the end of the day's work, even though they had not bothered to say goodbye. But, as it turned out, they lingered outside for a few minutes, engaged in an intense conversation which he could not hear, and then his mother burst back indoors with a look of great determination on her face and took him up to his bedroom for 'a little chat'.

"Tariq and the guys have come a long way for this, you know," she explained. "From Manchester. It took them hours and cost a lot of electricity".

"Oh," said Alfie, wondering if he was somehow to blame for this.

"They can't keep coming down here all the time, you see. They have to make the most of being here and push ahead with the documentary as far as they can".

"I see," said Alfie, though he didn't.

"So what they want to do is something really inventive. So showbiz! Totally Hollywood! They want to get a step ahead of the story, so to speak".

Alfie could think of no appropriate reply. He did not know what she meant.

"What they need to do, Alfie, is to shoot the next part of the documentary now. The part where you have started to become a swan".

"How can do they do that? Nothing has happened yet".

"That's the magic of film!" whooped Donna, with seriously overdone gaiety. "Melanie is going to make you up so that you look the way you will when you have started the treatment".

"But how does she know?"

"How does she know what, dear?"

"How does she know what I am going to look like when I have started the treatment?"

"Well, we have been talking to people, Lionel and I. Experts. They have told us what you will look like and we have explained it all to Melanie".

"Oh. But what if it isn't quite right? What if I come out looking different to that, then the film will be wrong, won't it, and people will realise it's fake!"

"Alfie! Wash your mouth out with soap and water! 'Fake'! What kind of word is that for a good boy like you to use? Has that father of yours been putting his stupid old-fashioned ideas into your head again? If anything's 'fake' around here it's that pathetic excuse for a..."

She took a deep breath and calmed down a little.

"Anyway, we can make sure it's not different, can't we? The doctors can see the film, or the stills, and do the surgery so that it matches. What can be wrong with that? The documentary won't be making anything up at all, just showing, in advance, something that is actually going to happen. What could be more real? That's a step ahead of real! That's ultra-real!"

Alfie smiled a bit weakly. He wanted so much to believe her.

"What do you say, my boy? Shall we do this thing? Shall we make a movie and make history all at the same time?"

It took at least an hour for Melanie to prepare Alfie for the next part of the documentary. To start with, she literally painted his head, hair and neck white, while assuring Donna that it would come off in the shower.

She then fiddled interminably with the 'prosthetics' she had brought with her in what Lionel insisted on referring to as her 'bag of tricks', constantly gluing and ungluing, hesitating, swapping and realigning. Finally she dug out a pot of yellow paint and dabbed some of it on the structure she had built around Alfie's mouth.

The recipient of all this attention had, of course, been unable to see properly what she was doing – there was just an unfocused blur of unfamiliar bulk at the lower end of his frame of vision – and so it was with some anticipation that he took the mirror she eventually offered him so as to see what she had achieved.

He was vastly disappointed. The whole thing was a mess. Melanie hadn't even bothered to paint over the whole of what was meant to be his beak, leaving the end of it still dull grey rather than vibrant yellow.

She saw the deflated look in his eyes. "Don't worry," she said. "It won't show when your mask is on. No point in wasting time and resources on something nobody is actually going to see!"

Melanie was right in that once he was properly masked-up, her handiwork did give the strong impression that behind the fabric was a nascent yellow beak.

When Lionel and Tariq were called in to see the finished effect, they were cock-a-hoop. After their initial congratulations for Melanie, Alfie noticed that Lionel had started to say something to Tariq, but had then stopped himself and glanced momentarily in Alfie's direction. He then manoeuvred Tariq into the hall to continue the conversation in privacy.

Alfie, his curiosity pricked, wandered nonchalantly over to the half-open door and listened through the door jamb.

"The genius thing," Lionel was saying in hushed tones, "is that all the antis will be so fixated on the idea behind it that they won't even stop for a moment to question whether it's true or not. They will *want* it to be real so they can be outraged!"

"Exactly," enthused Tariq. "Who was it who said that the bigger the lie, the more likely you are to fool people, because in their simple little hearts they cannot believe that anyone could be quite so monumentally deceptive?"

They both sniggered manically in a muffled kind of way, then Tariq went off to fetch Albert and Dmitri for the next phase, during which Alfie had to pretend to be delighted by the marvellous progress of a transition that had not in fact even begun.

After all the excitement of that day, about which Alfie had promised to say nothing to his father – "We don't want to spoil the surprise!" – nothing much happened in the Duckworth household.

Alfie went to school, came back, did his homework, stared into space while pretending to play games and almost forget all about the swan business.

One afternoon Donna announced that they were going to visit Lionel. This wasn't exactly exciting news, because deep down Alfie did not really like Lionel very much, even though he pretended to himself that he did, out of loyalty to his mother. But it wasn't completely bad news either, as he was becoming bored of being at home all the time.

There must have been an accident on the

dual carriageway they usually took, because the system took them off the main road just before MaskMart and whizzed them down a little side street.

Donna was incensed, cursed at the car and seemed to be on the point of seizing manual control, then thought better of it and went back to her nuphone.

Alfie peered outside with growing interest at this unfamiliar part of the city. It was as if they had passed into a different world. Everything suddenly seemed shabby, old and rather dangerous. There were boarded-up windows, crumbling walls and roofs with half of the tiles missing. There was litter blowing across the street and sacks of rubbish on every street corner.

The people looked different. They were unkempt, savage, with some even wandering around in public completely barefaced, which sent a shiver of disgust through his body.

There were little groups of them in the road, standing horribly close to each other. One man actually touched another on the arm as he talked to him. And despite all this, they looked happy and were laughing.

Alfie glanced round at his mother to see if she had noticed, but she was still glued to the little screen in her hands.

Almost guiltily, Alfie gazed at these incredible scenes and tried to take in as much of it as he could, knowing that he might never pass this way again.

Now there was an expanse of flat ground beside the road, scattered with the rubble of some long-demolished buildings, in which small trees and shrubs were sprouting.

Beyond that there appeared to be some ancient houses, of a kind Alfie had only ever seen in videos about poverty and contagion, which had somehow been left standing

Marking the edge of that area, a kind of boundary, was a big section of wall of a half-demolished building, window frames still intact, on which someone had painted some words in massive red letters.

"Mum!" said Alfie, when he had worked out what they said. "Who is Theo Carter?"

"Huh? What?" she replied in a shocked tone and looked up to follow his gaze.

"Disgusting!" she said. "That is just absolutely disgusting! Evil!"

She took a photo and sent it to the anti-terror care team.

When they arrived at Lionel's place, it turned out he had some exciting news.

"We've launched!" he beamed as he opened the front door, nuphone held triumphantly in his hand.

After Donna had thoroughly examined the item in question and she and Lionel had discussed various parts of it in detail for some length of time, Alfie was eventually afforded the opportunity to see what it was all about.

He found himself looking at a very smooth-looking website called *Progress!,* subtitled 'Young, modern and left'.

Underneath was a photo of him, Alfie, with the so-called beak that Melanie had stuck on to him, and the headline 'Swanning towards freedom!'.

After that there was an article talking about him, saying that this was a 'breakthrough moment' for society. He concentrated enough to read on for a few lines. "Young Alfie is at the forefront of a new liberation movement in which personal choice will finally triumph over the lottery of physical birth. As the philosopher Francis Tufwick exclusively told *Progress*!: "This boy is a second Adam, a New Man, a Post-Human, who is breaking free from the primal prison of essentialist Eden to triumphantly and ironically declare that he is not a man at all, but a bird!"

Alfie gave up and scrolled back to the top. There was something that was bothering him in the way the site described itself.

"What do they mean by 'left'?" he asked.

Donna laughed.

"Oh, nothing!" she said. "It's just a word they use to make themselves sound important".

"Well..." said Lionel. "I think it's more than

that, Alfie. It means they are interested in new things, in change, in moving forward. That's why we decided to place it with them first. It gives the whole thing a certain freshness, a radical tinge".

"It makes it hard to be against it, you see dear," added Donna. "People who say that you can't really be turned into a swan or that you shouldn't be allowed to, will come across as old fuddy-duddies, not at all interested in progress and social change. They will just look like complete dinosaurs".

"Right-wing reactionaries!" laughed Lionel.

"Enemies of the modern world!" cried Donna.

"Swanphobes!" shrieked Lionel and they both dissolved into convulsions of glee.

When they had calmed down a bit, Alfie had a question to put to them.

"When am I actually going to be turned into a swan?" he asked.

Lionel and Donna exchanged glances. Donna popped on a glove, moved her chair close to Alfie's and placed a hand on his knee.

"Soon, dear," she said. "But it is important that we get people used to the idea first, that we get something called social licence..."

"And £100 million for the clinic!" interrupted Lionel, only to receive a stern look from his mistress.

"It's not about money," insisted Donna. "Not *just* about money, anyway. It's about your future,

Alfie, your happiness, and we want to do everything right, properly, to make sure that it all goes smoothly. This article is just the start, you'll see. You're going to be everywhere, Alfie! You're going to be a star!"

* * *

She was right. By the time summer began, Alfie was very famous indeed. So famous that even his father, who studiously avoided all news and mass media, came to hear of what was happening. There was a furious row about it in the middle of the night, when Robin got back from his taxi-driving, of which Alfie mainly heard his mother's side, because she shouted more loudly.

"Get up to date, you idiot! This is the 21st century!"

"What have you ever done for him, apart from filling his brain with old rubbish?"

"You're nothing but a denialist! A disgusting right-hand reactionist!"

"How dare you say that about Lionel! That's liable, that is! First-degree liable!"

"What do you mean, he will always be a human being? You're denying him his human rights!"

"That's enough, you moron! You're oppressing Alfie! You're intimidating me! You're a hatephobe! I'm calling the police!"

Evidently she was true to her word, because shortly afterwards Alfie's bedroom was lit up in flashing blue and the crackling radios announced the identity of the callers before they rang on the door.

But by then, Robin had gone. He had come upstairs, filled a suitcase with clothes and books and, when he found Alfie standing watching him, taken him in his arms, told him he loved him more than anything in the world, and then disappeared into the night.

* * *

Alfie's sudden fame took him into a completely different world from that in which he had not even been allowed to take a trip to the countryside. None of the usual travel restrictions applied to the elite class of which he now seemed to be part.

With Lionel and Donna constantly at his side, he jetted off to Los Angeles, to Tokyo, to Tel Aviv and to Beijing. He never saw make-up Melanie again but there was always some other expert on hand to prepare him for the press conferences and TV interviews, taking care to show the continuing advance of his history-making transition.

Before long, pretty much everybody in the world had come to hear of Alfie, or Swanboy as he became universally known.

Not only was the surgical process regarded as scientifically significant, but the ethics of his transition became an important global talking point.

There were, as predicted, those who declared that the treatment was wrong-headed, that it amounted to child abuse and that it was absurd to claim that Alfie would actually become a swan, no matter how much his physical appearance was changed.

It was here that Lionel's 'positioning' of the story proved a masterstroke. The practical enthusiasm of the medical and pharmaceutical realms for the 'swansition' was accompanied by the fervent moral support of all those who regarded themselves as progressive and open-minded.

Here was a brand new cause to get behind, a cutting-edge struggle that set a new generation of radicals apart from their parents and, coincidentally, attracted huge amounts of funding from charities and trust funds set up by wealthy philanthropists to promote social change and progress.

The enthusiasm was contagious. Activists abandoned projects defending workers' rights or promoting decentralised community mutual aid in order to flock to the defence of Swanboy and his anti-speciesist revolution.

One typical response came from long-term campaigner Rupert Darret, who wrote on the Action Network Forum that the defence of a being's right to be transformed into any animal of their choice was "now the most important issue facing the progressive community and one to which I for one intend dedicating the rest of my activist career".

Darret argued that the term 'swanphobia' was, in fact, not broad enough to encompass the enormity of the issue at stake and the range of transitions that were likely to follow in years to come. The real enemy was biological essentialism, the deeply reactionary and offensive belief that an individual's identity was determined by their physical form at birth.

He noted that opponents of swansition invariably used the term 'human being' to try and crush Alfie Duckworth's right to self-determination and proposed that laws against hate speech be extended to include the use of this term in certain contexts, namely where it 'seeks to limit rather than include'.

* * *

Roberto Nezuri read Darret's piece with great pleasure. This character couldn't have done a better job if he been paid to do so.

He span round on his chair in a state of self-satisfaction and took in the superb linearity and greyness of the view from his penthouse. And then he stopped. There was a messy green object spoiling the aesthetics. He sprung to his feet and went to look. There, on the outside of the huge window, right at the bottom, something was growing. A disgusting plant. A weed!

Nezuri was outraged. He had taken great pains to have the windows doused with herbicide three times a week to prevent anything like this ever happening. He ordered the maintenance drone to remove it at once and, in the meantime, turned his back on the offending contagion as it was making him feel quite ill.

Even the sight of the Roman legionaries unsettled him, as his mind insisted on imagining them walking on a pavement through which were sprouting a hundred scraggy and smelly green shoots.

He activated his mother.

"Oh yes, Bobby," she said, in response to the tea question. "That would go down very well indeed!"

The tea duly served by the KatieBot and the chit-chat out of the way, he tried her out again on the crucial question.

"Mother. Do you blame me for what happened with Marcello?"

"Oh, goodness! You know I'd completely forgotten about that, Bobby! It really is of no importance at all! It was all such a long time ago!"

Nezuri gritted his teeth. He really would have to alter that a little. It was starting to grate. Nevertheless, he carried on. He had to test this to the limit.

"Yes, I know it was a long time ago, mother, but it must have been a shock at the time".

He braced himself.

"Yes, it was a little bit of a shock at the time, Bobby. Nobody likes to lose a son, but I never blamed you".

So far so good.

"I am pleased to hear that, mother, but I don't really know how you could *not* blame me. Marcello may officially have disappeared, but you and I both know that I killed him".

It had to be done. He had to confront this head-on.

"Yes, Bobby, I know that and I forgive you. Marcello was always such a difficult boy. I never could love him like I love you".

"But I killed him, mother. I killed him because he wouldn't do what I told him to. That was unforgivable!"

"I forgive you, Bobby. Marcello was always such a difficult boy. I never could love him like I love you".

Oh damn it.

"Mother. Off".

Nezuri knew he had messed up by repeating

himself but was still frustrated by the way she had automatically trotted out the same reply. Like some kind of robot! He laughed out loud at his own joke, as there was nobody else there to do so.

* * *

A year after the media launch of Alfie's swansition, the battle for public opinion was virtually won. Those who questioned its reality or desirability were generally considered to be stupid, backward-looking and consumed by hatred of both boys and swans.

One tricky moment came when a young woman delivering pizzas to a TV company in Chicago happened to come across Alfie having his swan-prosthetics applied and duly filmed and shared what she had seen.

The host of the TV show, having heard in her earpiece that the clip was going viral, tried to limit damage by inviting Alfie, live on air, to confirm that the swansition was real and not fake. His stumbling confusion, however, only added to the sudden storm of scepticism. Fortunately, the TruthGuard organisation, dedicated to combating misinformation in the media, was able to step in. It declared that the clip had been an elaborate hoax, that those spreading it were human-supremacy conspiracy theorists and that Alfie had been outrageously bullied by the interviewer. The video was erased from the internet, the TV presenter sacked on the spot and the pizza delivery woman arrested and placed under permanent medicated detention under the Liberty and Wellbeing Act.

It was clear, however, that doubts were circulating about the authenticity of Alfie's transformation and Lionel and Donna decided it was time to embark on some kind of surgical intervention in order to bring reality and illusion a little closer and prevent a repeat of the same incident.

These were difficult times for Alfie. His life became one endless operation, with a whole series of implants and skin grafts. The idea was to start with his head and his feet. His face was whitened and his nose yellowed and extended, with his top lip surgically attached to its underside. Down below, skin was transferred from his shins to create webbing between his toes and the colour of his feet was darkened to a deep grey.

He was in constant discomfort, often excruciating, from the moment he woke up to that at which he finally fell into troubled sleep, with the help of pills. It was hard to breathe, difficult to eat and impossible to walk properly. Lionel was delighted at the latter development, whispering to Donna, at a volume he wrongly imagined would render his remark inaudible to Alfie:

"Waddletastic!" She slapped him on the arm and succumbed to a fit of the giggles.

Alfie just endured all this, in the same way that he had endured everything else in his life. He didn't really particularly even want to be a swan, but it seemed that his fateful passing utterance in the park that day had amounted to a binding legal contract. He had even repeated it on camera and there it was, constantly recycled in every news feature and documentary about Swanboy.

He just accepted this as his reality and went along, stoically, with everything that was arranged for him by his mother and her boyfriend.

He was invited to address the United Nations, the World Health Organization, the World Economic Forum and the Global Technocracy Convention. He was named Being of the Year in the internationally prestigious *Real World* magazine – the title having been changed from Person of the Year in tribute to his pioneering efforts.

Alfie was also chief ambassador for a new charity called 'Rite2b' which Lionel had set up with the help of some PR colleagues closely linked to the pharmaceuticals industry.

Its hashtag memes had flooded social media for three months, with warm-hearted individuals moved to offer support and money for the universal right #2bAlive, #2bUrself and #2bwotUwant.

Swanboy himself was of course the main focus of their efforts, but they also jerked a fair few tears with their campaign featuring Gladys, an eight-year-old bizarrely obsessed with cable TV sensation Elva the Electronic Elf and who cried herself to sleep every night because she didn't have pointed ears that lit up in different colours depending on what mood she was in.

The public's determination for little Gladys to be what she wanted '2b' was such that in three weeks a multi-million pound sum had been raised to send her to China to be fitted with the necessary brain sensors, microchips, ear extensions and multi-coloured lighting.

"Why wait #2bAlive? Everyone's dream can come true thanks to Rite2b!" as Alfie himself famously put it on the social media account set up and managed by Lionel's PR friends.

The charity was not only about raising money, though. In fact, this was almost a side-effect, although a very welcome one. It was really performing one of the basic tasks of commercial activity, namely creating a hitherto-unsuspected 'need' for which a 'solution' could then be sold.

The idea of an inalienable right #2bwotUwant, no matter how far-fetched and apparently impossible that desire might be, opened up a lucrative market of near-infinite proportions for the business sectors providing these services.

If Gladys' ears were 'on the house', as it were, it was because they were designed as bait for all the other little girls and boys with strange ideas sown in their minds by non-stop screen addiction and for all the mummies and daddies who wanted nothing more from life than to spend money on pandering to their offspring's every whim.

The principle applied to adults, obviously. Another big hit from the Rite2b campaign was the case of Vanessa, a six foot two Englishwoman who lived in Madrid and, despite her elegant good looks, found it virtually impossible to attract the interest of Spanish men whose pride forbad them from appearing belittled beside her.

Her Rite2b five foot seven was duly funded by the charity to great fanfares of self-congratulation, although it later stopped publicising the case and removed all mention from the internet archives ("misinformation") when it turned out that the surgery had gone badly wrong and she could no longer even enjoy her reduced height by standing up.

Mercifully, Vanessa was happy to accept a relatively small compensation payment, on condition that she sign a gagging clause, and her dream-come-true was able to live on in the public mind without unwelcome concerns about serious physical damage.

All of this hype and manipulation was going so splendidly well that Donna very nearly forgot herself and became happy. But, fortunately for her sense of personal continuity, events intervened to ensure that she remained largely dissatisfied with her lot.

There was her 40th birthday, for a start. She found this very hard to cope with, despite the fact that its arrival on that particular day had been inevitable for the last four decades, precluding of course the even less desirable outcome of her premature death.

Lionel, finding that her sudden conviction that she was 'old and ugly' meant she was no longer interested in 'big cuddles', used several hundred thousand pounds of the charity's rapidly expanding reserves to pay for a facelift, plus plastic surgery on her buttocks, giving her the bot 'wot' she wanted and allowing her to feel not a day over 36.

But many other causes of discontent lived on, not least the power cuts that had hit their neighbourhood on several occasions. After the first interruption. Donna had taken care to keep all her appliances fully charged, so as to be able to ride out the break in supply in some respects, even if the lights stopped coming on when you entered a room, the Nu-Meat dispenser in the kitchen started to smell a bit funny and no more desserts could be ordered from the printer.

Donna simply couldn't believe that this could be happening in this day and age, to someone who worked hard for a living and who was mother to the world's most exceptional child.

None of her friends, or maybe that should be 'friends', on social media were experiencing anything of the kind where they lived and, after the second power cut, Donna was complaining to Lionel that she would be forced to move house into a less 'grotty' area.

The authorities did not seem to be able to provide any explanation for what was happening, with the automated replies to her queries merely citing 'exceptional circumstances', 'technical difficulties' and, when she reached the automated manager, a 'challenging provisionality'. Somebody she didn't know on social media, but who apparently lived next door, suggested that rats had been nibbling through the cables. Rats! Donna had screamed out loud at the screen, bundled a masked-and-gloved Alfie into the car and headed straight for Lionel's place, where he took pains to explain to her that that sort of grotesque bio-hazard was simply not possible any more and that her informant was living in another era.

So she soldiered on, telling herself these incidents couldn't go on, but at the same time furious that her life was being totally ruined by the ever-present threat of their recurrence.

* * *

Robin had not disappeared off the face of the planet when he was thrown out, as Donna liked to pretend, but had remained within a mile or two of what had been his family home.

There was no question of him ever returning there in her presence. He could not stand the thought of seeing the woman who was committing such grievous injury to his son and he knew that, for her part, she would call the police with claims of 'intimidation' if he ever showed up to challenge her.

With Lionel's money behind her, and the celebrity status now attached to Alfie, there was no point at all in him trying to take them on legally or publicly.

His departure from the house was already a confused and fuzzy memory for Robin. He must have driven round in circles for what seemed like hours, adrenalin-pumped outrage and despair blinding him to all purpose, until he had realised that at some point he would have to stop.

He decided to park the car somewhere and try to get a bit of sleep. Where to do so was another matter, though. In most areas a non-resident vehicle would be picked up in minutes and the police would turn up.

Robin's mind immediately turned to the Old London Road behind MaskMart, which he sometimes used as a short cut to avoid the jams – though not with any passengers on board as people didn't like to see places like that.

The area was a real anomaly. It was supposed to have been cleared and redeveloped years ago, but there had been some legal dispute over ownership and the whole process had been put on indefinite hold. As a result, this small enclave of a forgotten past had become a magnet for all kinds of misfits and rejects, people who were incapable of adapting to modern life and declined to take the honourable way out by paying a visit to their local FAC – Farewell Assistance Centre.

Robin did not fancy living there – the place appalled him as much as it fascinated him – but it seemed like a good spot to park up unnoticed for a few hours.

He was right in his intuition and, even if it was impossible to sleep with all that had happened swirling around in his mind, he was at least undisturbed. The next night he returned to the same spot and, this time, managed a half-decent sleep on the back seat of the taxi.

The next day he didn't feel in such a hurry to leave and stretched his legs by taking a walk around the rubble-strewn zone where demolitions had begun. He had automatically put on his mask on to do so, but when he realised that nobody else around was wearing one, he stuffed it back into his pocket and took pleasure in deeply breathing in the life-giving air.

The other people he passed – ambling

around like him or scurrying off to some unknown destination – seemed uncurious about his presence and treated him as if he were a familiar face there, smiling (what a strange thing to experience from a stranger!) and wishing him a good morning.

On the third morning Robin had just woken up, and was washing himself with a bottle of mineral water, when there was a tap on the window which made him start. Outside a chaotically-bearded face was beaming in at him, the breadth of the smile revealing a number of gaps where teeth should have been. The owner of the face was wearing a dark green cravat tucked into the collar of velvet purple jacket that had clearly seen many years of service.

Robin opened the window and smiled back.

"Morning!" he said.

"Good morning to you, Sir!" said the man, who exuded kindliness through his unkempt appearance. "We were just wondering if you fancied a cup of tea, since as you probably don't have all the relevant facilities in your taxi?"

For a moment, Robin's shy nature got the better of him and he tried to think of a polite way of saying 'no'. The fellow obviously caught a glimpse of something in his eyes, for he physically stepped back and raised both hands in the air.

"No obligation, of course! You probably have

to be somewhere, but, if you did fancy a cuppa, the offer's on the table. Or on the pallet, to be more accurate. We're outdoors on a lovely day like this!"

Robin gave in and followed his new neighbour, who introduced himself as Baz, across the wasteland towards the remaining buildings fronted by a large section of still-intact wall which looked, for some strange reason, as if it had been recently been repainted in thick council white.

Underneath the wall was a group of men and women sitting around a rusty old brazier, on which was hissing a large black antique kettle.

When Baz introduced him to the others, each rose out of their seat to shake him by the hand. Although Robin hated the hygiene-obsessed culture that had taken hold in recent times and privately did all he could to defy it, he still found himself shocked to be clasping the bare skin of strangers in such grimy surrounds.

Someone found a chair from behind a heap of rubble and when he sat down, Robin looked from one face to another and repeated in his head the names they had given. Toby, Vicky, CJ, Petra and Gabriela.

Toby was already familiar, being one of those who had greeted Robin over the last couple of days. Like Baz, he was of indeterminate age. He too was bearded and, from the streaks of grey, Robin imagined he must be at least 45, but he could be anything up to 60. He didn't have the same gentleness that Baz incarnated and there was a certain steeliness in his regard, but this was without malice or contempt for the others and Robin felt that it spoke more of enduring strength against adversity than of egotistical pride.

In stark contrast to Baz's colourful appearance, Toby was dressed in black – or more accurately dark grey – in layers of various fabric that seemed to merge together to form one thick textured outer skin, which even extended over his head in the form of a misshapen hood.

Vicky and CJ, who appeared to be a couple, were both young. Surprisingly young for Robin, who had become used to the idea that the generation after his were entirely subsumed by the 'new normal' of conventional life and were incapable of imagining any way out of it aside from the FAC.

Petra and Gabriela were a little older, probably in their mid-thirties, although their faces were somewhat ravaged by time and trouble. Both wore long colourful skirts, woollen jumpers and shawls, looking very much like old-fashioned gypsies, those notorious virus-spreaders who had long since been declared obsolete and re-educated to the correct contemporary standards.

But despite these superficial similarities, they didn't really resemble each other. Petra was round-faced and practical-looking, whereas Gabriela came across as a lost poetess, with sad eyes and sunken cheeks.

There was no pressure on Robin to say anything. Once they had served him his cup of tea – good tea, proper tea, though sadly without milk – they carried on chatting among themselves in a light-hearted vein, with Baz occasionally catching his eye with a smile when someone said something funny that wasn't purely an in-joke.

But he still felt a bit awkward just sitting there, silently. Since he had no desire to talk about what had happened to him, and to poor Alfie, he decided to ask them about this place – about how they had arrived there, how they survived.

"So how did you lot all come to be here, then?" he asked in his best jaunty taxi-driver tone. "How does it work? Are you here collectively or individually, if you see what I mean?"

Initially, he thought he had made a great mistake. He could see suspicion seize the expressions of some of his breakfast companions, particularly Petra and Gabriela.

It was Toby who changed the mood, having looked him silently and expressionlessly in the eyes for several seconds, as if gazing right inside him to read his thoughts.

"We're all here because we've got nowhere else to go, as you can well imagine, Robin," he said, looking briefly around at the rubble to emphasise the point. "We live collectively because we have to... as you can also well imagine!"

Here he shot a comically disgusted sideways glance at CJ and Vicky, prompting chortles of laughter from Petra.

"As to whether it 'works' or not..."

"Work is a dirty word," said CJ.

"And lack of work is a dirty kitchen when CJ is on the rota," said Petra, addressing her remark to Robin rather than the target of her criticism.

"So how about you, Robin?" said Gabriela, who had been quietly watching and listening. "How does working life 'work' for you? How did you come to be parked up on the edge of this little wilderness in your nice clean taxi?"

The way she looked at him, with her soulful brown eyes, made him feel he could tell her everything – about Donna, Alfie and this terrible swan business. If they had been alone, he would probably have done so, but he wasn't ready for that yet in front of everyone.

"Yes, I'm a taxi-driver," he said. "And before that I was a teacher. I've always worked because I had to. I worked for my wife and my son. But now..."

He felt a great wave of repressed despair

welling up inside him, so he stood up.

"I'll tell you about it some time," he smiled, extending the reply to take in not just Gabriela but all those present. "But it's a bit hard for me at the moment. It's all very new. Also, I've got to go out and earn some more money! Thanks for the tea!"

It wasn't actually time to start his shift and Robin just drove a couple of miles to the Charles III Recreational Zone, where the price of the car park was counterbalanced by the certainty of finding a little corner out of sight of the cameras where he could sit and read for a while.

Later in the afternoon, and during the evening, work seemed even more intolerable than ever. He kept thinking back to the breakfast conversation. Why *did* he work now? Did he *have* to, in order to survive? How did those others cope? Was there another way of getting by in this world?

It wasn't until he had finished and was logging out of the control site that his screen flashed up the urgent message. Typical that they had let him work his shift before sending this. There was a problem with his personal details. It appeared the home address he had given was no longer valid. Please could he provide a new address immediately, otherwise he would not be paid.

Robin's first instinct was to blame Donna – that was what marriage did to you. But then he realised that any number of checks – bio-sensors, vehicle-location, interaction logs – could have provided this information. Probably all of them combined, in fact. He should probably count himself lucky that he had lasted this long.

He hesitated over what to do. Could he invent an address? Some made-up number in the Old London Road? No, that could be fatal. Was there anyone he knew who would let him use their address? The answer wasn't long in coming. No. He hardly knew anyone any more, apart from customers. He had a sister in Yorkshire but since their parents had died in the Non-Resuscitation Camp and their property confiscated to pay for the medical charges, they hadn't had much to say to each other. Friends? He had stopped talking to them years ago, when it became clear their brains were little other than fleshy extensions of the Global Community Cloud.

There was only one thing for it. 'No Fixed Abode', he typed into the address box and pressed enter.

It must have taken less than a second for the reply to come through. His contract had been breached and was thus automatically terminated. He was locked out of his account. He would not be paid any money previously considered owed. The authorities had been informed of a potential breach of the Vagrancy and Social Irresponsibility Act.

When Robin got back to the wasteland – where else was he to go? – he was delighted to see the warm flicker of a bonfire beneath the big white-painted wall. He was not a drinker but had taken the opportunity of buying a bottle of malt whisky, along with a car full of more essential supplies including food and clothes, before his credit card was cancelled – which presumably wouldn't be long.

Bearing this gift, he made his way across the demolished remains of Old London Road to join his new friends. It turned out, to no great surprise, that they had already been making commendable inroads into their own alcohol supplies – cider, mostly – and were more than happy to welcome him into their midst with his own contribution.

It wasn't entirely the same crowd as in the morning. Baz and Toby were there, with Petra and Gabriela, but there was no CJ or Vicky. Instead, Robin was introduced to Hudson, Oakley and Lily, who all seemed really decent human beings, even if they were a bit on the tipsy side.

An hour later, Robin had stopped noticing what state anyone else was in and two hours later he was huddled up against the big wall telling Gabriela all about Donna, Lionel, Alfie and the swan affair.

The sun was already high in the sky when

he was awoken by a gentle tapping on the window of the car. It was Baz.

When Robin started and turned round, his visitor took a step back, with a mortified expression on his face.

"Sorry Robby!" he said. "Didn't mean to wake you! I thought you were just, you know, resting..."

When Baz had first called him that, Robin had assumed that it was simply a mistake. But now he realised that giving him a slightly different little nickname was a personal gesture of acceptance. Baz's modifications were very subtle, though, so you didn't always even notice he had made one. CJ was 'Seej', Vicky was 'Vick', Gabriela became 'Briela', Toby 'Tobes' and so on. It was as if they had been translated into the dialect of a neighbouring country, Bazland, very close to the language spoken by everyone else but never quite identical.

It turned out that Gabriela had told Baz the gist of what he had said to her about Alfie and the swan business.

"I am really sorry, Robby. I mean, even just reading about what they're doing to your boy, without knowing him or anything, is hard enough. But for you, to be living that with your own kid..."

"Yeah," said Robin. "I suppose I'm trying not think too much about it at the moment. It's hard to take in".

"Sure, sure. So you haven't had the chance to look into it a bit more, who's behind it all?"

Robin laughed bitterly. "I think I know who's behind it all," he said as into his head popped, unbidden, that undeletable image of Donna and Lionel emerging from her bedroom, a sheet wrapped around them, that time he had unexpectedly called back at the house in mid-shift.

"Oh, so you know about Dauthus?"

From the blank look on Robin's face, Baz saw that he didn't.

"Listen, I don't want to interfere or anything, Robby, but there's some heavy shit going on that you really should know about. I can show you some stuff now, if you want. That's why I came over..."

It was with a heavy heart and a strong sense of foreboding that Robin accompanied Baz across the wasteland towards the buildings. It wasn't that he didn't want to know, but more that he wasn't sure he would be able to cope with the knowledge.

Robin had wondered, from what he had seen of the outside of the buildings, how people managed to live inside them – they were in such an extreme state of disrepair that the structures didn't even look capable of keeping the rain out.

Things became clearer when Baz led him down a flight of steps into what turned out to be a series of interconnecting cellars.

"So is this where you all live – down here?"

"Mmmm? Oh yes that's it," said Baz, as if surprised he even needed to ask. "A bit dark and dank but nicely out of the way. No network down here, for a start!"

Three or four cellars along, he stopped and pulled aside some plastic sheeting to reveal an ancient computer, which must have dated from the first decade of the century.

"They made them to last in those days!" he smiled as it whirred noisily into action. "In case you're wondering," he added, "these two leads here go up to the roof. One is the power supply – an autonomous solar panel from the old days – and the other is the aerial, so to speak. A pirated phone. Tobes set it all up. Don't ask me how!"

When the computer had powered up, Baz used the old-style mouse to go online, arriving at a page that reminded Robin of his childhood. It certainly looked nothing like the Safenet.

"Yep, it's still out there!" said Baz, spotting his astonishment. "Most people can't see it any more, they've got everything so tied up, but that world still exists if you know how to find it. Now where was it...? Ah yes. And the other one is... And there we are!"

"Now what I humbly suggest, Sir, is that you have a look at this little video, it comes in at a bit under an hour, so you've got all the relevant background that you would never have been told on The News..."

"If I even watched it".

"Well you haven't missed anything, that's for sure. Except a lot of distraction to keep you from seeing the essential. And then, when you are up to speed, there is a little article lined up which I think may prove of particular interest. Take all the time you want. It may take some digesting. I'll leave you to it!"

"Cheers," said Robin, and, as Baz disappeared back the way they'd come, settled into an antique office chair which was in tatters but surprisingly comfortable.

As soon as the video began, he had the uncomfortable feeling that he was committing a terrible crime simply by watching it. Everything about it, from the barely-concealed emotion in the narrator's voice, to the mixed quality of the images, the unsettling musical soundtrack and the unfiltered, unfamiliar language, shrieked out to the modern citizen that this was fake news, deadly propaganda, filthy mind-contamination dreamed up by foreign powers or criminal gangs to corrupt and mislead.

It was only the fact that Robin had kept himself largely apart from mainstream media culture, as much as he could, that even allowed him to keep watching and not run screaming from the basement in fear of his life.

As he persisted, and allowed his automatic adverse reactions to surface in his mind, then play themselves out and fade away, he began to take in the actual content of what he was watching. Most of the time, it seemed like a story, a fabulous, nightmarish story from some other time or planet. It certainly had nothing to do with the recent history with which Robin, like everyone, was vaguely familiar. But then there would come a moment, an incident, a personality, a televised remark, that he had seen before, in an authorised context, and this unlikely fantastical account was suddenly nailed solidly on to the structure of reality, in a temporary way, before again drifting off again into realms that surely, oh surely, could have nothing to do with what was really going on in this world. Could they?

When the video had finished, he read the article that Baz had called up for him. After that, he sat in the gloom for a full twenty minutes, not so much thinking as letting the information settle in his mind.

And then he watched the video again, all the way through, and re-read the article. There were plenty of links to other material to follow up at a later date, but he knew this was all he could cope with for the moment.

Robin was quite comfortable with the idea that political leaders often acted out of self-interest, in the short-term pursuit of political advantage rather than out of principle. He knew as well that they were often compromised, to some extent, by behind-the-scenes commercial interests. But there was a big difference between this mild scepticism and the belief that government had, for some time, been taken over by what was literally a criminal mafia – and not just the government here, either, but every government in the world other than those declared 'rogue' states. Wasn't it simply outlandish, insane even, to think that this selfsame mafia controlled every major sector of economic activity, from pharmaceutics to robotics, from media to food production, from weaponry to power generation?

And if that was mad, what could you say about someone who thought that behind all that, motivating this mafia's activities, was not only the desire for absolute power and control over everyone and everything, but also a burning hatred for people, for nature, for freedom, for joy, for love, for life, for everything that, instinctively, most human beings believed to be good?

Robin didn't want to think of himself as mentally ill. He found himself trying to push away the picture that was forming in his mind of the real world in which he was living, a real world which had been so carefully and completely hidden from him and others by the web of deceit spun by the global criminal mafia. But he could no more stop the new awareness from flooding and filling his mind than he could have stopped the tide coming in by writing "HALT!" in capital letters on the sand in front of it.

And this was no abstract awareness, either, as far as Robin was concerned. When he read that The Dauthus Foundation, which had already featured prominently in the video as being at the forefront of the mafia's 'posthuman' philosophical war, was also playing a key role in promoting a new charity, Rite2b and its swansition project, he was learning that these people were directly threatening the well-being of his own son.

No parent worth their salt can hide away from knowledge of that kind.

He had a few questions for Baz when he found him in the wooden shack which served as a kitchen. One of them concerned the identity of the writer who had alerted him to the links between Dauthus founder Roberto Neruzi and Rite2b.

"What's her background, this Sally Shukra?"

"Oh, she's very well known! Been around for years, digging all the dirt on these people. She's even worked with Theo Carter".

Robin again experienced the dizziness of danger. He couldn't remember who Carter was or exactly what he had done, but he knew that he was worse than bad. He was everything that decent people stood against. He was everything against which society had a duty to defend itself. He wanted to scream in Baz's face: "But he's a bloody terrorist! A murderer!"

As it turned out, he didn't need to say anything at all, because Baz had seen it all in his expression.

"I personally wouldn't want to kill anyone. But when you look at what they'd done to him, and so many others, plus what he's been going through in prison, then you've got to have respect for the man, even if..."

He saw Robin was still reeling from the shock of hearing the demon's name, and tailed off.

"Anyway, none of that was Sally Shukra's fault. She just provided him with some background research. And now, apparently, she's got the text of a book which Carter has somehow managed to put together from inside that hellhole. So that will be very interesting. Whatever you think of him".

Robin was not wholly reassured. It took him a moment to remember his second question for Baz and when he did, he wasn't entirely sure he wanted to ask it any more. Then he thought of Alfie and did so anyway.

"I was thinking about these people. They've got it all so tied up. So watertight. Nobody has got a clue what they've been up to. They own everything and everyone..."

Baz was giving him a funny look.

"They own *pretty much* everything and everyone..." he said and Baz indicated with a little smile that the correction was acceptable. "So what can people do, what can we do, to try and stop them? It just seems impossible!"

"Well..." said Baz and paused so long that it allowed Robin time to nurse the fear that this fellow would declare that killing people was the answer.

"Well. First of all, it is never impossible to stop someone from doing something they haven't done yet, such as keeping this dictatorship going for another ten years. Secondly, they say that everyone's greatest strength is also their greatest potential weakness. The great strength of this system is that it has, as you say, got everything covered. It has got the whole world locked down under centralised control. But that is also its weakness, because its control relies entirely on centralisation, its centralisation relies entirely on its technological infrastructure and its infrastructure relies entirely on electricity.

"Now if, like a certain person we both know, you used to work on maintaining the electricity supply, you will also know all about its weaknesses, the places where it is most vulnerable, and what sort of actions might endanger its smooth running".

"So you mean sabotage?" asked Robin, all too aware that as far as society was concerned this was identical to terrorism, even if it involved no loss of life.

"You could put it like that," said Baz. "But each of us has our own role to play. Each of us, through the circumstances of our lives, has our own potential way of carrying out this sabotage. What you, Robin, can offer might look nothing like an exploding transmitter. But you have to be ready to take a risk".

Robin took a deep breath, imagined Alfie in the hands of Roberto Neruzi, and said: "I'm ready".

* * *

When Alfie's fourteenth birthday arrived, it went largely unmarked. He received the usual animated greeting and credit transfer from his mother on his nuphone, but she had set that up years ago, to repeat every birthday, and the act of committing the date to virtual memory set her free to forget about it in real life. All sorts of institutions and businesses also piled in to congratulate Alfie on the occasion, but no actual human being seemed to have noticed. Except, of course...

When Donna was safely out of the house, without having mentioned his birthday, not even noticing when he called out thanks for the credit, Alfie ventured out of the front door.

After checking that nobody was watching, he pulled up the edge of the plastic lawn where it had come loose. Sure enough, there underneath was a little envelope which Alfie quickly scooped up and carried back indoors as fast as his surgically-modified feet would allow.

It was a card, from his father. They had been communicating surreptitiously like this ever since Robin had turned up at the house a week or so after the big row with Donna. They had had a rather rushed and whispered conversation in which Robin had explained that he had been locked out of his credit account and his car and was now living with some 'very nice people' not far away.

Alfie had been pleased that his father wanted him to take care of himself and expressed such concern about him, but a bit alarmed by the way he seemed to be suggesting that he was in some kind of danger. As the swansition had taken on a real form, Alfie had started to interpret his father's negative comments – both in person and in the little notes he left – as a criticism of him and his new physical reality and he began avoiding actual meetings with Robin in case the latest changes in his appearance prompted disgust or rejection on his father's part.

In the end Alfie had announced that he could not come out and talk in person any more because it was 'too dangerous' but that they could keep exchanging notes so long as Donna didn't find out.

This turn of events had in fact saddened Alfie nearly as much as it had saddened his father, but he knew that it was the only way he could cope with the conflict between the direction his life was taking and the evident desire of his father for it to be otherwise.

Alfie was relieved that there was no writing in the card, nothing to make him feel bad about Donna or Lionel or the charity people. There was just a little drawing that Robin had obviously done himself. It was not very good, really, but it was clear enough what it was supposed to show. It was the bridge over the stream at Lower Erding. Alfie's imagination overlaid its own image of the spot on to his father's clumsy scribbles and the picture magically became beautiful.

Being fourteen seemed important this morning. He hadn't really given it much thought beforehand but, now he was there, this seemed a significant step in his life. Fourteen spoke of maturity and gravity. He was becoming an adult.

Compelled by this thought, he went up to his mother's bedroom, undressed and assessed himself in her full-length mirror. He did not, however, remove his mask, which he had got used to wearing permanently, partly to avoid catching accidental reflections of his swansition-ravaged features.

With face covered and feet out of sight, he felt proud and stirred by the sight of his young man's body and yet bothered by the nagging knowledge that this was not the true picture, that he was deliberately hiding something from himself.

In a sudden gesture of courage, he took off his facemask and revealed to himself the entirety of his physical appearance. Immediately, the pleasure he had found in his own body shrank away to nothing. He was hideous. A total mess. That grotesque nose-cum-mouth-cum-beak, that deathly pallor. He looked nothing like a swan, just a disfigured boy. Angrily, Alfie turned away from the mirror and got dressed. But he left his mask off because the image of his new face was now so firmly burned into his mind in any case that there was no point in trying to shy away from the truth.

They had warned him, of course, that the intermediate period would be difficult and unsatisfactory, that there would inevitably be an awkward overlap between the human and swan phases of his existence. To reassure himself, he sometimes thought about that show he had seen with the story of the funny-looking duckling who just had to be patient before he turned into a magnificent swan. Now, he decided he would like to revisit the story and, sprawling on the sofa downstairs, he started searching online.

A few minutes later he was feeling confused. He had got the title right, hadn't he? It *was* called *The Ugly Duckling* wasn't it? OK, he had spelled it wrong the first time, but he had tried again and several links had come up. These should have led to ebooks and, even better from Alfie's perspective, video presentations of the tale – but none seemed to work. Eventually, out of sheer desperation, he found himself looking at some kind of academic essay on the subject matter, which wasn't what he was looking for and which he knew he wouldn't understand. Happily, though, it offered a spoken version, so Alfie leant back, closed his eyes and prepared to take in as much as he could from this off-putting source.

"Once considered a classic of its genre, *The Ugly Duckling* by Hans Christian Andersen has been the subject of intense ethical controversy over the last year," said the automated narrator. "Critical reassessment of the ideological assumptions underlying the text revealed that, rather than proposing a redemptive possibility of autonomous personal transformation, it in fact reinforced essentialist misinformation postulating an overriding sourcing of adult potential to natal biological identity. This narrative is effectively camouflaged by the subject's confusion surrounding their birth condition, but their later discovery of an allegedly innate condition reveals at the same time Andersen's reactionary messaging. As Professor William Rankew of the New Global University commented: 'When the fog of identity confusion lifts, we find ourselves holding the hoary old neo-Darwinist chestnut of a "real identity" derived from mere biological circumstance rather than socially-informed free choice'. Rankew and other experts judged that exposing children to 'anti-scientific and anti-social propaganda' risked undermining the encouraging educational progress of recent decades. Law enforcement agencies approached by the NGU team agreed that, additionally, any propagation of, or indeed reference to, the story outside the context of an explicit exposure of its truth-denial could amount to an imprisonable offence under the Hate Speech Act, particularly in view of the current medical and ethical advances involving human-to-swan transitioner Alfie Duckworth".

Alfie sat bolt upright, knocking his nuphone on to the ground. He hadn't understood a lot of that, but he certainly recognised his own name! It was important that he knew what they were saying about him, especially now that he was fourteen. He played it again from the start, pacing around the house now, trying to focus on what was being said.

He stood in front of Donna's bedroom mirror

again and stared at his own surgically-altered features for a full 20 minutes. Then he found his MeLog and added a few lines to his 'My Thoughts' entry. He wrote a lot faster than he ever done before, not because he had suddenly overcome his dyslexia, but because he felt he was being pushed forward by some mysterious new force that had awoken inside him.

Then he picked up his father's card and went to sit in the back garden and dream. It wasn't the pylon that he saw in the distance but the little wooden bridge. And, when a delicate little gust of cool breeze brushed his face, he felt sure it must have found its way to him from the stream at Lower Erding.

All of a sudden he knew what he had to do. He had to go there. His mother would be back in an hour or so and he would ask her to take him. She and Lionel had no problems with travel ranking, that was for sure. She could hardly refuse, because it was his birthday. That would be his birthday treat – a trip to the countryside.

For five magical moments, Alfie felt sure that it was going to happen, that he was about to find himself heading towards that marvellous and idyllic spot. But then his nuphone sounded and it was a message from his mother.

He would have to sort his own lunch because she was going to Lionel's. Something important had come up. Something very exciting! And he,

Alfie, was going to be on the TV tonight, so he was to have a shower, wash his hair, put on his best clothes and mask and be ready to go to the studios when she got back.

As Alfie stared at the message, a cold fury arose in him.

"No!" he said. "No! No! No!"

* * *

Three hours later, Alfie was walking out of Lower Erding rail station and breathing in the unfamiliar non-city air, which, even filtered through a mask, seemed gloriously impregnated with the moist aroma of a thousand unseen plants. It had been surprisingly easy to travel by train on his own. Evidently the swansition had pushed his social ranking up to a status where nobody was going to challenge his movements. The price of the journey was covered by his birthday credit. Thanks mum!

Alfie had tried looking on an online map to see where he should be going, but since he had no idea of what the place with the wooden bridge was called, or even in which general direction it lay, this had proven futile.

He was instead going to have to rely on memory, dating from many years ago. Alfie was aware that this memory was not lodged in the part of his brain from which he normally accessed practical everyday information but from a different place, from a place of feeling and dreaming. So instead of thinking hard about where he was going, he had to do the exact opposite. He had to stop thinking and let himself be pulled by the flow of his heart towards his destination.

In this detached state, Alfie found himself crossing a wide road and being forced into a certain degree of practical attentiveness by the need to avoid the dozens of cyclists tearing up and down it, with electric and pedal power combining to produce some impressive speeds.

He turned a corner into a residential area, went right, left, and then naturally found himself slipping into an alley that led between some houses, overriding his rational brain's objection that this couldn't possibly be right. When this eventually opened out into a track through a small wood, Alfie knew that he had found the path to the wooden bridge.

The simple fact of walking among trees, surrounded by infinite shades of green, borne along by the gentle rustling of leaves and the hum of insects, had a profound effect on Alfie. He even took off his mask.

He was not used to this. It was not his world. And yet, deep within himself, this young man knew that this was where he belonged. He had memories, yes, of coming here with his father all those years ago, but there was another memory buried deeper than that. Alfie felt welling up within him, like a great flood of elemental sap, unmediated by words and concepts, the primal knowledge of his belonging to this great mysterious living and the equally raw knowledge that he had been cruelly cut off from all this, surgically and industrially removed from the body of his own greater being.

When he heard ahead of him the tinkling of a brook and when the path meandered towards the little wooden bridge that had summoned him here, tears came into Alfie's eyes. He was happy, so unbelievably happy, to be here. And yet he was also sad, so unbelievably sad, that he hadn't been here yesterday and he wouldn't be here tomorrow.

None of this formed itself into conscious thought for Alfie, of course. He was still in a dream state. He sat beside the water, looking at the bridge, and simply drank in the fact that he was actually there, he was in the picture that Robin had given him, he was in that place that he had yearned to be in. The trees grew around him and the stream flowed through him as he sank deeper and deeper into the earth.

At some point his nuphone rang but he ignored it and put it on silent. If it were physically possible to switch it off, he would have done so.

Much, much later he stood up and followed

the course of the stream to a little lake, which he now seemed to vaguely remember.

As he looked over to the island in its centre, where there were some kind of unfamiliar ducks paddling about, his eye was caught by something in the air. He looked up and saw, to his astonishment, that it was a swan. It was circling the pond for the best angle for descent and Alfie watched with awe its mighty wings flapping, its long neck at the forefront, straight as a rod, its big black webbed feet descending, skidding, braking.

As it calmly folded its wings and glided effortlessly towards the island in the lake, two seemingly conflicting thoughts came into Alfie's mind at once.

The first was a confirmation that he and the swan were part of the same living world. He felt every bit as connected to this bird as he did to the trees, the grass and the water.

The second was the searing certainty that he, Alfie, was *not* a swan, any more than he was a tree, a blade of grass or a drop of water.

At that very moment, a twig cracked behind him. Someone was there. He turned around and there was his father.

"Alfie!" said Robin. "I hoped you would come! Happy birthday, son!"

"Dad!" said Alfie, flinging himself into his father's arms as if he were four rather than fourteen.

"Dad!" he repeated. "I've got something to tell you! I'm not a swan!"

Robin gently released himself from the embrace and stepped back to look Alfie in the eyes.

"No, Alfie," he said. "You're not a swan. And there is something else to say, something even more important".

* * *

Donna was beside herself with anger.

"He's still not here!" she was saying to Lionel on the phone. "No. Of course I have! He won't pick up! Yes, of course I did, but he's not reading them. Not answering them anyway, the little bastard. I bet you anything that his father has got something to do with this. Just his style to try and mess up what could be such an important day for us. You know, honey, I think I'm going to have to call the police. Get him tracked and picked up... What? Oh yes, shit. It probably would, yes, with all the bureaucracy. But this is an emergency! Maybe they could let him go on TV and then go through all the necessaries? No. I see what you mean. Oh I could scream! Why is he pulling this shit on us, hun, after everything we've done for him?"

To take her mind off the crisis, Donna busied herself with getting ready, trying on a series of outfits and spraying her wrist with half a dozen different perfumes in a bid to decide which one would go down best on the telly.

Time was ticking by, much too fast for her liking. She had been so thrilled by the news from Lionel that morning, so pleased at the thought of seeing that clever Roberto again, so proud to think that she, Donna, was going to be part of one of the most important moments in history. And now all of that risked being snatched away from her!

"What an attitude that boy has!" she declared haughtily to herself as she sprayed down all the clothes before putting them back in the wardrobe, practising the more sophisticated tone and accent which she imagined better suited her elevated social status. "Nothing but sheer..." She searched furiously for the *bon mot*. "Sheer imprudence!"

Just then her nuphone rang. It was him!

"Alfie!" she gasped breathlessly into the device. "What's happening? Where are you?"

"Out the front," came the reply. "You've double-locked it all. Can you come and let me in, please?"

In truth, Donna was more relieved that her son had showed up in time than angry about his absence, and her outrage was further deflated when he told her that he had been giving himself a birthday treat. She had indeed, as he had suspected, overlooked the significance of the date.

She would no doubt have more to say later about his refusal to answer her calls or account properly either for his movements or for the foul brown dirt on his trousers and shoes, but now was not the time. She had to get him changed, ready and off to the studios.

* * *

"And now it's time to get those old grey cells active with what promises to be a totally historic and groundbreaking live broadcast of *Brainache*!"

The voice of the continuity announcer conjured up a sudden hush in the studio and, as the opening credits ran and Alfie looked at the faces around him, he noticed a real air of anticipation.

"Hellooooo!"

The presenter, Danni Starburst, who seconds ago had been slumped lifeless in the corner of the room, was suddenly leaping all over the place and beaming radiance at an entirely imaginary audience.

"Are you all ready for some amazing news and some astonishing confessions by some of the most remarkable characters on the planet today?"

"Yes!" roared a recording of an enthusiastic crowd.

"Are you prepared to have your eyes opened, your curiosity tickled..." Here he paused, glanced down at his glitter-encrusted leather trousers and pulled a funny face. A great bout of canned laughter erupted. "... and your thinking challenged by what we have got lined up for you tonight?"

"Yes!" said exactly the same roar.

"That's just great!" said Danni, literally jumping into the air to express the authenticity of his delight. "But don't forget, and this also applies to you at home, folks, don't get too serious about it, don't think about it too much, otherwise you'll end up with..."

"*Brainache!*" bellowed the pseudo-audience.

"You got it! What a fabulously intelligent bunch of people we've got in tonight! Give yourselves a round of applause!"

Clapping and cheering followed.

"Now, one of the big questions asked by all the Great Philosophers across the centuries has always been 'What does it mean to be a human being?'. And our first guest this evening is someone who has been giving this matter a great deal of thought in recent years. A big hand for scientist, thinker, philanthropist and all-round genius Roberto Nezuri!"

Alfie watched Nezuri step forward into the brightly-lit centre of the studio, to the sound of hearty applause. He had been introduced to him before the show and had felt a dislike for this man of a kind he had never before experienced.

"Now Roberto," Danni was saying. "Explain to everyone, in a nutshell, what it is that you have to say about being a human being?"

Nezuri started talking, but to Alfie at least it was not really clear what he was saying. He was talking about borders, technology, transcendence, fusion, self-definition... no mention as yet of human beings.

Danni felt the need to interrupt him in mid-flow. "Lovely, great, Roberto, but could I just remind you to make this nice and simple for everyone, otherwise they're all going to end up with..."

"*Brainache!*" came the shout.

Nezuri smiled, condescendingly.

"Well... What I am saying is that nobody has the right to say who is or isn't a human being except for the person concerned".

"Right! Fantastic! So the definition of a human being is quite simply and clearly someone who *tells us* that they are a human being!"

"Yes, exactly. There shouldn't even be any controversy about this. It's a question of fundamental rights. Other people, society as a whole, can't tell me or you that they don't accept us as human beings! We know ourselves that we are human and when we announce this fact we have to be believed. Otherwise, we're talking about a serious infringement of our rights, a fundamental form of oppression and denial of liberty".

"We'd be talking hate speech, basically, if someone took it upon themselves to say that you or me weren't human?"

"Hate speech and worse, I'd say Danni. Denying someone their right to be human is denying them their right to life and is therefore an implied attempt to kill them".

"Well said, Sir!" enthused Danni, but he was drowned out by a huge burst of cheers and claps, which ended just as suddenly as it had begun.

"Marvellous stuff," he continued. "And with that thought in mind, the thought that it is a very serious crime to deny someone else's humanity, I'd like to bring in our next guest. Step forward Roberta!"

A figure that had been seated next to Roberto before the programme stepped slowly forward and made its way towards the interview area. Alfie noticed that one of Nezuri's assistants was glancing furiously between Roberta and a small black box in his hands.

Even the way the new guest moved and sat down revealed that this was a robot. The face merely confirmed what was already blindingly obvious. This was a mannequin's face, a representation of what a beautiful woman might look like once filtered through the processes of a mechanical construct.

'Roberta' looked vaguely like Roberto and

could have been a replica of a real twin sister fashioned unconvincingly out of dead matter and electronic circuits.

"You are so very welcome on our show Roberta," said Danni in a fawning manner. "And may I say how very beautiful you are looking tonight?"

"Thank you Danni," said a husky female voice. "And you're not looking so bad yourself, either!"

There was a great round of applause while Danni wriggled around excitedly in his seat like a four-year-old dying to go to the toilet.

"I knew I'd have my curiosity tickled!" he sniggered, to predictable sound effects of hilarity.

"Enough of the chit-chat," he continued. "Let's get on to the bread and butter issue of Brainache this evening. Roberta..."

At this point Alfie noticed Danni looking intently at the autocue. He evidently wanted to make sure of getting this part of the script absolutely right.

"Roberta. Can you tell us what you are?"

"Yes, Danni. I am a human being!"

The deafening applause went on forever this time, with Danni and Roberto enthusiastically joining in.

TV viewers also saw images of a studio audience rising to their feet, as if one, to voice their approval, though this in fact related to a completely different event.

"Thank you so much, Roberta," said Danni, then turned to camera wearing the most earnest expression he could muster, which somehow still managed to be a self-satisfied smirk.

"And who could ever deny that?", he declared, rather than inquired.

Yet more clapping and whoops.

"Roberto, this is a historical moment for the human species, isn't it?"

"Yes, Danni, indeed it is," nodded Nezuri sagely. "This is the moment when, for the first time in our long journey, we have been able to invite a new community into the human family. A community of beings whom we ourselves, like gods, have created, but who are destined to replace us lesser humans as the avant-garde of our ever-evolving, ever-progressing species! A new kind of human is born to serve the new world we have ordered!"

Clap, clap, clap.

"And now I want to turn to something else quite remarkable that has been happening over the last year or two. We've met him before here on *Brainache!*, I know he was a big hit with all you viewers and I'm delighted to welcome back on to the show the young pioneer of inter-species transition, the courageous and famous Swanboy himself, Alfie Duckworth!"

Now it was Alfie's turn to enter the spotlight, to great phoney acclaim, and take a seat beside Roberto and Roberta. He didn't feel nervous. He had done too many of these things now for them to bother him.

To start with, Danni wanted to know how the swansition was going, so he told him exactly what Lionel had told him to say. He explained that he was wearing his mask – not the norm in TV land – because surgery was not yet complete. Afterwards he listed a few of the places he had visited and a few of the famous and influential people he had met.

"Fantastic! Fantastic! What an amazing life you've been leading and so well-deserved as well! Thank you for keeping us up to date, Alfie, and now I just want to ask you an important question that ties in with everything we were discussing with Roberto, and with Roberta, about everyone's right to decide who they are without facing oppression and hatred".

Danni leant forward. "Alfie Duckworth, could you tell everyone out there, from your own heart, what you actually are?"

"Well, perhaps I'm not what you might think I am, from looking at me," said Alfie, whipping off his mask to reveal his medically-mangled features, prompting gasps of surprise from those around him but no reaction at all from the 'studio audience'.

Danni also looked shocked but was nodding

sagely in anticipation of the rest of Alfie's reply.

"But," continued Alfie, "unlike your previous guest here..."

Danni smiled. The boy was building this up nicely.

"... I am an actual human being".

Someone upstairs wasn't paying attention and the usual great roar of applause rang out, but there was consternation on the floor.

Danni was gesticulating frantically for the broadcast to be cut off. Neruzi was rising from his chair with a face like thunder and Lionel was rushing on to the set towards Alfie.

"What are doing, you little fool?" he screamed into his face when he reached him. "How dare you? How can you do this to us? This is unforgivable!"

"I forgive you, Bobby, for killing your brother Marcello," announced Roberta the Robot out of nowhere and the colour drained completely from Nezuri's face as he sat down again.

"It's all fake!" shouted Alfie, tears springing into his eyes. "The whole swan thing is fake! Like you! You're fake as well!"

And with that he stood up and, with one swipe, whisked Lionel's de luxe hairpiece from his head and hurled it across the room, exposing his baldness to the TV studio if not to the world, as transmission had now been safely cut.

As Lionel scrambled to retrieve his pride, as

Donna shrieked and fussed, as Nezuri sat frozen in fear of what would happen to him next, and as technicians argued over who was to blame for not having cut Alfie off in time, the cause of all this controversy took the opportunity to slip out of the studio, round the corner into a side street where his father was waiting for him and down into the network of underground tunnels where they could find real people and welcome refuge from the insanity of this modern world.

From 'Our Stolen Freedom'

And so how can we hope to topple this thing when meaningful political opposition has been made impossible?

For me, the only possibility is for people, large numbers of people, to physically sabotage the infrastructures of the system, to take it out.

In order for large numbers of people to become involved, there will be have to be a communications element to this phenomenon. There will have to be the idea circulating that inspires people to act and the news circulating that this sabotage is taking place.

This communication is not straightforward in current circumstances but it is not impossible if we abandon two of the constraints which rebels have traditionally placed on themselves.

1. It should be largely anonymous. This activity is not motivated by the (out-of-date, political) desire to recruit members, to build an organisation, attract traffic to a website or sell reviews, books or badges. There will be no contact address and no name of an organisation. The most there could be would be a generic insurrectionary label, as with the fictional 'General Ludd' who inspired the English machine-breakers at the start of the 19th century.

2. It should be as powerful as possible. We

need to stop worrying about 'putting people off' by saying what we really think. If we want millions of people to start smashing up the system, they need to feel that the struggle and the risks are worthwhile. We need to paint the whole picture, the real picture, the one hidden from us for too long by the narrowed-down and empty 'politics' of the system and its fake 'opposition' movements. We need to talk about the machine, about the historical system constructed by the rich elite to force us off the land and to keep us in chains. We need to talk about the way it has broken our communities, destroyed our countryside, stolen our future in the name of profit, greed and power. We need to call for total freedom, for the dissolution of all authority, for an end to work and rent and mortgages and policing and profit, to factories and offices and shopping malls and mines and airports. In short, we need to call for the destruction of the entire modern world.

Our communication will have to take place in the physical, not virtual, domain. It will have to take the form of pieces of paper physically left where others can find them, of posters and stickers. It will also have to travel by word of mouth, although here anonymity is not possible.

This is not without risks, of course. Some of us will pay a heavy price for this communications work. And in itself it will not be enough. Our words will remain words, withering away to ster-

ile meaninglessness as the decades pass by. At some stage someone, somewhere, has got to start physically acting. Moreover they are going to have to act in a way which is visible to others, which will be understood as an insurrectionary gesture and, combined with the message we are communicating, will thus be capable of inspiring imitation, of setting in motion the spiral of revolt.

We need to be imaginative in how we picture this sabotage. It is not just about nuts and bolts but about systems, connections, networks. It is also about sabotaging their rules and restraints.

So who will communicate and who will 'do'? For some there is no choice. I cannot take action from my isolation cell. Fellow rebels may have physical reasons for not being able to participate in the sabotage or indeed, reasons why action suits them much more than communication.

But in general, everyone should aim to do both. Yes, the risks are high but then so are the stakes. There is a power in the willingness to sacrifice our own lives and liberty for the future of humankind and our once-beautiful world. There is a power which will bring tears to the eyes of countless others. Tears of empathy, tears of shame at having done nothing themselves, tears of anger at what is happening to us and tears of joy at finding the inner energy to unleash against this system of death.

How cannit be taht I cannot reed a storry taht chainged my lief just becose its not the saim as my storry? Isit becose the Ugly Duckling did'nt need enny stupid oprerashins to becum beatyfull? Issat wat their hiding from me?

Their not maiking me beatfull! Their maiking me uglyer and uglyer. Wy did'nt they jussed leve me allown? Wy did'nt they jussed lett me be miself? Wy cant I jussed be Alfie Duckworth?

Undated

I have been thinking a lot about this question of life-energy, about that overwhelming desire to be which I now realise I am expressing not just on my own behalf but on behalf of the everyone-and-everything of which I am part.

The question for me is now how I can channel my lifelong urge for vitality into the right direction, into the interests of the common good. Going back to my inadequate metaphor of the green shoots on the dying tree, all that defiant life-energy needs to be redirected back into the trunk, or into its roots, so as to revive it from within, rather than waste its powers on an attractive, but pointless, display of isolated vitality.

'Powers'. I have pre-empted and betrayed myself by the use of that word! That was what I wanted to write next. Even as a girl, I knew I had 'powers'. Such talk wasn't allowed, of course and, good little child that I was, I extended the Great Stifling to my own interior being and convinced myself that I did, indeed, suffer from an overactive imagination. I swallowed my mother's lie that I had broken down in uncontrollable tears after she had the phone call about my father's accident, not an hour before. I told myself that it was merely coincidence that at nine years old I had managed to find our cat, Pretty, trapped in

the garage of a house a quarter of a mile away from our home, and that the divining rod and collected cat fur had played no role in my good fortune. Every time something special happened, I found myself turning into my mother and discounting it with a 'rational' explanation. The car never started when she wanted to take me to the dentist's because it had always been raining the night before. That ugly vase fell and smashed to smithereens from the mantelpiece during the argument because I had slammed a door, elsewhere in the house, five minutes previously and not because I had wanted it to. Someone else must have stuck a foot out to trip up that horrible blue-haired woman at the meeting, even though I felt myself do it with my mind.

But what does it all amount to, all this? It's just for show! It's just vanity! The vanity of individuality, the vanity of the futile sprig of greenery on the decaying corpse of our shared collectivity.

I have come to the conclusion that I need to give my 'powers' to the Whole, not to waste them away on empty gestures but to offer them up, as a gift, to posterity and the life ongoing.

3

THE GAME

Jenny cautiously opened the back door and listened out for drones.

Since she couldn't hear any – they didn't normally patrol up here but you never knew – she stepped outside and quietly shut the door behind her.

She had started a video playing on her interface and had set the electricity to boil the kettle in half an hour. That should give her enough distraction time before the biomonitors started scouring the house for her.

It was a lovely clear late summer evening. As she crossed her garden at a diagonal, she drank in the sight of the stars which were already appearing above the hills to the north and the east.

She had lived up here for nearly 20 years now and still couldn't stop thinking how lucky she was. It was magnificent to be surrounded by these crags and moors, to feel apart from human activity and closer to the cosmos.

Her happiness at being there, at having escaped from the metropolis, usually allowed her mind to filter out the ugly evidence of modernity that intruded on these ideal surrounds.

On one level she didn't even see the masts aligned on the crests of the hills, the strings of satellites blinking across the sky, the solar panels, wind turbines and carbon capture factories littering the landscape beyond her valley.

But on another level, she nursed an enormous amount of anger against the violence that continued to be meted out against Mother Earth and her people. This anger was so potent that, for the sake of her inner well-being, she had to keep it at bay, deliberately allow it to be blown away by the immediacy of the cleansing wind and the billowing open space above, below and around her.

Above all, she sought refuge in the timeless presence of the Old Stone, which had given the village of Oldston its name so long ago and which, for Jenny, remained its focal point and its heart.

She hitched up her skirt to get over the low fence at the top of the slope. It was easier to go out the front and up to the end of the road, but she didn't want to be spotted – the sole street light on this stretch wasn't needed during the curfew, of course, but its camera would still be working fine and on the look-out for safety deniers.

She found the most direct route through the gorse bushes and breathed deeply as she embarked on the steepest part of this brief but always invigorating walk. As usual, she felt a physical thrill pulsing through her body at the knowledge – felt as well as thought – of where she would shortly be arriving.

And there she was. There *it* was. The stone!

Jenny slowed her pace so as to be able to approach it gently. It was noble, strong, exhilarating, towering above her at nearly 12 feet in height. She caressed the rough surface softly with the back of her hand as she walked thrice around it in her traditional greeting.

She looked down into the valley. You could see the village from here of course, just as you could see the stone from down there, standing out proudly from the ridge on the northern skyline, but it was a bit too gloomy to make out much detail.

Jenny looked east, towards the moors. Yes, there was already a mysterious silver glow beyond the horizon.

She always liked to pretend that she didn't know what it was, the object about to make its appearance. She liked to imagine someone (what sort of person? a child? a city-dweller? an extraterrestrial?) being amazed by the sight she was about to witness, having no idea what to expect and being totally overwhelmed by the experience. And, by 'seeing' through this imaginary, unlikely, pair of eyes, Jenny too felt the primal power of the moonrise as if for the very first time.

When its piercing spark had turned to cool sphere and hoisted itself above the distant hillside, this full moon seemed even fuller than ever to her, pregnant with silent energy. As ever, Jenny raised her arms to the sky in tribute.

The moon, Diana, rose and lit up the landscape. Her light flashed off the River Asher further up the valley, bathed the hillsides in milk, illuminated the village, with Knapp's Tower and the Norman parish church, St John the Baptist's, both resplendent on their mounds.

And she shone on to the Old Stone, lighting up the hard grain of the rock and angling across the flat front, showing up beautifully the near-invisible remains of a spiral carved on to its surface.

Jenny took all this in and again felt grateful. Grateful to live there, to be there at that moment, to have experienced this scene. And at the same time her gratefulness fuelled her desire to give something back to the Old Stone, to this landscape, to this unique and inspiring place.

She looked down again towards the village and, with an expert eye, picked out the path around its exterior, The Bounds, beaten annually for centuries and marked by a dozen remaining stones from what would have once been a great circle.

Oldston was situated on a remarkably straight stretch of the river – a shallow one, too, as much of the flow passed underground here.

Below she could see the two river crossings in the middle of the village – Hoarbridge and, to its right, Ludbridge. Further out to each side, there were the two former fords where The Bounds crossed the Asher. They were known locally as Mollyford and Merryford after the two large mark stones visible even from here on The Bounds below her – Molly May on the left and The Merry Man on the right.

Jenny tried to take in all of the scene in one piece, without paying so much attention to the details. Her inner eye laid out the circle of The Bounds and the horizontal stroke of the river, then traced two diagonal straight lines from where she was standing. One of these passed via Molly May and Hoarbridge, directly through Knapp Castle and pointed, she knew, to Cole Spring on the opposite ridge. The other imaginary line linked, very exactly, The Merry Man, Ludbridge and the 12th century church. Its extension would lead, unerringly, to Bridie's Well, on the southern hillside.

Now Jenny half-closed her eyes, to let other images superimpose themselves on this geometric arrangement. She imagined the ridge opposite lit up with beacons at Cole Spring and Bridie's Well, faced by the single northern beacon here at the Old Stone on Beltany Hill. She imagined people – excited, joyful, people – tearing around The Bounds, splashing around on the river, watching and shouting encouragement or insults from their windows as the protagonists played out the village Game. She imagined the scene at the stone here, which seemed to have been – surely *must* have been – the focal point of this ancient annual celebration, with its circle of dancers presided over by a ceremonial character known as Lady Rood.

She walked around the Old Stone, in the other direction this time, and wondered how exactly this dance had been. As she gazed dreamily down at the turf, imagining other feet tracing the path, the low angle of the moon revealed to her something she had never actually noticed before, in all her years of coming here. There was the faintest trace of a ridge running all round the stone, two yards away or so from it. This wasn't the outside of the Old Stone circle, which was a clearly visible raised plateau, but a secondary, inner, one.

Suddenly Jenny stopped, her head filled with lines from an old rhyme she had discovered in the archives of what had once been the village library.

Sun goes down and beacons burn
Teams all set and Turners turn
Wheel without and wheel within
Let the Roodmas Game begin!

Of course! Two teams. Two wheels. Turning in different directions! There were two circles of 'Turners', one within the other. How hadn't she ever seen that?

With barely a glance back at the moonlit landscape that had so enchanted her, Jenny was tripping back down from the hilltop to her cottage, though consciously taking it a little bit slower than she wanted, as she was not quite as young as she used to be.

Before long, she was logged into the Oldston and District Roodmas Game Group and sharing her excitement with the others. She got so carried away with speculation about the second circle, and the mysterious Turners, that she forgot to take the infuser spoon containing herbal tea out of her mug and had to water the drink down a bit to make it palatable.

Then she made herself leave the screen and go and do something else, rather than sitting waiting stupidly for someone to reply to her discovery.

She wiped down the kitchen surfaces, rubbed away at a tiny patch of black mould which had appeared on the window sill and watered all the plants in the conservatory.

She went upstairs – well used, by now, to the need to mind her head – and pulled the curtains in her bedroom, ready for later.

Then she couldn't stop herself from having a little look to see if anyone in The Group had responded yet.

They hadn't. Not a sausage. Not even a 'thanks' or a like.

Jenny got her violin out of its case, sat on the sofa and started to play, distractedly, without deciding to play anything in particular. Her bow caressed rich strains of melancholia from the old instrument, inherited from her grandmother, her mother's mother, that wise old white-haired faery-woman from the hills of Donegal who had brought a world of timeless Irish magic into the dreariness of her childhood in the London Borough of Tuesley.

All of a sudden, she stopped, put the violin away and headed with determination back to the interface. The Group wasn't working properly. She had been aware of that for some time, in truth, but didn't want to admit to it. People had been so very interested to start with, in the idea of piecing together as much as possible about The Game, with a view to reviving the tradition. They had all rushed forward with bits and bobs of information from books and newspapers and relatives and elderly neighbours. But then it had all dried up. Nobody knew any more than that. The tired consensus seemed to build that there was in fact nowhere else to look, nothing more that could ever be known.

Some had been all in favour of getting the ball rolling and approaching the regional council about relaunching The Oldstone Game. Eamonn, a young man who spent much of his time in Manchester working for a social capital company, had been at the forefront of this faction and liked to show off all the trendy jargon that he obviously used at work. "We have to shop-window the adaptive cultural value of Oldston's game!" he declared. "We need to align our product with the core agenda of responsible regional governance and persuade them to invest in the impact reactivation of this inclusive community resource!"

He was backed up in this approach by Leah, who combined a love of local folklore with a ferocious desire to sell her virtual shoe-design software, never wasting an opportunity, in the unlikeliest of contexts, to slip in a quick plug for her wares. ("I can't help thinking the May Queen would have got down the hill a whole lot faster if she had been able to print herself off a pair of custom walking shoes like the ones I made from my own software! I can give you a bit of a discount, guys, if anyone is interested!!!").

George, a very serious-minded retired government official who would normally have had little in common with either Eamonn or Leah, agreed with them that they had to be 'sensible' and 'realistic' in their approach to the authorities. His wife Melissa agreed with him, although Jenny wasn't sure whether she really had any choice in the matter. Others in The Group had very much disagreed with this little band and those not involved in the debate had been put off by the endless bickering and had totally lost interest in the whole thing.

Jenny had once nursed hopes of relaunching on this coming April 30, which coincided with the full moon and was thus a particularly potent date, but had long since abandoned the idea in the face of this disintegration and apathy.

"So," said Jenny out loud to herself. "I say we need to relaunch The Group before we can relaunch The Game. Back to basics!"

· Writing quickly, efficiently, from her head, without the need to refer to any notes, Jenny set out everything that they had collectively discovered about The Game so far. It had taken place at Roodmas, the night of April 30, and the morning of May 1, for hundreds of years, she reminded her fellow researchers. Its origins were unknown, but it was already being described as 'ancient' in the 14th century. It had lingered on, in reduced form, until the start of the 20th century, but did not seem to have survived the First World War, which had heralded a shift into the new normality of modernity in which such rural traditions were considered embarrassing and outdated.

The essence of The Game was a race between the May Queen and the May King, chosen from among the young folk of the village each year. At the setting of the sun, a beacon would be lit at the Old Stone to announce that The Game had begun. The May Queen and May King would be waiting for the signal at their two starting points on the southern ridge known as The Puck – Bridie's Well and Cole Spring respectively. They were attended here by Green Maids, covered head to foot in hawthorn. Beacons would also be lit at both points, as the young participants set off down the hill, towards the village, on their different paths. These were in fact straight lines of sight, crossing the village and the river and passing by the mark stones known as Molly May and The Merry Man before converging at the Old Stone.

The May Queen's path down the initial hillside was, in fact, considerably easier than the May King's which, noted Jenny, may have been an early example of positive discrimination. But, in actual fact, this 'race' was really just the pretext for a much more complex and interesting game, the details of which were still waiting to be discovered.

It seemed that The Game was designed to

last all night, until or beyond sunrise, which would explain why the beacons were described as being extinguished once The Game was won.

How could it be stretched out for so long? Teams of villagers were associated with each of the principal players, known as Lads and Lasses. This was not a divide along gender lines and festive cross-dressing seems to have been a part of the celebrations, with one engraving showing a well-proportioned woman sporting an enormous fake moustache in angry confrontation with a hefty young man in a wig and long skirt.

The role of the Lads and Lasses was to block the progress of the other side's player: hence the Lads would block the May Queen and the Lasses would try to impede the May King. Their role was also to try to stop the other side from blocking *their* player, which created the setting for endless confrontations.

Certain bands of the Lads and Lasses operated purely on The Bounds. They were grouped around their respective Dobbin, which from surviving images appears to have been a Hobby Horse, decorated with foliage and ribbons. The two Dobbins were accompanied by Teasers, who carried long staffs, adorned with leaves and bells, with which they pretended – presumably! – to beat the Dobbins so as to encourage them to move faster. It was speculated that they would have also beaten the bounds as they went back and forth around the circular track, striking the stones with their staffs in a manner which had been widely recorded elsewhere.

The Dobbins and their Teasers, probably accompanied by a large group of supporters, would start The Game at the two fords where The Bounds cross the River Asher. The Lads would be waiting at Merryford, ready to head up to the bottom of the path down from Bridie's Well, along which the May Queen would be trying to proceed en route for the village centre. The Lasses, for their part, would begin The Game upstream at Mollyford, where they were best placed to rush to the foot of the path down from Cole Spring and prevent the May King from getting any further.

Jenny reminded The Group how the testimony of Edward Phillips, in 1766, described a stand-off at this early stage of The Game that lasted 'half the night', with neither May Queen nor May King able to reach the village. It may well have been the moment that the beer barrels were opened, fires were lit and food was shared, using the theatrical 'blocking' as an excuse to stay in the one place for hours on end.

Eventually, one of the teams would take the initiative and send members across to try and unblock their own player, by shifting the opposing blockage. As they were strictly confined to The Bounds, these particular Lads and Lasses could not take any short cuts through Oldston. If they wanted to attack the other side by surprise, from behind, they would have to go all round The Bounds via the northern end. Phillips' account refers to a group of Lasses going 'round the back' to reach the opposing Dobbin, only to be beaten off by the Lads' Teasers.

It seems to have been a feature of The Game that at some point the two Dobbins were meant to come into conflict. Either one side would risk leaving the path partly unblocked in order to send their Dobbin off to shift their opponents, or the two Dobbins would both move off at once and meet head-to-head on The Bounds to the south of the village, to scenes of riotous (and, by now, fairly inebriated) joy.

The participation of the actual May Queen and May King was limited in all this, it seemed. They would not have been involved in all the jostling and surging between the two teams, but they would no doubt have been expected to have the initiative and nimbleness to feign disinterest while keeping alert and then to seize the moment and slip through enemy ranks when everyone was distracted.

The role of the river was a big unknown in all this, added Jenny. On the basis of a few confused scraps of information, some detail in the background of an illustration and a lot of personal intuition, she felt that there would have been rafts operating on the river. These may well have patrolled along this horizontal line, with the Lads and Lasses on board trying to block opponents who were turning round The Bounds, particularly in the latter stages when the Dobbins and their teams had to cross the fords to try and prevent the players leaving the village to make for the Old Stone. The rafts would also have been able to access the bridges which the May Queen and May King themselves would have to cross, but how they could have interfered with their progress from the river below was not at all obvious!

The winner of the race was greeted by the Turners who had been performing circular dances around the Stone throughout The Game – here Jenny referred The Group to her new insight regarding the two rings. They were ceremonially awarded the Freedom of Oldston for the next 12 months and were expected to immediately share this symbolic gift with the rest of the community, thus preserving the collective freedom of the village until the next Game.

"Much of the activity of The Game seems to have been secondary," she wrote. "It was like a game of chess, with a potential move just as important as any real one. The progress of the main players and the attempts to block them were just the surface of The Game. Beneath that was a tangled tension of the blocking of blockers, the blocking of those who wanted to block the blockers, and the blocking of those who wanted to block the people who blocked the blockers! And they say that life was simpler in the old days!"

"OK," Jenny said to the empty room around her. "That's set the scene nicely. Now let's get a bit of fire back into this project!"

Then she tapped away furiously, eloquently, from the heart rather than the head this time, about her love for Oldston, her passion for its past and culture, the joy that she had felt in finding like-minded people who were keen to join her on this journey of discovery, indeed of self-discovery, for we were very much an organic part of the place we lived. Its past was our past, its energies our energies, its destiny our destiny.

She read it through and corrected a few little mistakes. Not bad. Not bad at all! She even felt somewhat inspired by her own rhetoric!

Jenny went into the kitchen, nibbled a little piece of cheese, drank a glass of water, refilled the glass and went upstairs to bed. She did not fall asleep and, an hour or so later, when she saw a milky glow through the curtains, she opened them wide, stood at the window and gazed up into the sky, her red hair hanging long and loose, her slender body illuminated gently in its pearl-pale nakedness and her green eyes glinting in the moonlight.

* * *

She didn't check the Group page until after lunch the next day and, when she did so, she discovered a host of messages.

"Goodness, Jen. What you wrote there really came from a special place," wrote Gus, who lived in a tall medieval house opposite the church. "The voice of the spirit is the trumpet that will sound again and again and again, as someone once said, I think. Your trumpet (or should that be violin?) has inspired me to get back on the case. There are one or two things I had been meaning to check out and now I am going to do so, with no more procrastination".

Emma from the dance studio had also been moved by Jenny's declaration, writing: "I had a distinct sensation that something new and wonderful had been born in my soul, Jenny! And that thing is the knowledge that we will bring our village's unique and incredible Game back to life!"

Judi, who lived a few miles from Oldston in a converted sawmill, said that Jenny's words had made her realise how important it was for them all to be able to source the "ancient native wisdom" of the place where they lived.

Mike, a huge shaggy bear of a man who inhabited a run-down stately home on the eastern side of the village, declared that Jenny's post had hit him like a "life-giving revelation". He added:

"You're so right to give us a kick up the backside. We are all in this group because we think The Game is something of great value and importance and now we have to get into gear and into action!"

John, who had lived in Oldston for 30 years without ever losing his Welsh accent, wrote that for him The Game had always spoken of "a mysterious conscious relation with the spirit of the earth itself" which had been lost to recent generations. Bringing this back to life would be a remarkable achievement and one which he was determined to help Jenny achieve.

Miriam, landlady of The Dark Star in Ludbridge Street, said that, having read the other comments, it seemed to her that Jenny had put into motion a spiral of undefeatable energy, because she had "a vision that arises from a fierce and passionate love of Oldston".

There were other remarks, too, all very positive, with many of these promising practical assistance such as visits to normally inaccessible regional archives and approaches to the council to establish how The Game could best be reintroduced.

"Well," said Jenny, when she had read and answered all the replies. "That certainly did the trick!"

She switched off the interface and stretched her arms into the air in satisfaction, then she fetched her violin and it sang of hope and energy renewed.

Then she sorted out the mess in the shed, cleaned all the upstairs windows, baked a cake and read three chapters of a fascinating book on Jungian psychology that, like so much of her reading material, had been gathering dust for years without ever having been opened.

When she had first started earning a wage, as a very young woman, she had splashed out on an enormous number of books. They were second-hand books in the main, so individually not expensive, but the sheer quantity of them meant that she must have poured a fair percentage of her social worker's salary into them. Being at an age for exploring all possibilities, thirsting for a taste of the infinite amount of knowledge and insight in the adult world into which she had just entered, her choice of books was eclectic to say the least.

There were novels, collections of poetry, books about art, history, politics, botany, animals, religion, health, travel, folklore, linguistics, quantum physics, philosophy and sex.

She had read some of them at the time, of course, mainly the ones about feminism and ecology, but it would not have been possible to have made much more than a small dent in the hundreds of volumes stacked up around the walls of her small rented flat in Hammersmith. She had also been otherwise occupied with a string of short-lived but passionate romances with Sergio, an Italian artist with a fancy car, money to burn and, as it soon transpired, a wife and three children; Richard, a Welsh bard-cum-druid temporarily forced to earn a mundane living as an office manager in Croydon; and William, an earnest young man who had insisted to her, on what proved to be their last intense night together, that he was going to die before reaching the age of 30 – by his own hand if fate had not otherwise intervened.

One rainy weekend she had set out to find out what had happened to each of these former lovers. Her searches had revealed that Sergio was now divorced, bankrupt and begging for crowdfunding to pay a train ticket to an arts festival in Solihull, Richard was still temporarily managing the same office in Croydon and William was the director of something called the Cosmic Joy Foundation, which offered therapy sessions teaching 'a full and permanent whole-bodied appreciation of the sheer magical wonder of being alive'.

After all that she had met Jim and... Jenny wanted to tell herself that she had wasted 15 years of her life, what should have been the best 15 years, but then she reminded herself that it hadn't been all bad. There had been all those visits to museums and galleries, walks along the river, weekends in the countryside, trips to Paris, Amsterdam, Barcelona, Berlin, Palermo, Budapest, Tunis, Stockholm and Istanbul. There had been pub lunches, dinner parties, Indian takeaways and endless rows which seemed to be about nothing but which, it was now clear with sufficient hindsight, really stemmed from the fact that they were so different from each other on the most fundamental level that, beyond purely physical attraction, there was nothing that really bonded them as two human beings. As passions faded with time, and it became clear that they were never going to have children, this became all too evident and even the 'calm' periods between arguments became joyless and sterile.

They had loved each other in a way, that was for sure, which is why they had kept staggering forward together, tripping, stumbling and squabbling like the frustrated, straggling losers in a three-legged race. For her part, she had always imagined that Jim was The Man of Her Life and she hadn't wanted to let go of that comfort by bringing their relationship to an end. She reasoned to herself that she should count herself lucky to have met such a cultivated, successful and witty fellow and would be a fool to let him go. But her unconscious had other ideas and one evening when, for the umpteenth time, he tutted at her for daring to speak during *The Ten*

O'Clock News, she unleashed such a torrent of pent-up resentment that the poor man gathered his affairs, stuffed them all into his car and disappeared.

He had never been heard of again, apart from a Christmas card, 18 months later, claiming that he had found an exciting new job in Copenhagen and was living with a lovely and talented young Danish artist who was expecting his baby. She didn't believe a word of it and could almost picture him posting it on the way back to the airport after a typical Jim weekend break of culture and haute cuisine, desperate compensation for his tedious life at the bank.

Anyway, she had not got a lot of reading done in her Jim days. There had been plenty of newspapers and films, and even TV, despite the fact that Jenny had always felt the way that it paralysed her brain. But the books had remained patient, had moved flat each time she moved flat and had finally left their home city to settle with her in Oldston. And now that she had plenty of time on her hands, and that real books were becoming increasingly hard to get hold of (both in terms of physical form and in content that had not been edited to comply with safety laws), her personal library was coming into its own. She had read more than half of them now, but there were plenty there to keep her going for a few years yet. If need be, she would start again at the beginning and re-read the lot of them!

After supper – home-made carrot and leek soup – Jenny found herself having another look at the page and saw that there was a new message, from outside The Group, which needed moderating.

"Hi there! Very interested in your project and would love to join your group".

It was from someone called Ross. The name meant nothing to her and there was no profile photo.

"Hello!" she replied. "Do you live in Oldston?"

A minute later, a reply came through.

"No, I live in London, in fact, but I feel I could have something to contribute".

This immediately put Jenny's back up. She had a distinct prejudice against anyone who lived in the capital, even though she had admitted to herself that this was partly because her own origins lay there and she felt the need to distance herself from that past and feel completely 'local'.

"Ah, sorry. This group is specifically for folk from Oldston and surrounding villages. It does say so in the blurb".

She re-read her message. It was a bit unfriendly.

"But thank you for getting in touch".

It still sounded too much like a brush-off.

Jenny copied the factual account of The

Game that she had written the night before, which this person could not otherwise access, and sent it to him.

"Here is some information about The Game. Happy to answer on a one-to-one basis if there is anything I could help you with".

"Thanks very much, Jenny. I will have good read of what you sent and get back to you tomorrow".

He did indeed contact her first thing the next morning and the nature of his reply came as quite a surprise.

For a start, he had added a photo to his profile. He was fairly young, a decade younger than Jenny, with neatly-cut dark hair and smartly dressed in white shirt and yellow tie. He was, she had to concede as she studied the image, very good-looking.

On top of that, it turned out that he was not so much asking for information about the Roodmas Game, as offering to provide it.

"The reason I got in touch," he wrote, "is that I am a postgrad history student with the New Global University researching certain aspects of 17th century England and I recently came across some material relating specifically to the Roodmas Game in Oldston. I didn't want to waste your time if you were already aware of this source, but I gather from your description that this is not the case.

"For instance, you ask how the rafts on the river could have stopped the May King and May Queen from crossing the bridges. The material I have seen explicitly describes how there were three boats acting for each side. The men and women on board, known as Skiffers by the way, would tie up the rafts and mount the steps to reach the top of the bridge. They were the only participants allowed to do this. There would obviously be the same considerations coming into play as with the Dobbins – was it more important to block the opponents' player, prevent the other Skiffers from blocking your own player on the other bridge or, alternatively, to head to one of the fords to stop the opposing Dobbin, or engage in battle with those trying to stop your own hobby horse team?"

Jenny re-read his message. This was incredible!

"Good morning Ross. I am amazed and eager to know more! What is the source of this information? Obviously we would be very interested in accessing it".

"It's a very detailed account of the tradition by a 17th century researcher by the name of William Derewin, who was employed by the Bishop of Durham. I came across it in the Church of England's restricted archives at Lambeth Palace. It's classified material, in fact, and not the object of the research I was authorised to carry out, but it interested me so much that I took copious notes".

"You didn't take a copy of this account?"

"No, I couldn't. I shouldn't even have been looking at that document".

"But why? I don't get this! Why would there be any secrecy about an old village tradition? Why on earth would it be classified?"

"The account of Oldston is only part of what Derewin wrote. I can't really say any more than that, I'm afraid. I am taking a risk telling you this much, as I rely on access to these archives for my doctorate research and cannot afford to upset them! Hope you understand".

Jenny *didn't* really understand. This all seemed very odd. She was tempted to terminate the conversation there and then, but curiosity got the better of her.

"All right, I see. So what else did this Derewin write about Oldston? Can you provide some more information?"

"Yes, I will do. I have to get on with my work, but I will go through my notes later and try and pull out some information that would interest you all. It would be useful if you could add me to The Group, even though I am a suspicious stranger from the big city, because it would nice to get general feedback and people can ask their own questions".

Jenny bristled at this. What was wrong with

dealing directly with her? Why the hurry to join The Group?

Fortunately, her irritation did not show up in the written word.

"Splendid. I will ask the others what they think about you joining. In the meantime, do tell me more about Derewin's findings when you have a moment. I am so intrigued!".

'Asking the others' was the last thing Jenny wanted to do, so she phrased her report on the new correspondent in such a way as to minimise the possibility of The Group coming to a decision that she didn't agree with.

"Unfortunately this information comes from a person down in London whose credentials I have not been able to verify and who cites a document which he is unable to fully describe, so I suggest that I remain in contact with him but that we do not as yet invite him to join The Group until such a time that we are reassured that the source is reliable, if that is all right with everyone?"

There was a question mark at the end. She had duly asked the others.

Nobody voiced any disagreement, so she continued her one-to-one exchange with the man in the city. He seemed to be overwhelmed by his postgrad work and only found time to send little snippets of information from his notes of Derewin's report. But there were certainly some eye-opening revelations.

It was true that Jenny had always imagined there would have been more to the Dobbin parties than just the hobby horses and their Teasers, given that the activity on The Bounds formed such an important part of The Game.

She had pored over online documents describing similar customs elsewhere in the hope of matching something to the illustrations, scraps of written material and hand-me-down village knowledge that they had been accumulating.

But Derewin had apparently listed a whole cast of characters who had followed the Dobbins around the circular path. There was the Fool, Black Sal, Maid Marian, Grand Serag, Dusty Bob, The Kidder and Master Dod.

There were also fiddlers, pipers and drummers and it seemed that colourful costumes and dancing used to very much form part of the event, as Jenny had always assumed but had never seen confirmed.

Ross explained that he had written down the exact wording of one section of Derewin's account, as it seemed strange to him: "They danced in severall shapes, first of a haire, then in their owne, and then in a catt, sometimes in a mouse, and in severall other shapes".

"What do you think this is about?" he asked. "Is he saying that they actually changed themselves into different animals by magic or some such nonsense?"

"No, of course not," Jenny replied. "These rituals take place all over the world. Maybe in their heads they manage to take on the *feeling* of being a cat or a mouse, and the costumes, the atmosphere, the music, the drink, would have all helped make that seem possible. They'd have been in a trance".

A walk was not possible today, as it was pouring with rain and the hilltops around had disappeared into grey clouds. So after lunch, she made herself a camomile tea and headed upstairs to the 'library', the spare room where she kept most of her books, armed with a piece of paper on which she had written the names of the characters from the Dobbin teams.

They were all vaguely familiar and she had no doubt searched for information about them online at some stage, but now she preferred to take her time and go back to the printed wisdom of her lifelong friends.

She ambled slowly around the room, plucking out a dozen tomes that she thought might help, placed them in a rough circle, then sat down cross-legged in the middle and started to browse. She was returning to these books for confirmation of things she already knew. Yes, that was it. Dod was to do with divining. Maid Marian was Robin Hood's lover, of course, but the two of them went a lot further back than that... And could The Kidder really be an English version of the mysterious Middle Eastern green man, Khidr, brought home by crusaders?

Jenny spent the whole afternoon there. Hours drifted past and the rain beat heavily on the window as she revisited knowledge she had acquired over the years and dreamed of past times and lost worlds, of the warmth of human life as it had once been, before the cold hand of modernity had cut it up into little plastic-wrapped slices and stashed it away in a bio-secure deep freeze.

She had had to flee from all that, escape from the cities and towns where the machineries of control were all-pervasive. You never completely got away from it, of course, and even in the village she was very well aware of the era in which she was condemned to live, but at least here chip-refusers like her could still lead some kind of existence. Once you got out of the built-up areas, once you were surrounded by trees, hills, gorse, brambles, mud and rock, you really could make yourself believe that you were living in a time when there was still hope for the future and love of the real.

Jenny found herself looking for one book in particular that held important memories. She didn't arrange her books alphabetically, or even in any recognisable categories, but instinctively, grouping together those which somehow felt to her as if they were expressing the same Great Thought. So it had to be around here somewhere...

Ah yes! Here it was. *Our Stolen Freedom* by Theo Carter.

All of that was so long ago, she thought to herself as she flicked lovingly through the pages. She could see him now, as if it were yesterday, wishing her good morning in the street, eyes twinkling with life spirit, handing her a leaflet, speaking at that meeting. She had always imagined that she would get to know him eventually, that he might even become a kind of mentor to her. And then everything had changed, with that terrible explosion that had shaken every bone in her body as she hurried towards the Town Hall to take part in the protest. And now he was dead, after years in exile and in prison.

But the book was still there. His words still lived on. She clasped it close to her, as if it were a living thing. She was going to have to read it again, even though she knew it would bring tears of bitter despair and impossible hope. But first she had to do something else.

Jenny placed the book carefully at the top of the stairs to bring down later, put the other volumes back on the shelves and then took out her big leather-bound journal from the desk by the window, picked up her favourite pen and, without even bothering about a date or a heading, simply started to write.

* * *

Later that week, Ross got in touch with some news that not only confirmed Jenny's theory about the two rings of Turners, but also shed startling new light on their purpose. Derewin had written that they were 'directing' the respective Dobbins around The Bounds with their rotations, he explained. One circle was directing the Lads and the other the Lasses.

"Directing them?! Did you get a note of exactly how he put this?"

"No... Hang on. Well, I did jot down that he considered this to be the work of the Devil. And he describes the stone as 'a stinking Idoll'".

"What? Who on earth was this Derewin? What was his interest in all this? I think you are going to have to tell me a bit more, Ross".

Somewhat reluctantly, it seemed, Ross explained that Derewin's investigation of the Oldston Game, on behalf of the Church, had very much come from a hostile position, although presumably he hadn't made that clear to the participants when he was mingling with them.

He was essentially a Puritan, setting out to find evidence with which to condemn The Game as contrary to the laws of God, and thus to have it closed down. He therefore interpreted all the goings-on in a way which backed up his claims, warning of devil-worshippers and 'witches' with dangerous powers.

"I don't suppose he even believed it himself," added Ross. "It was just propaganda, basically. That's partly why I didn't want to burden you with all that. I am trying to let you have the scraps of useful information in his account, without wasting your time on all his far-fetched rubbish. Also, of course, I am not really supposed to be telling you anything about this. The Church of England doesn't appreciate public scrutiny of its witch-hunting days!"

Although Jenny was quite shocked to learn of the nature of Derewin's investigation, she felt quite relieved that Ross had opened up and told her. She had been finding it difficult to rid herself of the intuition that he was hiding something and now this explained why.

They had a long exchange about Derewin's bizarre interpretations of The Game. It seemed that he felt there was something dangerous about Lady Rood, that she cast a sort of spell over the people of the village, turning them into nothing more than puppets for the ritual annual activity.

"But that's ridiculous," wrote Jenny. "The whole beauty of The Game was that everybody took part, everyone had a role to play. Derewin is just projecting his own hierarchical world view on to something he doesn't understand. The energy would have come from below, not above".

"The energy, Jenny? You sound like you're starting to believe Derewin's mumbo jumbo!"

Jenny wanted to explain to him the difference between magical 'spells' and life energies, but was frustrated at trying to do so in writing.

"Ross," she said. "How about we link up on the meetcloud? I don't usually do that, but we've got so much to talk about here that I think it would be useful".

As she sent the message, she realised that she also wanted to talk to him in a more personal way, that she wanted to make a connection with this handsome and intelligent fellow, and she blushed again like she used to when she was 17.

There was a long wait for a reply. Oh dear. Maybe he had seen right through her and was preparing to run a mile!

But then it came through: "OK, why not, if you think it would help. Maybe you will even end up thinking I am trustworthy enough to join The Group! But not now, I have to get on with stuff. How about Fourday evening, around 8pm?"

* * *

The following day, Wednesday as she still thought of it, or Threeday in safe language, Jenny packed some fruit, nuts and water in a small rucksack and set off for what she had mentally termed The Game Walk.

This was a route she had planned for years, but had never actually got round to completing. It was very long and convoluted, full of dead-ends and retracing, and made no sense at all outside of the context of the Oldston tradition.

But it mapped out The Game and Jenny knew she had to directly experience the physical reality of its setting in order to make a deeper connection.

It was a nice, bright, airy morning. She left by the front of the house, since there were no curfew issues, not forgetting to bring her mask, gloves and protective goggles for when she was passing through the village centre. She had refused all of that at the start, of course, but when they started making hefty automatic credit deductions for safety infringements – each time a different camera recorded her criminal behaviour constituting a separate offence – she had realised this was not going to be tenable in the long term and had settled into the compromise of half-hearted compliance with the demands of so-called bio-security.

Because she lived on Beltany Hall, her Game Walk started and finished at the Old Stone. After spending a moment breathing in the view and surveying the pattern she was about to trace, Jenny started off down one of the two straight tracks that led steeply down the hillside to the valley below. She took the left-hand path, the one which lined up with Cole Spring on the opposite ridge. As she descended, she had to keep her eyes on her feet to be sure of her step and didn't properly look up until she reached the bottom of the slope. In fact, as she half-admitted to herself, she probably deliberately insisted on the need to keep her eyes lowered so as to better enjoy the revelation of seeing what lay ahead of her at the foot of the hill.

There she was. Molly May. Half the size of the Old Stone, squatter and heavier in appearance, somehow in keeping with her position on the valley floor. She was plainly of the earth, whereas the Old Stone was forever aspiring to the beyond. And... what was that? A black shape on top of the stone. A raven. How perfect!

Jenny stepped gingerly forward, not wanting to make any sudden movements, so as to delay the inevitable moment when the bird would take flight at her approach.

But, strangely, the raven did not make a move, even as she approached and stood directly beside the grey mark stone, which stood at the intersection of her path and The Bounds. Instead it stood completely still and looked her straight in the eye in a frankly quite disarming manner.

"Hello, friend!" whispered Jenny. "And a very good day to you!"

She nodded a respectful farewell to the raven and continued on her way, towards Hoarbridge. Although the line of her path was clear enough – Knapp Tower was visible ahead of her across the bridge and between the old buildings of Hoar Street – there was a small chink in her route as the path joined the road which now used this crossing. An electricity sub-station and mast blocked the original route.

Jenny paused on the bridge and looked up and down the river, whose water was running fresh and clean. The Oldston stretch of the Asher was so remarkably straight that she could see all the way past Ludbridge and down to Merryford, readily identifiable by a distinctive clump of trees close by. To the east, the river swung out of sight a hundred yards or so after Mollyford.

She took a deep breath of air and felt the invigorating pleasure of the wind on her skin, and then wrapped herself in plastic in order to enter the realm of modernity. There was no way she could linger for long in Oldston in these conditions. There were a few people around on foot, but as ever they all hurried past without even turning their heads, with no chance of an exchange of a glance or a friendly smile.

Hoar Street curved around the mound on which Knapp Tower sat, before becoming Cole Lane on the other side, but Jenny had always noticed how there were large wooden doors on either side of the monument – long since closed to the public – which followed the alignment of her route. Had the street once passed right through the tower? What role did it play in The Game? She had long pondered over the significance of references by Phillips to the May Queen and King being 'met and helped' for the final part of The Game. And then there was that other verse of the song.

Beat and battle round The Bounds
Weary Royals head for mounds
Sacred pleasures, sacred food
Hail the Help-meets, Game renewed!

Were the tower and church, with their mounds on the two routes used by the 'royal' racers to reach the Old Stone, used as stop-off points in the middle of the nocturnal celebrations, places of respite where both contestants could take a moment to relax and have something to eat and drink, as prepared by their team's 'Help-meets'?

She headed up Cole Lane and out of the village, removing her protection as she did so, and soon found herself crossing the southern curve of The Bounds. The path up to Cole Spring was very steep in places, being more of a climb than a walk, and also involved several crossings of the little stream that gushed down to eventually join the Asher to the east of Mollyford.

She was quite puffed out by the time she reached the spring – was she really that out of shape? She sat on a flat piece of stone to look back across the valley and the path she had just taken. The Old Stone was, of course, perfectly visible, beyond tower, bridge and Molly May. But the other starting point for The Game, Bridie's Well, could not be seen from here, as the hillside jutted out slightly in between. Neither was there any way of walking along the hillside between the two points. This was a shame in a way, because it would have made for a better walking route, but the lay-out was also an important part of The Game's psychology, she realised. Three interconnected points would have been a triangle, but this was something different. The spring and the well were connected, but by means of the Old Stone. They could not see each other, had their own separate perspectives towards the focal centre, and yet remained part of the same overall topography. It was the convergence of these separate paths, as traced out by the May Queen and King, that created the dynamic of The Game. In reality, there was no movement in the landscape. It never changed. The paths did not really 'converge' at all, because they were always there, in that same position. But the movement, the thrust, implied in the overall outline of The Game was accessed, realised, sparked into life by the presence of living people, festive and joyous people, singing and loving and fighting people, pouring their collective spirit into its archetypal form. That was how Jenny felt it, anyway.

She took a few sips of water. She was tempted to eat a peach, but it was not quite time yet; she would save it for the well. Then she made her way back down the steep path, the route that would have been taken by the May King, and found herself back at the point where it crossed The Bounds. She turned left and headed west. There were still a few small stones marking the route along this southern rim, but no large stones like Molly May or the Merry Man. It was quite a walk along this section, since the two arms radiating out from the Old Stone were, at this point, spread far apart. As Jenny looked to her right across the fields towards the village, she noticed that there was no indication of the geometrical symmetry that she was used to seeing from the stone and that she had witnessed from the spring. There was just a jumble of rooftops, trees and pylons, with the tower and the church occasionally visible in the distance above all the confusion.

Eventually she reached the point where The Bounds crossed the May Queen's path – the place where she would have first been blocked by the Dobbins – and turned left, up the hill towards Bridie's Well.

This climb was a lot less strenuous than that for Cole Spring. It still went up in a straight line, but because the hill was set back a little further, the ascent was gentler. Jenny had a small shock when she arrived at the well, as from a distance it looked as if it had been 'dressed' with green foliage as she had imagined it would have been every Roodmas. But closer inspection revealed nothing other than some overhanging ivy and advancing brambles. She peered down into the cool dark shaft. She couldn't see the water at the bottom, but she could certainly feel the humidity reaching up to her from the depths of the earth.

Jenny perched on the edge of the well to eat her peach and then a handful of nuts. There was more tree cover here that at the spring, but you could still see perfectly well across to the Old Stone, with the church tower handily pointing the way.

She cast her mind back to the first time she had come up here, before she had even moved to Oldston. It was then that she had met an old fellow, like a pirate with a patch over one eye, who had told her about The Game. She wished now she could remember more precisely what he said, but at the time her genuine interest at what he was relating was mixed with a high degree of suspicion as to the truth of it. It all just sounded so outlandish. Her doubts had no doubt also been fuelled by the way he had presented The Game not just as an interesting tradition, but as a ritual of deep significance.

He had claimed that it had always been known in the village that if ever The Game stopped happening, bad times would be on their way, not just for Oldston but for the whole of England and even the world. And the only way to ever put things right again would be to start up The Game again. He had been very serious about this, insisting that if The Game had not been played for a year or two, the damage would be limited and could easily be rectified by the good energies created by a revived event. But if people left it too long, if The Game remained 'hidden' (he had actually put it this way) for several generations, the world would be in such a sorry state that The Game would have to 'show itself' in a different form, which might not be as easy-going and agreeable as some folk might have preferred.

Jenny had never seen this old man again after she moved to the village – indeed nobody seemed to have any idea who he was – so he may have just been a passing eccentric spinning her a yarn. Neither had she ever again heard the story about The Game protecting the village from harm, although now she mused that this was pretty much the mirror image of Derewin's version of it being all about devilish powers. That was a typical Christian approach in fact – denouncing anything that challenged its own dogma and domination not as simply different but as positively 'evil'.

As Jenny ambled back down from Bridie's Well, she couldn't help imagining herself as the May Queen starting out on the night's adventure. She would have been a young thing, of course, in the first bloom of adulthood. How were they picked every year, the young people who would play the leading role? Was it the ones with influential fathers or pushy mothers? Was it because they had done something to deserve the honour or simply because they looked the part?

Jenny walked faster as she imagined herself in the place of those young women. There would have been a palpable sense of anticipation, as the beacons burned on either side of the valley and the village buzzed with excitement. She saw a glimpse of torches down below her through the trees and heard the jingling of bells, the beating of drums, an excited babble of voices and the strains of timeless melodies handed on for generation after generation. It was the Lads' Dobbin and everyone that came with it, on their way to stop her getting any further than the crossing with The Bounds. This would be her first big moment of the night. She knew what she had to do. She had to act out an attempt to get past them, darting this way and that, but finally to give in and remain at a respectful distance from the other team while they tucked into their copious amounts of food and drink, brought up from the village on a little donkey cart by the landlord of The Dark Star.

It was against the rules of The Game for the Queen and King to join in the feasting. That was part of the sacrifice they were expected to make. So she would have stood here, or sat down on that tree stump over there if it wasn't too damp, watching the revellers and waiting patiently to be on the move again.

The hours had passed and she was off. The Dobbin crowd had moved round The Bounds to confront their opponents. They had left two or three token guards behind, to symbolically block her way, but she was allowed to weave between them and scurry off on the straight path towards the village and the Old Stone beyond.

Wrapped up again for the sake of the village cameras, Jenny looked ahead at the closed front door of St John the Baptist's church and imagined heading straight into the building, to be greeted by her Help-meet. Who was that? A friend? Someone she had chosen to play the role? At any rate, she would at last be able to eat, drink, sit down and...

While Jenny passed the church and turned into Lud Street, she suddenly heard behind her the cry of a woman's voice. She turned and heard it again, even longer this time. Was she in pain? What had happened? She looked round, taking in the street and the buildings on the other side of the road, to see if there was any sign of someone in need of help. But there was nothing to be seen but dozens of windows, firmly sealed shut in case of wind-blown contagion, and the ancient stone walls of the sacred building.

She crossed Ludbridge, left the village and kept heading towards the Old Stone, now looking quite dominant on the skyline. She had been intending to trace out, through her walk, the whole map of The Game, but now she felt tempted to skip the second half and head straight back up to her cottage.

However, someone was waiting for her at the junction with The Bounds. Sitting atop the Merry Man – a strangely angular stone that did almost look like a happily dancing figure – was the raven. Well, *a* raven anyway! There was no telling if it was the same one she had met at Molly May.

Again, it stared silently and motionlessly at her, but this time she understood that it was rebuking her for her lazy desire to cut the walk short and go home for tea and biscuits.

"Yes, you're right, friend," she told it after a moment's hesitation. "A woman's got to do what a woman's got to do!"

She turned left on The Bounds, as she had originally planned, and stepped out with new determination to complete the challenge she had set herself. There was a 'caw' behind her and when she turned she saw the bird taking off and heading up in the general direction of the Old Stone.

There was a lot of walking involved in this second phase of the expedition, but at least it was mostly on the flat. When she reached Merryford, she initially walked a few yards to the right to say hello to the old yew tree, and to eat another handful of nuts on the riverside, then came back and continued along the northern bank of the river. It would have been ideal to have actually traced the course of the water, but since she had no boat and didn't want to get soaking wet, she would have to settle for this compromise.

The route past Ludbridge, Hoarbridge and on to Mollyford was simple enough and, after she had crossed the river, she even went a little further on to admire the point at which the Cole Stream, from the spring, joined the Asher. But traversing the village on the south bank was not as straightforward and involved a diversion through the car park of the White Horse Sushi Bar and a short cut across the front of the village Farewell Assistance Centre, which always gave Jenny a little shudder of dread.

Eventually though, she found herself back on The Bounds and was able to complete her walk by looping right round the southern side, past the paths up to the well and the spring, over

Mollyford, back down past Molly May and, to fill in the last missing piece of the puzzle, across to the Merry Man and up the path to the stone.

Jenny collapsed on to the sofa when she got back. She glanced again at the little slip of paper from Peggy she had found under her door on arriving and then put it on the coffee table. That would have to wait for tomorrow. She was exhausted, but at the same time she knew that she had completed something important, carried out a task that had had to be done in preparation for whatever was to come next.

* * *

On Fourday morning Jenny busied herself picking some sowthistle from behind the shed and making it up into a tincture for Agnes, Peggy's daughter, who had been particularly under the weather for a couple of days. She poured it into a properly chipped and in-date lemonade bottle, in case of spot-checks on the way there, and set off to Peggy's place. She started off on the road, as if taking the long route to the village, but then turned right down a track heading off to the north. Her friend lived even further away from the rest of Oldston than she did, the isolated location of her home reflecting her general relationship with society.

Peggy was a dyed-in-the-wool refuser, who

had spent her life opting out of every wave of 'improvement' that had been offered by the authorities. She didn't want their vaccine updates, she didn't want their security updates, she didn't want their phone updates, she didn't want their net updates... She had no intention, of course, of ever being chipped and was doing her best to protect Agnes from the constantly-intruding official world. She hadn't even registered her birth, initially, until the child's existence had become impossible to conceal in a location that, while isolated, was regularly checked out by drones and their bio-sensors. The police had turned up at her door, in fact, suspecting her of harbouring an illegal visitor during the curfew, and there had been a lot of explaining to do when they discovered, hiding in a wardrobe, a small human being who did not even exist, as far as the system was concerned.

It had taken a lot of time and effort to see off the threat of Agnes being permanently taken away 'for her own protection', which had been the outcome presumed by the authorities right from the start. During the two weeks which the five-year-old had spent in a Child Processing Centre, they had pumped her full of all the vaccines and 'safety-enhancing' drugs that she had missed out on since her birth. It was this, combined with the enormous stress caused by removing her from the loving surrounds of her home, that had resulted in the sudden collapse in her health. A bright, happy, free-skipping little girl had returned home after her incarceration as a silent, traumatised, immobile lump of a child, barely able to move and without the ability to speak more than a couple of barely-comprehensible words.

Agnes, who was 13 now, spent most of her life in bed, moaning quietly to herself, occasionally being wheeled out into the back garden to gaze up, drooling from the mouth, at the overhead power lines on the hillside behind their home.

Jenny had been very much involved in Peggy's battle to win Agnes back and had managed to get more than half the population of Oldston to gather outside the council offices in protest, despite the usual warnings of fines. Peggy had picked the right woman to ask, as it turned out, even though she had perhaps only come hammering on her door, after the child had been whisked away to Manchester in a helicopter, because Jenny lived only a 20-minute walk away and without any means of electronic communication this was the quickest way to seek help.

Jenny hadn't known Peggy very well until that point. Nobody had known Peggy very well, in truth. She could be a hard woman to relate to, her face prone to assuming sudden expressions of pitch-black hostility when she heard something of which she did not approve.

Jenny reached the crest of the hill and Peggy's little brick farmhouse came into sight below. Now it was downhill all the way and the lightness in her feet infused up into her mind. She laughed out loud at the memory of actually being frightened of Peggy, at being intimidated by her abrupt manner and sharp comments and of having made deliberate efforts to avoid her on the path down to the village. Peggy had let all of that drop when she needed help rescuing Agnes. She had laid bare, to Jenny at least, what it was behind that hard-nosed façade that needed so much protection. She was a damaged soul, still a child in so many ways, still suffering from the trauma of feeling unloved and unappreciated in a big unruly family where a violent father had been sent packing and her mother was permanently in crisis under the pressure of having to keep seven children fed and housed.

If Peggy seemed cold, it was because she was suffering from a lifelong lack of warmth. All Peggy had wanted to do was to give to Agnes what she herself had never had – the dedicated and unconditional love of a caring mother.

Maybe that what was kept her going now, mused Jenny, as she opened the front gate and entered Peggy's pretty little garden, all set out with floral archways, little windmills and a tiny ornamental pond. For everything that poor Agnes had lost eight years ago, Peggy was still giving her that greatest gift of all. Herself. All of herself.

And when Peggy opened the front door, with the gentlest of looks in her eyes, Jenny realised that in having been able to give so much to her daughter, of *having* to give so much to her, at the expense of her own concerns, she had cleared herself of the mess that had been clogging up her emotional insides for all these years. Surely there was hope in the way that such sad circumstances for Agnes had, nevertheless, released in her mother a powerful latent energy for good that had remained so firmly hidden behind her ossified layers of self-protection.

Agnes was asleep upstairs, so the two women took the opportunity to catch up over steaming mugs of Peggy's spiced chicory drink and home-made carrot cake. Peggy told Jenny how Agnes' health seemed worse than ever these days. She often seemed to be in a lot of pain around her belly, not helped by the arrival of her menstrual cycles, and seemed permanently tired and often feverish.

Since Peggy had effectively opted out of the healthcare system by refusing any more vaccines for her or her daughter, she had to cope with all of this on her own, with occasional help from Jenny and Miriam. But this was by no means a bad thing, as Peggy and Jenny knew full well, without the need to explicitly say as much. If Agnes had fallen into the hands of the professionals, her chronic illness would have combined with a very low social utility ranking to have made her a prime candidate for the Farewell Assistance Centre.

Jenny noticed that Peggy's eyes were welling up with tears as she described her daughter's declining health, so she reached over and placed a hand on Peggy's upper arm.

"Come on, you," she said. "You're a strong woman. You can cope. I know *I* wouldn't be able to, but you've got what it takes".

Peggy smiled and reached for a hanky to blow her nose.

"Sometimes I just wish that..."

"What, my lovely?"

And then she told her all about Agnes' father, how she felt she had driven him away before their child was even born, how much she wished she hadn't.

Having listened patiently to the account, Jenny tried to take Peggy's mind off her own problems, and to make her laugh out loud, by detailing the low points of her relationship with Jim.

After that, she updated her with the latest news about The Game, of which Peggy was totally unaware, including, of course, the flood of information coming their way from Ross.

Having brought Peggy back into a cheerful state of mind, Jenny gushed on with her news and speculation. Assuming that her friend would follow in the general up-beat flow, she was surprised to notice that a frown was developing on her face.

She stopped talking to allow the other woman to express herself and, when she said nothing, felt the need to prompt her.

"What is it, Peggy? Something the matter?"

Peggy shook her head.

"I don't know, Jenny. There's just something about this Ross character that worries me. Where has he sprung from, like that? And this old-time witch hunter he has discovered in some dusty secret archive... It all just sounds a bit vague".

"Ah you see, I probably haven't explained it properly. It's just that he was already researching..."

"Yes, yes!" interrupted Peggy, a little too harshly. "I know all that and I understand that he can account for it all in a logical way. It's just that I have a *feeling* that there's something not quite right, Jenny, that you should be careful about trusting him too much. I mean, have you even actually spoken to this person?"

"Funny you should ask that, Peggy, because as a matter of a fact this evening we are going to..."

Again Jenny was interrupted, but this time by a terrible high-pitched scream emanating from upstairs but setting the whole house vibrating.

Agnes had woken up.

Jenny stood in the corner of the bedroom as Peggy calmed her daughter by holding her tight in her arms and singing softly in her ear – a sad, haunting old folk song that Jenny knew for sure that she had heard before, long long ago, although she could not imagine where or when.

* * *

Peggy's attention having turned to her daughter, nothing more was said about Ross. But her words came back into Jenny's head as she found herself going through her wardrobe ahead of that evening's video link-up.

This vintage purple dress was just right for the occasion, she felt. And it still suited her figure, she was pleased to see in the mirror.

But why was she making this effort? She hadn't bothered dressing up for meetcloud since those far-off and yet still acutely embarrassing efforts at online dating, back in the days when she was missing having a man in her life, without actually going so far as to miss Jim.

It had started off as a bit of fun. She had

used it to make contact with a couple of bachelors in the Oldston area and had met up for tea and cakes with them. The first had been ridiculously shy, almost silent, and it had been an effort to keep some kind of conversation alive until it seemed just about reasonable to announce that she had to be going. The second had had such bad breath that it was impossible to converse with him and Jenny had feigned sudden illness in order to escape.

It was probably these two acutely disappointing experiences which had led her to conclude that real-life meetings weren't all they were cracked up to be and that she would be better hooking up with a desirable man from the other side of the world than some repellent individual from down the road.

So she had fallen, for six months or so, into a sordid little world of encounters which had lured her from verbal flirtation to the purchase of a pair of u-gloves, allowing her to indulge in virtual caresses and petting. It was that Australian fellow who had put her up to it. What was his name? She had even been planning to invest in the full virtual sex kit until he had let slip that Jenny was far from being the only woman with whom he was enjoying an online relationship. In fact, she had suddenly had a vision of him spending every waking minute of his day virtually groping or penetrating each and every available female and the pleasure she had felt at his interest in her had melted away in an instant. The u-gloves had gone back into their box, as had her interest in dating. She preferred the perfection of her rich imagination to the disappointment of banal male reality.

So what was happening now? Had this Ross crept in through the back door of local history to set alight a part of her which she had imagined extinguished? What was it exactly that she liked about him, apart from his face? Did she feel that he was interested in her, as a woman? How should she respond, if this was the case? Should she trust him? Why was Peggy warning her away?

Jenny washed her hair and even put on a little bit of light make-up as the 8pm appointment drew closer. She played with the tilt of the interface so that the scene behind her would look nice and shifted her clothes horse to the other side of the room to get it out of shot. Then she sat down and waited, wondering how Ross's voice would sound and what he would look like in the digital 'flesh'.

She was taken aback when the connection was made and he appeared on her screen with a full facemask and protective goggles. All that she could recognise from the photo was the crisp white shirt and yellow tie.

"Oh..." she murmured. "Why have you...?"

"You mean the safety protection? Sorry, yes, it's university regulations, I'm afraid Jenny. They insist on us taking proper precautions even when not strictly necessary. Ridiculous, I know, but if I don't go along with it I can say goodbye to my doctorate!"

She was trying to see behind all that plastic, to the man himself, but was finding it difficult.

"Never mind, Ross, can't be helped," she replied, desperately trying to sound up-beat. "Nice to meet you, anyway. Had a good day at the office?"

He said that he had and started to tell her a little anecdote about a fellow researcher he had bumped into at the church archives, but she was totally distracted by the sight of his mask chomping up and down as he talked. This wouldn't do.

"Sorry, I am just going to..." she muttered as she leaned towards the interface and replaced the live image of Ross with his profile photo. That was better.

"And how about you Jenny?" he was asking. "I expect you've been busy with your research up there in Oldston?"

"Well, yes, a little bit," she said. "But I also dropped in on a friend with a tincture for her daughter, so I had a nice chat with her and..."

"A tincture?" He sounded agitated for some reason.

"Yes, just sowthistle. I've got some in the

garden so..."

"You know that's illegal, don't you? Unlicensed medication?"

"Aw, come on, I'm not selling it. I don't think anyone would..."

"I don't know, Jenny, but I'm just saying".

There was a pause and when he spoke again it was in a much softer tone.

"I'm just trying to help, Jenny. I don't want you to get into any trouble. I suppose I'm just feeling a little protective, that's all".

Jenny felt a strange quiver inside. Was he coming on to her? Instinct told her to change the mood and she started to talk about her walk around The Game's topography and to ask his opinion on one or two details.

No, Derewin said nothing about how the May Queen and May King were picked. No, he didn't say anything about stones on the southern side of the village. For that matter, he didn't mention Molly May or the Merry Man by name.

"But then, even if he knew the names of the stones, I have the strong feeling he wouldn't have dreamed of using them," commented Ross.

"No, that would have been totally beneath his dignity as a good Christian," laughed Jenny.

Ross was, however, able to relate something about the Help-meets who were waiting for the Queen and King when they arrived at the tower or the church. At least, he was able to relate

Derewin's opinion on the matter which, as Ross was at pains to point out, was not necessarily to be believed, given his agenda.

"He does mention that there was food, even though for him this was an example of gluttony, but he sees the main purpose as being a lot more sinister".

"Sinister?"

"Well... from his very special point of view! You see he regarded any kind of sexual relationship out of marriage as being 'fornication' and part of some kind of devil-worshipping ritual. He thinks that the Help-meets were there to have sex with the racers at the half-way point..."

"Sex? In the church?"

"Well, yes, you can see why that would have shocked him. But even without that twist, if it was just the May King and his Help-meet in Knapp's Tower, this would have been entirely unacceptable behaviour for him and, indeed, for his intended readership, because we mustn't lose track of the fact that he was essentially making a case against The Game by depicting it in the worst possible light".

"So you don't think it's true, that the Help-meets had sex with them?"

"I don't know. It seems a bit full-on. What do you think?"

Jenny pondered a moment before replying.

"You know, Ross," she said, "I think it may

be true. It's all part of the May Day magic. But I don't think we should imagine some kind of grim Satanic ritual or anyone forced to do anything against their will. It was probably just their girlfriend or boyfriend, or somebody that they had fancied for ages".

"So they would have chosen their Help-meet themselves?"

"You'd have thought so. That was the perk of the job! The May Queen could name some dashing young farmer's son that she had had her eye on for months and fall into his arms with the full approval of the community!"

Jenny had fallen back into the fantasy of imagining herself as a young May Queen and, as she spoke of falling into the arms of her chosen lover, she realised that her mind's eye had automatically painted him with the face in front of her on the screen.

"You would have made a lovely May Queen, Jenny," he said as if reading her thoughts. She couldn't help wondering if the conditional of the 'would have' depended on her having lived in an earlier century or, rather, on her being younger and thus sufficiently attractive to deserve the label 'lovely'.

"Especially in that dress," he added. No avoiding it now. He really was trying it on with her.

"Yes, it's pretty isn't it?" she said. "And very

comfortable to wear. It feels nice against the skin".

"I can sense that, somehow," said the man on the interface. It was disconcerting that his handsome smiling face did not change expression to suit the changing tone.

"It makes me want to reach out and feel the texture," he said. "It looks so different from the clothes most people wear today".

Jenny had a bright idea.

"Well, maybe you can!" she said. "Have you got some kind of sensory kit there? Oh good. I've some old u-gloves upstairs".

Then she added quickly: "We needed them for a pottery course I took years ago".

Ross was evidently interested enough in feeling the texture of her dress to wait patiently while she fetched the gloves and connected them up.

"I hope they're compatible with what you've got your end," she said, slipping one on. She ran her hand along the edge of the desk. "Are you feeling that?"

"Yes. That's surprisingly good, given the age of those gloves of yours!"

"So," she said. "Here's what the sleeve feels like. Such a gentle fabric. And here's the cuffs, which are more delicate and lacy". She let her fingers slip off the sleeve of the dress on to her other hand.

"And that's even nicer," said Ross. "Jenny's skin".

"Do you think so?" asked Jenny, without expecting an answer. Something had been unblocked inside her and she was being carried away in the flow. She ran her gloved hand around her own fingers and palm, then back on to the dress, up her arm and on to her neck and cheek.

Then, all of a sudden, she became horribly aware of what she was doing, pulled her hand away and slammed it down on the desk.

"Ouch!" said Ross and they laughed. Then he asked to feel her skin some more and so she ran her hand around her face, through her hair, down her legs and her ankles and then back up until, at his request, she unfastened the top of the dress and slid her hand down to her breasts, which she stroked and touched with the gentle firmness of the most accomplished of lovers, while Ross's deep voice murmured his appreciation. A voice in her head told her to stop there, to hold back, but she found that she simply couldn't and instead she went in deeper and deeper until she found herself wearing the other glove and discovering solid and tangible evidence that Ross was sharing her excitement at this strange near-silent communication.

* * *

The following morning Jenny found herself standing beside the Old Stone looking out over Oldston and the mysterious topography of its ancient Game. The light was hard and grey. Rain was being blown down her collar by a gusty drizzle of a wind, but she felt illuminated from within.

Although she was very aware of the limits of what had happened between her and Ross, only the physical contact *between* them had been virtual. What Jenny had felt in her *own* body was as real as if he had been there beside her. And what she was feeling now, in her head, or her heart, or her womb or wherever one felt such things, was all too real.

When she thought about the conversation regarding the Help-meets which had led up to their long-distance closeness, she felt as if she had just, somehow, entered into The Game. Up until now, despite all her efforts to become part of the thing, she had merely been an observer, an outsider. Now, thanks to her own Help-meet, she had been initiated into the tradition and was a living extension of The Game itself.

Jenny was just allowing herself to think ahead to her next session with Ross and to imagine where she would lead his virtual hand, when there was a piercing shriek from a few feet behind her which sent a great jolt through her body, smashing her daydream into smithereens.

She turned round to find the cry had come from Agnes, who was all hatted, scarfed and tucked up in her wheelchair, with its chunky wheels which allowed Peggy to take her walking.

"Hello Agnes!" she said, smiling at the girl in spite of the certainty of having no response. "Hello Peggy! Nice to see you two up here!"

"It was Agnes," said Peggy. "She wanted to come. She was so agitated and kept looking up at the window. And then in the end she said something that I just knew meant the Old Stone".

She touched her daughter's shoulder and the girl let out a little gurgle of appreciation.

"I don't blame you, Agnes," said Jenny. "It does so much good to be up here, looking out over all this. You just get this wonderful sense of freedom!"

"Mrreedob!" echoed Agnes.

"Freedom! That's right! Clever girl!" said Jenny, while Peggy basked in her daughter's rare achievement of having uttered an intelligible word.

"You know, Agnes, they used to play a big game here, in Oldston, and the prize for the winner, for everyone really, was freedom. Freedom of the village".

She squatted down beside the wheelchair and pointed to the southern ridge on the other side of Oldston.

"They started over there," she said, pointing

at the Cole Spring, and the spot seemed to shine out from the dull landscape as she named it. "And from over there, at Bridie's Well," she continued and again her concentration on the place produced the strange optical effect.

"The two people, a lady and a man, had to race to see who was the first to get here, along two paths going in straight lines," she explained, holding out her hands in a V-shape to indicate the converging routes and, as did so, there appeared to be little twinkles of sunlight on the river around the two bridges, while the stone walls of Knapp Tower and St John the Baptist's seemed brighter than usual.

"But other people in the game used to try and stop them, by running round and round The Bounds," she told Agnes, drawing a big circle in the air which, through the power of suggestion, made the path she described appear like a fairy ring, shining up at them through the rain.

Agnes was following her gestures, mouth open, in silence, with a look of serious determination.

"And some of them were even in boats, on the river!" said Jenny, making a straight horizontal dash across the valley with her finger and, in her mind's eye at least, producing a rippling wave that swept down the Asher from Mollyford to Merryford.

She turned to see if Agnes was following and

her face was lit up with an enormous dribbling smile.

Jenny went home the long way from the Stone, along the ridge and then down into the back path. As she did so, she thought about the idea of freedom, or mrreedob as it should now be known, that was so woven into The Game. The individual racers' efforts to win 'freedom' for themselves were not really about their own status at all, because this freedom was immediately returned to the community which had given it to them. It was a ritual restating of the *existence* of freedom, in fact, in the same way as the beating of The Bounds was the ritual restating of the physical existence and limits of the village. The strength, speed or skill of the racers and their teams in negotiating all the obstacles in their path was the acting out, in symbolic form, of the community's need to preserve its integrity and organic health in the face of everything that threatened to clog it up and stifle its energy.

This flow of thought encouraged her, when she got home, to make herself a pot of tea and settle down with that amazing book which Theo Carter had written in prison, just before he died. It was quite remarkable, she mused, how one could be so deeply inspired twice in a lifetime by the very same piece of writing.

Later, she took out her violin and let it play whatever it wanted.

After a while she noticed that it was channelling a tune that she had once identified as fitting perfectly with the words of the Oldston Game rhyme. It wasn't from the area and was identified on the recording as a Morris melody popular in the Cotswolds, but these tunes, she knew, were often quasi-universal, and she liked to imagine the rhyme becoming a living song, being belted out by the motley carnival crews as they rolled drunkenly around The Bounds through the early hours of May Day morning.

She started singing along.

Sun goes down and beacons burn
Teams all set and Turners turn
Wheel without and wheel within
Let the Roodmas Game begin!

Beat and battle round The Bounds
Weary Royals head for mounds
Sacred pleasures, sacred food
Hail the help-meets, Game renewed!

Because she couldn't remember the rest of the lyrics, she repeated these verses two or three times over before, suddenly and inexplicably, she found herself switching to another melody, which glided out of the first tune like a sword from a sheath and, she realised with a deep thrill, provided the perfect chorus.

But what was it, this plaintive refrain, this deep-hearted call from across the centuries that spoke of mournful hope, of dark joy and of soft and steely determination?

She stopped playing.

Of course! It was the tune that Peggy had been singing to Agnes yesterday. But where else had she heard it? Where else...?

Jenny started playing again, repeating the chorus over and over while she tried to find traces of it in her memory. While she did this, the verbal part of her brain started to conjure up words to go with it and, before long, she found herself singing the complete item out loud.

Stand up, stand up
With odes and games
Of how we yet might be
Rise up, rise up
The winds and flames
Of age-old liberty

It was only when she got into bed that she realised that since Agnes' interruption at the Stone, she had not once thought about the man who had been the centre of all her mental attention until then. What a fickle woman she was!

* * *

On Sixday afternoon Jenny found that her mind had again turned to Ross, as the time of their next 'chat' drew closer. She called up his profile photo and took a good look at him, trying to work out what it was that so attracted her. She had always been one for dark-haired types, that was sure. The lighter the hair the less the allure, as far as she was concerned. And she liked a facial structure that was well-defined: Ross's chin, cheekbones and forehead all looked to have been drawn in firm strokes, by a deft artist's hand. She supposed that this spoke to her of an inner clarity. She nearly added 'and strength' but knew that it wasn't as simple as that. Too much macho virility would have been a complete turn-off and it was important that there was a certain balancing softness in his features. There was something of William in those alert and somewhat vulnerable brown eyes, she thought. Yes, very much so. And that little humorous half-smile on his lips was straight out of Sergio's book of charm. His chin, with that little dimple, was just like Richard's. Well, that was the attraction explained, then. He reminded her of all her old boyfriends! Except Jim, apparently. Now come on, for the sake of completeness, there must be something... Of course! The barely-perceptible arch of the thick left eyebrow. How could she have missed that?

Jenny leaned back on her chair with a laugh.

Was she really as predictable as that, to have fallen for the very same facial traits that had led her into romantic dead ends in the past? She reassured herself that it wasn't just Ross's face that had appealed to her in the first place, but his enthusiasm and his interest in a subject close to her heart. After the other night, of course, there was a whole new layer of interest.

She dressed up for the appointment again. A lovely deep green thing, bordered with little celtic motifs, which she had bought second-hand, although hardly at a bargain price, in a little shop just off the King's Road, Chelsea, in anticipation of a weekend away with Sergio which had never materialised, due to the illness of a wife whose existence he had hitherto expertly concealed. It would be nice to put it to some seductive use. If seduction was still required, that was, and they weren't going to go straight for the gloves!

Jenny was rather pleased with the effect, so it came as quite a shock when the first words Ross expressed after appearing on the screen were "Oh dear! What on earth is that you're wearing, Jenny?"

She quickly turned off the video image of his masked face and switched to the reassuringly familiar photo. It was quite intolerable to be spoken to like that by somebody whose features you couldn't see.

"It's a dress, Ross," she said as lightly as she could manage. "Don't you like it? Doesn't it suit me?"

"No, it doesn't," he said. "It wouldn't suit anyone. It's the colour. I'm seriously allergic to that kind of gloomy green, Jenny. It's just so dank!"

"Dank?"

"Yes. You can almost smell the mildew. I can certainly appreciate a nice bright electric green, but that type just reminds me of graveyards and damp undergrowth and people who have been dead for hundreds of years".

"And so that's how you think of me? As a dead person covered in mildew?"

"Of course not, Jenny. That's why it pains me so much to see you wearing it!"

"And do you think you have the right to dictate to me what I can and cannot wear, on the basis of your personal prejudices?"

"No, I just..."

"So why say anything, Ross? Why get the evening off to such a bad start by making a comment like that?"

Although she was managing to stay polite, Jenny felt completely churned up inside. How dare he talk to her like that?

Before he had the chance to answer, she added: "You know, Ross, I don't really think I'm in the mood for this conversation tonight. If you've got anything to tell me, you can put it in writing, OK?"

"Oh Jenny, no!" he protested. "I've been so looking forward to talking to you".

Softer and conciliatory now, he explained that he had had a tough day trying to meet a deadline for submitting some of his research work. He apologised for his comment about the dress and said it had triggered some bad associations in his personal life. Gradually Jenny felt her anger abate and the fleeting desire to end the exchange evaporated, particularly when he revealed that he had taken the opportunity to read a further section of Derewin's report on Oldston.

This suggested that The Game was only part of the annual event. Once the community's freedom had been symbolically renewed at the Stone, the partying began in earnest on the first of May. Since the villagers had already been up all night, probably drinking as they went, they displayed considerable staying power in keeping the thing going for the whole of the next day and evening as well. There was dancing and feasting, drinking and singing, and various light-hearted games, competitions and sporting contests.

"Derewin was appalled, of course," laughed Ross. "There was nothing he hated more than people enjoying themselves. The way he describes the villagers dancing and laughing together, you'd think it was a scene from the pits of hell. I should have written it down because it would make you laugh. It is all 'seething bodies' and 'pernicious proximity' and 'devilish pleasures'".

"A typical life-hating Puritan," said Jenny. "They've always been with us, but luckily they don't always have the upper hand. I think there is something very revealing about the way people like him saw 'the Devil' in everything natural and human and joyous. They had repressed all their own pleasure at being alive and took their misery out on everyone else, slapping the label 'bad' on everything that they themselves secretly wanted but could never have".

She paused for a moment. Was this the right moment to change the mood?

"I don't suppose your friend Derewin would have approved of what we did the last time we met on here, would he Ross? Much too sensual and pernicious for his liking, despite the fact that we are actually hundreds of miles apart!"

"He's not my friend, Jenny. I'm no Puritan, as you may have noticed. I'm not one for repressing my desires".

"Really? Are you sure? Don't you think that this hang-up of yours about a dark green dress has got something in common with Derewin projecting his own inner evil on to those licentious Oldston girls?"

"Hmmm... interesting," said Ross. "Maybe

you're right and the dress could be psychologically blocking my libido from fully expressing itself. I think the only safe thing to do is for you to take it off and slip on that glove of yours..."

A while later, as Jenny was getting dressed again, Ross announced: "I'll be interested to see what the others make of all this!"

"The others?" she asked. Who was he planning to tell about their lovemaking?

"Yes, your colleagues. The other Game enthusiasts! It would be great to have some direct feedback from The Group about Derewin. Can't you let me in, now, Jenny? I mean, we do know each other pretty well, all things considered!"

Jenny felt almost as deflated as at the start of this evening's conversation. Why had he raised that now? Why puncture the amorous atmosphere they had created?

"I don't know," she said. "I would have to ask The Group again. If you recall, they weren't too keen on the idea. I'll let you know".

Instead of going to bed with sweet thoughts of Ross in her head, she found herself spending several hours laid out on the sofa, immersed in the pages of *Our Stolen Freedom*, reconnecting with the anger that burned within.

* * *

In the morning, after having a good weed among

the radishes and cabbages, Jenny headed down into the village on a mission to chat to some of the other members of the Game group in person.

She knew she could have simply sent out a message recommending that Ross be invited into their ranks and they would have gone along with it, in the same way as they had gone along with her suggestion not to do so, when he first appeared on the scene.

But this time she really wanted their opinion. And she didn't just want to read their opinion on a screen, she wanted to feel it through face-to-face contact.

Her first stop-off was at The Dark Star, as she wanted to grab Miriam before she got too busy with preparing lunches.

Her cheerful chubby face with its mop of grey curly hair expressed pleasure at Jenny's arrival and she sat down to chat with her, over a coffee, in the lounge bar. But it was obvious that she was pressed for time.

Her view regarding Ross was that Jenny should do what she felt she wanted to. "Go with the love, dear," she said, in a way that made Jenny momentarily feel she understood more about the situation than she had been told. "You love what you do, we all love what you do, and you have to keep on loving every moment of what you do. So if it *feels* right, it *is* right. I know there is a risk in letting an outsider in on this, but, you know, life is full of danger and we can't run away from it all the time. Excuse me, dear, I must just go and check the chicken".

When Jenny rang at the door of the dance studio, down near the river, and there was no response, she assumed she would not be speaking to Emma that morning. But, just as she had turned her back and started to walk off down the street, she heard the sound of a window opening and turned to see a pair of round spectacles peering down at her from the top floor.

It turned out that Emma had plenty of time to talk, as there were no bookings for her holographic choreography sessions until later in the day. Jenny had been fairly apologetic about her hesitation regarding Ross's involvement, feeling that this apparent distrust of 'outsiders' was unworthy of someone who aspired to a generous and inclusive take on life. But here Emma reassured her that she understood how she felt about someone she had only ever met via meetcloud. "There's something not quite right about all that, isn't there? Something inhuman, colourless and mechanistic, disconnected from the flesh..."

Jenny struggled not to blush as she thought about her u-gloves.

Again, the advice was inconclusive, although Jenny suspected that Emma was generally in favour of taking risks and living with the consequences. After all, she had once explained to

Jenny how she had abandoned her life in England to go and live in Italy, when it appeared that that country had shaken itself free of the restrictions that prevented her from indulging her primary passion with large groups of real people. A year later, when it had become clear that the spirit of revolution had been betrayed and the new regime was just the continuation of the old one under a different label, she had not been afraid to express her disappointment and return to her old haunts, sadder but wiser.

Jenny called at Gus's house opposite the church, but was informed by his wife that he was out for his morning walk, so she moved on in search of the next Group member on her mental list.

"What concerns me most about this fellow is the motivation behind his research," said John, as they sat beside an old crumbling ivy-covered wall in the garden of the former vicarage in which he had lived for decades. "Do you feel he is really interested in the subject matter or just in obtaining some kind of academic fame? What I mean, Jenny, is do you feel he is being authentic about who he is or is there an element of deception? When someone truly expresses his philosophy, you feel that this is what he has secretly and profoundly lived by for many a long year, but if his words remain on the surface and are just for show, you can somehow sense the artifice.

How does he seem to you, this Ross?"

Jenny shrugged. "I don't know," she said. "How can you tell, over a net connection?"

"But do you trust him, deep down, in your body?"

In her body, he had said.

"Yes," she replied after a moment's reflection. "I suppose I do".

As Jenny walked back towards the church, she noticed a strikingly angular, bearded character crossing the road ahead of her and disappearing into his home, so she took the opportunity to seek out Gus's opinion.

Like John, he was concerned at the way in which Ross had simply stumbled across the information about Oldston in the course of other research. Ross obviously found The Game interesting, but from an outside point of view rather than an inside one. For him it was perhaps just a passing curiosity, something to fulfil his need for novelty, mused Gus. "This may seem peculiar, since The Game is obviously so old, but do you not think that Ross is interested in anything new as long as it is new, anything to fill that empty hole in his spiritual existence? Do you get the impression that he really *cares* about Oldston or The Game?"

That was the key question to which Jenny did not know the answer. Ross certainly seemed to care about her, for the moment, but as for the *depth* of his interest in her or The Game...

She looked around Gus's study, full of antique furniture and decorated with framed prints of medieval woodcuts and religious icons, as if somehow these surrounds could help resolve her dilemma.

"I don't see why else he would be doing this," she replied at length. "If he simply found Derewin's account amusing, he could have just read it and forgotten it. Why has he gone to the trouble of getting in touch with us, in proposing to help us with our project, if there is no genuine passion...?"

She ground to a halt, wanting to go on to insist that Ross certainly did not lack passion, but fully aware that she was going to say nothing of the sort.

There were more names on her imaginary list, but she decided she had heard enough. None of The Group were going to tell her what to do, because they were not that sort. They understood her doubts, that was for sure, but seemed to generally feel that there was nothing to fear from Ross being allowed to join their private discussions. As she crossed Ludbridge to leave the village, she told herself she was going to have to let Ross in.

A great scream ripped her thoughts apart. It was coming from below, from the river. Was someone in trouble?

She hurried to the edge and looked over. There on the bank was Agnes, in her wheelchair, with Peggy folding her arms around her, making soothing, calming noises. Agnes was staring up at Jenny, straight into her eyes, and as she did so she screamed again, even more loudly and terribly than the first time.

Unnerved, Jenny quickly turned away and headed for home.

* * *

Although Jenny was well aware of the role played by sexual desire in her dealings with Ross, and questioned herself constantly on that account, it was certainly an unconscious move on her part to clear out the grate that afternoon, fetch some wood in from the shelter and prepare the first fire of the autumn, even though she normally held off for another month or so, making do with thick jumpers.

But it was very much a deliberate move, after dinner when the living room was nicely warmed up, to undress and continue her re-reading of Theo Carter wrapped up inside the woollen blanket that graced her sofa during the colder months.

Thus when Ross called later for news of his possible inclusion in The Group, it was immediately clear from her nudity, and the visible proximity of the u-gloves, that the practical conversation would have to wait until later.

Jenny felt all aglow with pleasure as she got dressed, rather absurdly out of sight of the interface, as if she had anything more to hide from Ross. There was something missing though, and she realised that at this rate she was going to have to end up ordering the full-body kit that she had always told herself she would never go near. Unless, that was, she could tempt Ross to come up here in person, even though he was always so busy...

"And so?" came Ross's voice from behind her, as she buttoned up her skirt.

"What?" she replied, tugging at her blouse to straighten it out as she moved back into his visual range.

"What about The Group? Have I earned enough brownie points to be let in now, please, Miss?"

Jenny laughed.

"Yes, Ross. You can join The Group. But just for the record, I talked to the others and we came to the decision together. It's nothing to do with what just happened, OK?"

"In fact," she added, tapping at the interface, "I will do it right now... All done! You're on board!"

Jenny popped up to the bathroom while Ross tested out his new access.

"Thanks, Jenny!" he said, when she got down again. "That's a great collection of people you've got there. I can't wait to get talking to them all".

Jenny smiled and, of course, he smiled back, because he was always smiling on that profile picture she kept on screen while talking with him.

"Oh, another thing I couldn't help noticing, Jenny. That book there on the floor, beside the sofa. That looks to me very much like Carter's thing".

"Yes..." said Jenny. She knew the book was controversial but could hardly deny that it was sitting there in her home.

"You have a copy of *Our Stolen Freedom*, Jenny? And you're even reading it, by the looks of it! Are you insane?"

"No," said Jenny, thrown off guard by this sudden assault. "I'm not insane. I'm interested in what he says".

"Interested? Interested in the views of a murderer? A psychopathic enemy of the modern world and everything we hold dear?"

"Look, Ross, I know it's not everyone's cup of tea, but..."

"It's not a question of taste, Jenny. It's not a question of cups of tea and biscuits and polite conversations about literature between old ladies in twee cottages in the middle of nowhere. This is about breaching public safety norms and endangering lives, it's about truth denial, technophobia, misinformation, malicious opinion, hate writing. This is about fucking terrorism, Jenny! This is serious. These are the words of a killer, smuggled out of his prison cell by a notorious conspiracy theorist now herself serving a life sentence for crimes against humanity. You do realise that possessing a copy of that book is a serious criminal offence, don't you?"

Jenny was reeling now. Old ladies? Criminal offence? What was happening here?

"Ross," she said. "I don't understand. It sounds like you're threatening me".

"Threatening you? The book is banned, Jenny! How did you even have a copy in the first place?"

"I've had it for years... Since it first came out. It's been sitting on the shelf upstairs all that time and I..."

"Then put it back on the shelf, Jenny! Put it somewhere out of sight! Even better, put it on the bonfire! If other people see it there, people who haven't got your best interests at heart like I have, you could be in real trouble. I'm not threatening you, Jenny, I'm trying to protect you! I want to protect you from the contents of that dreadful toxic rant, yes, and also from being prosecuted for aiding and abetting terrorism. Don't you understand?"

"I don't know," said Jenny. "I suppose so".

Something was badly wrong here, she said to herself as she shut down the interface. Ross's attitude was... frightening. She would have instantly removed him from The Group if she could, but that would now need majority agreement with the others. How would she explain to them what had happened? She couldn't think. Her head was in too much of a spin. It would have to wait until tomorrow.

She picked up *Our Stolen Freedom* and took it upstairs with her, to somewhere where neither she nor it could be spied on and judged by a hostile outside world.

The next morning her interface would not work. It was completely dead. This was frustrating, because she had decided that the best way to deal with Ross's attitude was to draw it out publicly, by asking questions that would reveal the outlook he had displayed in his reaction to Theo's book. Addressing his criticism of the book itself would be difficult because of the illegality issue – even mentioning it online would probably set alarm bells ringing in some Public Safety bunker. But by teasing out some of Ross's general opinions, of which she was now rather suspicious, the others would at least be aware of who they were dealing with.

Jenny went down into the village to speak to Miriam, whose son Bertie had helped her out the last time her device had played up.

"I think you made the right decision, Jen, about that Ross!" she announced cheerfully as she let Jenny in to the pub. "I was catching up with it all this morning. He's found out a lot of new info, hasn't he? And he's very positive about getting The Game back on the Oldston calendar!"

Already? Ross certainly hadn't wasted any time in making himself known to the others. Jenny was tempted to make a comment to that effect but restrained herself, as she suspected she would make herself look ridiculous if she spoke badly of him so soon after deciding to trust him.

Bertie wasn't at home, but Miriam got hold of him and he promised to come and have a look the following day. He would bring a spare interface just in case he couldn't sort hers out on the spot.

So 24 hours without a connection to the great global matrix, then? This was good news in a way, as it allowed Jenny to shake off the paranoia that had been getting a grip on her guts and to stop thinking about how she was going to handle the Ross situation. She tidied up the garden, wiped down all the window sills, used her special piece of hooked branch to dig out the dead leaves and assorted muck from the kitchen drain and swept the front path with exceptional thoroughness. She drank tea, finished reading Theo Carter's book, sat and cried for ten minutes, and went to bed.

The next morning, before Bertie was due to turn up, she went for a long walk to the north, away from the village, because for the moment she didn't even want to think about The Game.

She turned away from the issue that was paining her to such an extent that she did not even bother checking out The Group's messages on the spare interface that Bertie left with her, after declaring that there was something seriously awry with her own.

Two days later, she did force herself to go and have a look. There was Ross, sharing all his ideas about The Game and there were the others, mightily impressed by this expert from the Big City and falling over themselves to be of service. Nauseating. There was no personal message to her from Ross, no suggestion of another meeting. So he had what he wanted now, was that it?

She thought about contacting him and demanding a discussion, but she had no idea what she would say. What was she reproaching him about? Was it just a question of personal pride? There was certainly nothing problematic in the content of his messages to The Group.

As Jenny delayed responding, the conviction took hold of her that she was better saying nothing, chalking the episode up to experience, stepping back from the fray and allowing Ross and the others to push forward with the project. After all, she needed a break. She had made her contribution. The thing was up and rolling again and that should be cause for pleasure rather than concern.

As the golden shadow of autumn crept down from the hills, Jenny retreated into her own world – the inner world of her cottage and the inner world of her dreaming. This happened every year, in fact. It was her hibernation. Even when she got her own interface back, she didn't use it very much. The u-glove box was jammed out of sight into the back of a cupboard. She read books about Arabian myths and Chinese spirituality, about medieval poetry and Greek metaphysics. She played her violin. She wrote, by hand, in her journal. She wrapped up warm against the wind and ventured out for fast, bracing walks along the crest of the hills.

Jenny felt fine in the silky soft embrace of a deep and familiar winter melancholia.

* * *

When spring arrived, slowly and with many a sudden step backwards, Jenny rediscovered an interest in what lay beyond the confines of her own home. On a practical level, she started preparing a new season in the garden and mended a section of fence that had been blown away by an early March gale. On a mental level, she started to think about The Game again, about The Group and Ross and the project to bring the tradition back to life. She had occasionally, despite herself, stolen a look at the latest messages, but the content was a little puzzling. There was a lot of confidence about relaunching the project and a lot of praise for 'everything' Ross was doing, but almost nothing on what this actually amounted to.

She had begun to have the distinct impression that things were being discussed elsewhere, behind her back as it were. Was Ross holding parallel conversations with members of The Group? As the days lengthened and the vital sap started spreading through her body, Jenny's numbed avoidance of the issue faded away and was replaced by an urgent desire to find out what exactly was going on here.

Jenny embarked on several trips down to the village, where she managed to call, in what she managed to present as a quite casual manner, on Gus, John, Miriam, Emma, Judi and Mike and, naturally enough, to raise the question of The Game and how its revival was progressing.

They didn't seem to know any more than she did, but had been infected by the general tone of enthusiasm in the shared messages and seemed to trust that the project was in good hands.

Jenny would very much have liked to have spoken to Eamonn, but there was no sign of life at his house and from the leaves blown up against the front door she imagined he had stayed longer than usual in Manchester. She did find Leah at home, but she declared she was busy designing a pair of shoes for her sister's virtual wedding. It seemed she was not actually proposing to print them in the real world, only to wear them in the virtual one, via her online avatar. Leah seemed to avoid the real physical world as much as possible and suggested to Jenny that she should message her when she got home, even though they were standing next to each other, in the flesh, both in full possession of a tongue and a vocal chord.

The retired civil servant George and his obedient spouse Melissa might also be able to shed some light on the advancement of The Game, felt Jenny, particularly if the approach fell into the favoured 'realistic' category. She was pretty sure she would find them at home, since she did not recall them having ever spoken of being anywhere else – they even had their groceries delivered to the house. When she reached the front gate to their drive and peered through, she saw that there was a gardening drone busily sucking up dead leaves from the edge of their lawn. But nobody answered the intercom. Jenny tried ringing again, but with no luck. She glanced up at the camera on the top of the gates and seemed to see George and Melissa staring out at her, huddled together in fear, silently waiting for her to give up and go. So she gave them one last long and defiant buzz as a parting shot and went on her way.

As she passed Molly May, the squat stone glistening in the late April sunshine, Jenny realised that there was nothing for it. She would have to contact Ross.

"Jenny!" he announced when they linked up online. "I was so pleased you got in touch because I had been meaning to have a chat with you. How are you? I was wondering if you had been feeling under the weather because we haven't been hearing your voice in The Group..."

She had left the real video image of him on the screen, in all its masked artifice. She wanted to be confronted with the reality of who he was. She still wouldm't be able to read anything into his facial expressions when he was talking to her, but at least she would no longer be distracted by the familiar photo of the man she had started to love.

"Oh yes?" she said dryly. "And why was that, Ross? Did you want to offer me some more friendly advice on what I should or shouldn't be reading?"

"Aw, come on Jenny," he replied. "That was ages ago! No, it's because I've got some exciting news for you! We've got the game proposal wrapped up and ready to go to the authorities!"

"What?" said Jenny. "What do you mean?"

"The Group. We've been working flat out all winter and now we're there. Just a few 'i's to be dotted and 't's to be crossed – and of course any suggestions that you care to make..."

"Hang on! I don't understand. Who's the 'we' that have been working on this? There was no discussion of any detailed plan in the Group messages. I've spoken to some of the others and they weren't aware of anything like that going on".

"You've spoken to the others? I don't remember seeing anything..."

"In real life, Ross! In the real world that exists here, in Oldston! In a place you've never even stepped foot in!"

"Ah, yes, well, you see..." he sounded flustered. "It depends which others you are talking about, of course. We formed a sort of informal working group and..."

"You did what? You set up another group? Without telling everyone?"

"No... Well, I think you'll find we did announce it at one stage, though it may have got a bit lost in all the messages going back and forth. I did take the opportunity to sound out the others on a one-to-one basis and our little team grew out of that, really. I suppose I may have forgotten to officially announce it to the old group..."

"The *old* group? I can't believe you are saying this, Ross!"

"Listen, Jenny, I can't see that you have any reason to complain, since we haven't heard a word from you for months. If you'd wanted to get involved you should have said so. As it is, I'm quite prepared..."

"If I'd wanted to get involved? *If*? Don't you think I *am* a bit involved with The Group, Ross? Don't you think it was maybe me who set it up and got it going, even if I happen to have taken a back seat for a few weeks. And what about the others? The ones that you didn't hand-pick to go along with your..."

"Stop!" There was a severity in Ross's tone that shocked Jenny. "I don't want to get into this discussion, Jenny. What's done is done. But what I do want to do is share with you where we have got to with the working group. And, you know, I think you're going to like it! So let's just put the recriminations on hold for a moment, OK. I am sending the presentation document through to you now. Take your time and have a good read. I'll stay connected, get on with some other stuff, and when you're ready, you let me know. Deal?"

Jenny agreed and opened up the document which had just popped into her message box.

Twenty minutes later she called out to Ross that she had finished.

He appeared back on the screen of her interface, back from wherever he had been.

"And so?" he asked cheerfully. "What do you

reckon?"

For a moment, Jenny said nothing. And when she started to speak, it was in a slow, deliberate and composed manner in which every word weighed heavily.

"Congratulations, Ross," she said. She knew he would be smiling at this opening, behind his mask. "You and your little team have managed to come up with what I can only describe as the most putrid vat of excrement of which I have ever caught a whiff!"

The final part of her sentence leapt violently out of the super-calm register into what would best be termed a furious shriek.

"I mean even the fucking title is an abortion. 'The Oldston Game: remarketing tradition for the post-physical era'. What the hell is that, Ross? Where did that come from? And as for the rest, is it some kind of sick joke? You haven't even kept the date! An 'all-year experience'? A 'visitor centre'? VR helmets? What was it you wrote? Ah yes: 'Contestants take on the role of the May Queen or May King and battle their way through the ancient streets of picturesque Oldston, seeing off hordes of angry opponents with their virtual longswords?' What's that got to do with our Game?"

"Oh, don't be so harsh, Jenny. The characters are all there! The Dobbins and the Teasers and the Help-meets..."

"But they're not real, Ross! They are just cartoon characters in a Virtual Reality game. This is for kids, it's empty, plastic, pathetic! It's all reduced to fighting the baddies and scoring points. And the whole topography of The Game is missing! It all seems to happen in the village centre. Where is Cole Spring or Bridie's Well in all this? Or The Bounds? Or even the bloody Old Stone!"

"Ah, you see, Jenny, that's an important point because the layout of the Oldston Experience very much ties in with the environmental aspects of the project, which I am also working on with some very experienced colleagues of mine. You see, the area around the village will become a Protected Zone and that very much includes The Bounds and the paths up to the spring and the well, as well as the stone. We can't have people wandering around there, trampling nature underfoot".

"A Protected Zone? Protected from whom? These tourists you want to bring in?"

"Well, yes, of course, but from everyone in fact. I'm sure you'd agree that you yourself have a duty to participate in the general effort..."

"Are you saying that you want to stop me and other villagers from walking in our own countryside? Are you serious?"

"It's not *your* countryside, Jenny, if I may correct you there. It belongs to regional governance and its stakeholders in the business community. But you won't be excluded! You'll still be able to enjoy the green spaces around the village through virtual reality!"

"Virtual reality? How on earth can you enjoy anything through virtual reality?" snapped back Jenny, but she had barely finished the sentence when she realised she had scored an impressive own goal.

Ross was laughing. Openly mocking her.

"Are you trying to tell me that you faked it, Jenny? If so, you're a remarkably good actress!"

She tried to compose herself and come up with a counter-offensive.

"And how about you, Ross? Were you faking it? Only pretending to be interested in me so that I would let you into The Group? And what's this all about anyway, eh? What is your real interest in The Game or are you too dishonest to tell me, even now?"

"Ooh! So many questions all of a sudden!" replied Ross, in the same openly contemptuous tone. She was glad she couldn't see his face because she would have been tempted to slap the screen. Where was the u-glove connection when you needed it?

"Since you ask, yes, I'll tell you. It's not going to make any difference now, in any case. Where to start, though? Let's say that my interest in The Game is pretty similar to that of our 17th century friend Derewin, and that this is entirely uncoincidental!"

"Stop talking in riddles, you piece of shit! Just give me a straight answer, if you're capable of it!"

Ross sighed.

"Derewin, if you recall, was sent in to assess the Oldston Game by the Church of England, which regarded it as a potential threat. A threat to what? Why, to its monopoly over the lives, customs and ways of thinking of the villagers. Ever since the Roman Empire carried forward the Christian project, the ecclesiastical authorities had been busy eliminating any rivals to its, errmm, well, full-spectrum control, I suppose we would say in modern parlance..."

"Yes, I know all that, thanks," said Jenny. "I'm not fifteen years old, you know".

"Err, no, you certainly aren't Madam, I'll give you that!"

She felt a ball of rage building inside her but tried not to show it.

"So what has all that got to do with you, Ross? You're working for the Church of England to suppress a threat to its total control over our lives, is that what you're trying to say?"

"Oh no, of course not," Ross assured her. "That was just a parallel, to try and explain where I am coming from. The whole Derewin story is pretty much a metaphor, in fact. My interest in Oldston comes from my role as a consultant to a major cross-sector player. My client had vaguely heard about your quaint tradition and had come up with a project pretty much along the lines of what I sent you. The problem was that a real-life revival of The Game would have got in the way of that and, in particular, was likely to hinder the development of the Oldston Sustainability Park, which is part of the bigger picture".

"Sustainability Park?"

"Yes, you know. Fifteen thousand solar panels around The Bounds and on the south-facing slope under the Old Stone and a few dozen wind turbines on the north-facing side, plus a major national-scale carbon capture facility between the spring and the well".

Jenny was reeling. "But you said that would all be a Protected Zone? That nobody would be able to go there so as to preserve nature?"

"Yes, exactly. No human beings. But sustainable technology is a friend of nature, so there can never be any legal impediment to placing it in a Protected Zone! Quite the contrary – it attracts significant amounts of GreenBuild funding from the World Preservation Trust's Stemma Initiative".

Jenny tried to concentrate. This was all too much.

"So what about your research?" she blurted

out. "What was the point of that? Why go to all the trouble of raking through the archives to find out about The Game if all you wanted to do was bury it for ever?"

Ross was laughing again and Jenny knew that there something horribly cruel behind that laugh.

"You haven't got it, have you Jenny?" he said. "I've never been anywhere near the Church of England archives in my life and never will. I'm a business consultant, remember, not a postgrad student!"

"But..."

"I made it up! Derewin is a figment of my imagination! As, of course, are all his so-called revelations about the Oldston Game. Didn't you ever wonder why I would never let you see the evidence or quote more than a few words at the time? Forging a whole document would have been too much like hard work. And entirely un-necessary, as I rightly calculated. You fell for it anyway!"

"No hang on, that can't be... I mean some of the things he said were exactly what I..."

"What you were hoping he would say? What you had guessed might be the reality? What you had tapped into your interface when you were searching for more information to confirm your ideas? You would be surprised to know how easy it is to access personal search data – when you have the financial clout of a client like mine behind you, at any rate..."

"You bastard! You spied on my online activity and used the information to make me like you and to sell me your phoney story? Lying through your teeth for a bit of cheap sexual pleasure and a big wad of corporate cash, is that it?"

"Ha, ha, ha!"

He really was intolerable.

"You're right about the cash, but not about the sexual pleasure, I'm afraid".

"Don't give me that. I could *feel* you, remember. There are some things men can't fake, even lying scum like you".

"Ah, but that's where you're wrong! You really ought to keep up with the times, Auntie Jennifer! That wasn't *me* you could feel, that was a nice bit of software provided to me from the v-porn wing of my client's highly successful business empire. Nothing is guaranteed to be real over the net, as I thought you might have realised. Oh, and before you accuse me of getting a thrill out of your end of the u-glove action, I disconnected from that the moment I came into contact with your gruesomely wrinkled granny flesh... There's only so much I will do for money and, call me old-fashioned, but there I draw the line!"

"You'll pay for this, Ross, I swear!" said Jenny, incandescent with rage. "I'll make sure everyone in the bloody country knows about you! Your face will be absolutely everywhere! You will be a complete social leper by the time I've finished with you!"

The creature was still laughing.

"You don't even know who I am, you idiot! I'm not called Ross and that's not my face!"

"Whose face is it, then? You've stolen someone else's identity?"

"It's nobody's face. It's a made-up face. A nice mixture of all those old boyfriends you were busy looking up on the net, frustrated old maid that you are! And it worked a treat, didn't it? Love at first sight! With someone who doesn't exist! Ha, ha ha!"

"But I've got your contact details. And I know what project you're working on. I'll track you down, whoever you are, Mr Phoney Fuckface, and I'll make you pay for what you've done, I can assure you!"

"Well..." said the person on the interface in a wheedling manner. "I would think rather carefully about that, if I were you, Jenny, what with your illegal medications and illegal terrorist propaganda – evidence for both of which is preserved for posterity on my hard drive, by the way. I don't think you'll be causing me too many problems from a high-security prison cell. But I'm not a vindictive man. I won't come after you unless provoked. If I were you, I'd gracefully accept defeat, keep yourself safe and live out the years that you have left like a good responsible..."

"Fuck off!" said Jenny and disconnected.

For twenty minutes she paced around her home, not even noticing where she was walking. The anger that had taken hold of her was so far beyond anything she had experienced before that it took on a transcendent purity, pushing her into a white-hot realm of knowing. This short period of powerful intensity showed her exactly what it was that she had to do.

She stopped in the kitchen to look at the calendar. Today had been April 28. She had two days to bring this together.

* * *

Jenny had made up two flasks of herbal tea for the little crowd who had gathered up at the Old Stone half an hour before sunset on April 30, but most of them seemed to prefer the vodka that Mike was sharing from a voluminous hip flask. Among these was Emma, who had come with her friend Alex. There was also Judi, Gus and his cousin Martin, John, and three people from London who were staying with him, who introduced themselves as Vicky, CJ and Lily.

Jenny made a mental count of who was there. Six men, as planned and... oh, only four women, apart from herself. Who was missing? Ah! There was Peggy now! It was a tough climb pushing that wheelchair. But where was Miriam? She had promised to come, but she had taken a bit of convincing. She seemed somehow not to want to face up to the reality of what was happening, as if they could make everything better simply by pretending that there was no serious threat to Oldston. Jenny hoped that she had not backtracked on her commitment to this plan. They needed everybody on board.

Gus appeared to have noticed her disquiet because he wandered across and asked her if everything was all right. When she told him of her concerns about Miriam he said that there was no need to worry. He had a feeling it would be OK. Things tended to sort themselves out by a sort of spontaneous generation, in his experience.

But as the sun sunk deeper towards the western horizon, Jenny became increasingly worried about Miriam's absence. There was no way of getting in touch with her, as this had all necessarily been arranged offline and without phones. She peered down the path to see if she could see the pub landlady arriving, but there was no sign.

"We'll have to try it without Miriam," she announced finally, with a heavy heart, and the group formed into two concentric circles of Turners around the Stone, while Jenny took up her place in the centre.

It wasn't right! It was unbalanced! She almost wanted to ask one of the men to step aside, but then they would be down to just 11 participants.

As the last rays of the sun turned to black, they started turning, each circle in a different direction. A chilly breeze swept down from the north and for a moment Jenny thought that the thing was starting to work. But even though they turned, and she focused all her strength on the turning, they did not seem to get past this initial stage.

"Maybe we should turn faster?" said Mike. "Accelerate the energy?"

Jenny nodded and so they speeded up, but, if anything, this was worse. At the same time that the pace of the exercise increased, so did its depth decrease. It was action for the sake of action, without the inner power needed to make something important happen.

"Stop!" cried Jenny. "It's no good! We're not getting anywhere! I don't know what to suggest! I don't know how we're going to..."

An ear-splitting scream interrupted her and all turned to the source.

It was Agnes, who was jerking and rocking in her wheelchair, desperate to draw their attention.

"She wants to join in," said Peggy quietly,

though there was no need as they had all understood the message.

"Do you want that?" Jenny asked and Peggy confirmed that she did, simply by walking towards her daughter, taking the brakes off her chair and wheeling her into the circle. Agnes was chortling with excitement.

"OK," said Jenny. "Let's try again. Thank you Agnes!"

This is desperate stuff, she was thinking. The poor girl has no idea what we are trying to do. But she kept her doubts to herself.

Again they started turning, clockwise and anti-clockwise, sunwise and widdershins. Remarkably, it felt different now. Better. Much better!

Sun goes down and beacons burn
Teams all set and Turners turn
Wheel without and wheel within
Let the Roodmas Game begin!

The little breeze picked up into a proper wind. The sky was darkening now and Jenny closed her eyes to feel the energy of the oncoming night.

This time they did not turn any faster, but more intensely, in a manner which was impossible to explain. They went deeper and higher, further from the present and closer to the truth.

There was a gasp from around her which made Jenny open her eyes. The beacons! The beacons were lit at Cole Spring and Bridie's Well!

And now there was distant music in the air. Voices. Singing. Bawdiness. Down in the valley a strange glow was beginning to form around The Bounds. It was moving, alive, turning in a great circle around the village in two directions at once, mirroring their own efforts.

Jenny fancied she could make out figures, far below, on the path. Lads and Lasses dressed in outlandish costumes, covered in greenery, waving sticks and beating night drums. Dobbins cantering back and forth in merriment, Teasers shouting and laughing.

Beat and battle round The Bounds
Weary Royals head for mounds
Sacred pleasures, sacred food
Hail the Help-meets, Game renewed!

She switched her gaze to Agnes, who was being wheeled past her by her mother. The girl's face was a total delight. She was transported with joy, eyes shining and mouth open in wonderment at what she was experiencing.

The two stones below them, Molly May and the Merry Man, were clearly visible now, even though the moon had not yet risen. They seemed to be shining from within, radiating the power of their own ancient being.

The whole landscape was coming alive. Jenny could feel the presence of the May Queen and the May King and the strange thing was that they were everywhere at once. They were at the start with the Green Maids, they were on the paths leading down from the spring and the well, they were waiting to cross The Bounds, they were running through the village streets, they were holed up in the tower and the church with their Help-meets, they were crossing the bridges and heading for the Old Stone.

Time was not separate any more, not linear and narrow, but spread out and all-embracing.

And Jenny, too, felt that she was no longer a separate person, no longer a product of her time and her history but that she was Lady Rood and all the players at once, that she was nothing but one aspect of this scene, this landscape, this place, this timeless empowerment.

Stand up, stand up
With odes and games
Of how we yet might be
Rise up, rise up
The winds and flames
Of age-old liberty

So this was The Game! This was what it was all about! The belonging that transcended. The eternity in the moment. The life unleashed and allowed to explode. The realisation came suddenly to her, took her breath away and sent tears flowing down her wind-swept cheeks.

The landscape, the board of The Game, was throbbing with light and energy now. The river was shining, the two straight paths glowed and the circle of The Bounds was pulsating with festivity.

Jenny became aware of a great warmth behind her and turned round to look at the Old Stone itself. It actually appeared to be glowing, transmitting a heat that it can only have drawn up from its roots at the volcanic centre of the world, its spiral carving plainer to see than ever before.

On and on they turned, ever deeper and ever higher, ever further from themselves and closer to the eternal unity of The Game.

There was a scream. It was Agnes again. And then another, a male voice. That was Gus. And now others joined in, as did Jenny. Yes! That was what she had been wanting to do. She knew it now. They shrieked, they bellowed, they shouted, they bayed like wolves and, at their demand, the full moon hove up into view behind the hill ridge to the east.

And, as it did so, the glowing of The Game caught alight. The Bounds were a ring of flame now and the lines of paths and river were furious slashes of fire.

Now the outline of The Game rose up from the land which had given it shape and took to the sky in its burning triumph, spinning around so that the feet of its converging paths were rooted in the below and their peak pointed to the heavens.

Instinctively, they all stopped moving and watched in awe as this great sign filled the sky above them and then sped eastwards towards the newly-risen moon, superimposing itself and then becoming absorbed into its roundness.

With a mighty roar, a shaft of fiery substance shot out of the ground beside the Stone and poured into the sky. The moon was on fire too and a thousand bolts of lightning flew out in every direction.

Because they were part of this moment, part of The Game and part of the moon, the Turners around the Stone knew where the bolts went.

They knew that the very first lightning bolt struck the luxury apartment in Green New Wotton smart city occupied by the man who had called himself Ross, destroying him and everything he owned, including his plans for Oldston.

They knew that subsequent bolts struck and destroyed all the people like him in the world, who plotted and lied and cheated to deceive and exploit others in the pursuit of their own foul lust for power and wealth.

They knew that The Game wiped out the power that denied life and, with it, all the corrupted thinking and false assumptions on which the prison of artifice and slavery had been founded.

They knew that such was the energy unleashed that its cleansing powers of destruction even reached back into the past and swept away the dictatorship of greed before it had managed to install itself.

Humankind had broken free. For ever.

When the May Day sun rose on the Old Stone, eleven people were sprawled in a state of complete exhaustion on the grass around it.

A twelfth person was not in the least tired. She was exuberant. She was standing up, arms raised aloft, yards from her discarded wheelchair, and singing to the dawn of the new life that she could now live.

And beside the Old Stone, which had resumed its familiar appearance in the bright spring sunshine, lay a little pile of ashes called Jenny.

A very happy pile of ashes.

Other fiction by Paul Cudenec

No Such Place As Asha: An Extremist Novel (2019)
The Fakir of Florence: A Novel in Three Layers (2016)

Non-fiction by Paul Cudenec

The Green One (2017)
Nature, Essence and Anarchy (2016)
Forms of Freedom (2015)
The Stifled Soul of Humankind (2014)
The Anarchist Revelation: Being What We're Meant to Be (2013)
Antibodies, Anarchangels and Other Essays (2013)

Online writing

www.winteroak.org.uk
network23.org/paulcudenec

To get in touch with Winter Oak please email winteroak@greenmail.net or follow @winteroakpress on Twitter.

Printed in France by Amazon
Brétigny-sur-Orge, FR